Th
Debt

D A Latham

DEDICATION

To my dearest, darling Allan

CONTENTS

D A Latham

ACKNOWLEDGMENTS

I'd like to thank Iris Winn for her
unwavering support and enthusiasm
and
Brian Schell for his sense of humour and
terrific pep-talks.

CHAPTER 1

I sat in abject misery, unable to believe that I was actually in Bromley County Court's waiting room. People like me don't get into debt, and we don't get taken to court; only I had been. A series of bad decisions plus some bad luck had landed me there. MVDI, the credit card company that had given me a shiny gold card five years previous, on my 19th birthday, had finally lost patience and wanted to find a way to make me pay up with money I didn't have.

I glanced around furtively, praying that I didn't come face-to-face with anyone I knew. The shame would've been crushing. There were single mothers with children at their feet, no doubt trying to make ends meet and failing miserably, just as I had. They didn't look ashamed, just sad. Numerous nationalities were represented in that snapshot of the poor of Bromley. A duty solicitor sat behind me, trying to communicate with an African woman, attempting to steer her through what would happen while not being able to speak the same language. I wished I had a solicitor. Someone to represent me and hold my hand would've helped. Unfortunately since I worked, albeit for a low wage, I wasn't entitled to free legal help, nor was I able to pay for it, so I was all alone.

I'd challenged the amount of my debt, having read online about cases where excessive charges and interest had been disallowed by sympathetic judges. I was pinning all my hopes on getting the interest frozen and the charges wiped off. Without it, I just couldn't see a way of paying back the amount I owed. My fingers clasped the handle of my document carrier, my knuckles white from tension. I prayed that the credit card company would forget to send anyone along, and the case would be dismissed. There was only ten minutes till my turn, so it was not long to wait.

I surveyed the room, wondering what all the different people were there for, when a man in an expensive suit strode up to the check-in desk and spoke to the lady booking people in. She pointed at me, making my heart sink. The Suit nodded at her, signed in, then made his way over. In happier times, I would've said he was handsome, attractive even, but in that place, he was almost the devil himself.

"Miss Higgs?" The Suit enquired. I nodded. "May I sit down?" His voice was quite posh, not upper class, but educated. I nodded again. He sat opposite me and plopped his briefcase on the chair next to him. "My name is Mr McCarthy, I'm from Alpha, the law firm representing MVDI. Can I ask why you're contesting this claim?" I was glad he kept his voice down. I didn't want the whole waiting room knowing I was there because I was in hopeless debt.

"I'm not contesting that there's a debt," I murmured, my determination and bravado failing me, "but there's been excessive charges and interest applied unfairly. I found out online that some people have successfully challenged them and had their debt reduced."

I glanced up at him; his face was impassive. "In the cases you've been looking at, people were in a position to pay a reduced amount in one lump sum, which is why the company accepted it. I have a copy of your credit agreement that states in the terms and conditions how much the charges would be for late or non-payment. I'd urge you to accept this judgement now, before you rack up more costs by going in front of the judge."

"I'm here now, Mr McCarthy, so I may as well try my luck. None of those cases said anything about a lump sum payment being involved. You won't scare me out of walking into that room." I tilted my head towards the doorway to the judge's chamber.

"You won't win, I can tell you that now. I do a lot of these and the law is on the side of the creditor." He held my gaze with bright blue eyes.

"We'll see," I said, looking away, cursing him inwardly for being so damned attractive. I stared down at my document bag. It'd been my old college bag and had seen better days. Like everything I owned, it was frayed and scuffed.

"As you wish," he said abruptly. He stood, grabbed his pristine briefcase, and moved to another seat several rows down. I watched as he played with his iPhone, noticing how his long fingers flew over the screen with a practiced ease. He was no stranger to luxury.

By the time we were called into the judge's room, my palms were sweaty and my heart was pounding. The Suit directed me to sit on a bench to the right-hand side, while he sat on the left. The judge was a tiny, dark-haired lady, who sat behind a large mahogany desk, on which there were a few thick legal books laying open.

"Let's get started," she said in a no-nonsense way. "Higgs versus MVDI. Is that correct?"

I nodded.

"You are Miss Higgs. Is that correct?" She pinned me with an intense glare.

My mouth went dry. Even saying "yes" to her felt as though I was mumbling through a mouthful of cotton wool. All thoughts of getting away without paying my debt vanished. I wished that I'd just admitted it to begin with and avoided the hearing. I debated running out of the room. "Are you unrepresented?" She asked.

I nodded. "I don't qualify for free legal help as I work, but I couldn't afford a lawyer."

She didn't answer, just turned to the suit, "You must be Mr McCarthy for MVDI?"

"Correct," said the Suit.

The judge flicked through a file of papers slowly. "So tell me Ms Higgs, on what basis do you dispute this debt?" She fixed me with rather kindly brown eyes.

I swallowed. "At least five thousand pounds of this debt is made up of charges and extortionate interest. I found some other cases online where this had been successfully challenged." I'd stumbled a bit over my words, but had gotten my point across.

"Which cases were they?" She asked. I'd printed off the case notes secretly at work. I began to recite the names.

"Ambleford versus MVDI, Foster versus MVDI, Benson versus MVDI. That's just a couple. There've been a lot more." For the first time since walking into that room, I felt a glimmer of hope.

"May I see them please?" I stood and walked up to the desk to hand her the notes I'd printed off. For the following few minutes we all sat in silence as she read through them carefully, then consulted a large legal book in front of her.

"Mr McCarthy, are you aware of these cases?" She eventually asked. She held the papers out to him. He took them from her and flicked through them quickly.

"Every single one of these cases involve a historical card agreement, at least twenty years old, lost by the company. Plus, the defendants were able to offer a reduced lump sum settlement. It's not relevant in this case. On page two of your bundle is the agreement signed by Miss Higgs. Clauses 4, 5, 5a, and 5b relate directly to late payment fees and charges, and clause 8 covers interest charges. It's an agreement approved by the FSA. Miss Higgs was given another copy when she received her card on the third of March 2009. The cases are not relevant to hers." His voice was deep and confident.

"Agreed. The debt is upheld." The judge barely looked up. Ice flowed through my veins at the verdict.

"I request costs at four thousand and seventeen pounds," said the Suit. My mouth dropped open in horror. We'd been in there five minutes. Nobody was worth nearly a thousand quid a minute.

"Denied. Costs shouldn't go above three thousand pounds for a hearing, you'll cap costs at that level," the judge snapped. "Session is dismissed."

I stood up in a daze, my mind a fog of despair. Not only did I already owe twelve thousand pounds, in five minutes, I'd racked up another three thousand quids' worth of debt. I had no hope at all of ever paying it back. I was a fuck-up of monumental proportions.

I fought an almost-overwhelming urge to scream in a toddler-tantrum kind of way. The sheer injustice of the robbing, greedy credit card company, and the way they'd brought me to my knees, made me want to howl with the unfairness of it. I would be in total poverty for the rest of my life trying to pay them back.

All my hopes for a better future crumbled away at that moment. I'd wanted to be one of those career girls I'd watched on Sex and the City. I'd wanted a nice apartment, a great wardrobe, expensive shoes, and a gorgeous man on my arm. Instead, I had a County Court Judgement, a tiny bedsit, and I was all alone in my predicament.

Stumbling out of the courthouse in a dream-like state, I tripped on the last step. My humiliation was complete as I landed on my knees in front of a gaggle of rough-looking girls. They erupted in peals of laughter as I floundered on the floor, trying to ignore the pain in my knee and the blood flowing down my leg. I felt my face burn even brighter with the fresh embarrassment. I limped away to find a quiet bench round the back of East Street and let the tears flow.

I knew my debt was merely a drop to a huge company such as MVDI, but the judgement meant bailiffs ransacking my tiny bedsit, or worse still, my boss being told in the form of an earnings attachment order. Given that I worked in a position of trust, I'd probably get the sack. My job was all I had, so to me, losing it meant my life was over.

I sat there for half an hour or so, letting all the tears out. Eventually I was dry-sobbing, like an empty petrol tank trying to power a car. In my own mind, I knew I was one of life's losers; one of those people who never gets it quite right. Some people sail through life easily, not experiencing crushing defeat or gaggles of girls laughing at their misfortune. All my life I'd been the butt of jokes, the one who slipped up. I'd been the girl whose parents had died, leaving me at the mercy of the state care system. I'd been the girl whom the social workers "forgot," and the one who didn't get the help I'd been due. I'd been on my own since the age of eight in reality. Ill-prepared and ill-equipped for the world around me. I was the girl with the scars.

I'd thought that as I'd entered adulthood, that somehow I'd change, that I would stop making the bad decisions and learn to fit in with all the winners. MVDI, assisted by the Suit, had effectively slapped me round the face and reminded me how inferior I was. Now the company would own my future, helped by the same government who had shoved me into a terrifying and cold children's home, and then forgotten to give me a social worker or try and find me a foster home. They just left me there, ignored and afraid.

I stood to begin the walk home. I could've caught the bus, but knowing that every single penny would need to be used for paying back my debt, I decided that I'd have to get used to a frugal existence. My misery was complete when it began to rain. Within almost no time, the water had oozed through my thin coat, and seeped into my shoes via a hole underneath the toe. I cursed Primark for selling cheap, inadequate products that didn't do their job. Another sob erupted when it hit me that I'd never be able to afford good shoes again, or even a pair of winter boots. I'd have cold, wet feet forever.

I squelched along, the rain concealing tears streaming down my face again. In that moment, I made a decision. I would escape once and for all. I would thwart the evil card company. They wouldn't get their money. I'd end it all in a two-fingered gesture to a world that had never given a shit whether I was there or not.

With the decision made, I relaxed a little. I pondered the best way to enact my plan. I knew overdosing was risky, since too few people actually died from it. Hanging would be difficult in my tiny box of a bedsit. I spotted a sign for Bromley South Station and decided it would be a speedy, efficient way to do it. There were plenty of fast, through-trains, so I wouldn't feel a thing, it would be so quick.

I had to buy a ticket at the station to get through the barrier. I used money that should've gone to MVDI to purchase a single to London. Nobody noticed me as I wandered along platform three waiting for the right moment. I sat down on a bench to wait and contemplate my last moments in a cruel, uncaring world. A train pulled in slowly, the announcer saying it was a Herne Bay service. I remembered going there once with my parents, in happier times, before the accident happened. My memory was hazy, but I recalled having chips on the beach and an enormous candy floss. It was one of very few early memories I had, having mentally locked away all vestiges of childhood happiness while in the bleak, oppressive orphanage.

I watched a family get on, cheerful in their tight foursome. I no longer found seeing families painful, especially knowing my own pain would be ending soon. The train pulled away, leaving just me on the platform. Groups of people were on the platform next to me, probably heading into London. I ignored them all and sat quietly, waiting for my chance.

"Fast train coming through at platform three. Stand well back," said the announcer. I stood, leaving my handbag on the bench. I began to walk towards the edge, ready to fall at the right moment. I could hear the train in the distance, different from the norm, as there was no slowing down. I stood, waiting for its approach.

As it neared, I began to tip forward, my mind blank.

I felt an arm round me, yanking me back. "I've got you," said a deep voice. I opened my eyes in surprise. I'd expected oblivion, but instead I could see an arm, wrapped in a wool coat, firmly holding me round the waist.

"What did you do that for?" I snapped at the arm, angry I'd have to wait for the next train.

"Because nothing is ever that bad," he said in a voice I recognised. I tried to prise his arm off me, but he held firm. "I'm not letting you go all the time we're near this train track," he added. I sagged, tired beyond belief from all the emotion. "We're gonna go over, get your bag, and then we're gonna walk out of this station and get you some help," he said quietly.

I didn't reply. With his arm firmly grasping my waist, he frogmarched me out, up the escalator, and back onto the high street. Without stopping, he guided me into a Starbucks, and up to the till. "What would you like to drink?"

"I haven't..." I began. He stopped me.

"It's on me. Large latte? You must be frozen." He turned to the barista, "two large lattes please," before plonking his briefcase down to use his free hand to fish around in his pocket for some money. I carried our coffees to a table in the back. Finally, he released me, and we sat down. It was then that I noticed he had my document bag strapped across him. I'd left it in the courtroom in my haste to escape.

"Would you like to tell me what all that was about?" He said.

"Mr McCarthy, I don't really think that's any of your business." The man had wrecked me once that day; I didn't really feel like justifying my decision to him.

"It's Andy... My name, that is. And I think it's very much my business when you walk out of a room and try and kill yourself. It's only a credit card debt."

"Only?" I spluttered. "That three thousand pounds you just earned in there represents my food money for the next three years. I have nothing. Now I know I never will, either." A fat tear rolled down my face. I swiped it away.

"They won't take your food money," he said softly. He seemed genuinely concerned. His kindness and my own embarrassment at the situation caused more tears to leak out. "You said in there that you worked," he said, pointing towards the court with his chin. "What do you do?"

"I'm a veterinary nurse," I told him, "but my hours were cut last year, so I'm on a lot less money than I was, hence the trouble I had paying MVDI." I played with my napkin, twisting it between my fingers, praying that he'd hurry up and drink his coffee.

"So how come you weren't represented? Any lawyer worth his salt would've stopped you going to court today, racking up costs."

"I couldn't afford it." The truth was that I hadn't even tried to get help; too ashamed to admit how badly I'd fucked up. I wasn't about to share that nugget with him though. He was clearly one of life's winners: good-looking, great hair, and immaculately dressed. He was wearing what was obviously a good quality navy wool coat over his suit. I doubted his feet were wet. Mine were like blocks of ice.

He interrupted my pity party. "Did you try Citizen's Advice or National Debtline?"

I shook my head.

"They could have helped you, even though you work. There are benefits available for people on low incomes. They can guide you to what you're entitled to." He smiled tentatively.

"I don't want to be 'entitled,' thank you. I just want to work, earn and pay my way like everyone else. It seems I can't even do that." I paused. "Mr McCarthy."

"Andy... please."

"Andy. Thanks for your fake concern, but I'm sure you have better things to do than deal with a fuck-up like me, who you've just shafted for every penny I'll earn for the foreseeable future. You may think it's 'only,' but to me it was everything. You've had your gawp, assuaged yourself by saving my life. Your good deed for the day is done. I'd appreciate some alone time now." I stared down into my coffee, resisting the urge to walk out and leave it there. Lattes were a rare treat, and I was enjoying mine. It was too hot to just gulp down though; I wanted time to savour it.

He rolled his eyes. "First off, it's not fake concern. Secondly, you just frightened the shit out of me back there. I watched you crying outside the court. I followed you to give you back your bag, I just didn't know how to approach you. I knew from the case notes that you lived by Bromley North, so when you headed south, I followed. I didn't realise you were planning to fling yourself under a train though. I need this coffee as much as you do." His eyes flashed anger as he spoke. "I could've got you sectioned by mental health back there." He tilted his head towards the station.

"Why don't you?" I challenged.

"Because I happen to think you've got enough problems going on. Getting locked up in a mad-house won't help."

I couldn't fault his logic. I watched as he took a sip of his coffee. His mouth was perfectly sculptured. The man had just about everything going for him, lucky bastard. "Thank you," I said, figuring that if I played nice, he'd congratulate himself and be on his way, leaving me with my latte. He nodded, his eyes boring into me. It made me a bit uncomfortable, as though he was trying to see into my head.

"It's a permanent solution to a temporary problem," he said eventually.

"What is?"

"Suicide. No amount of money is worth a life."

"That's easy for you to say," I snapped, "you're not the one who's gonna have bailiffs taking your telly."

"That won't happen." He was self-assured as he spoke.

"Will they tell my boss about this?" I asked. He shook his head.

"No, not for an unsecured debt."

I relaxed a little. "So what will they do?"

"They'll send you a form to fill in with your income and expenditures. They aren't allowed to take your rent, bill, or food money. They have to accept what you can spare. They'll ask you every six months if it's changed."

"I see." I began to feel stupid for reacting as I had. I wished I'd used Citizen's Advice; I wouldn't have felt so scared.

"I can help you," he said.

"I'm sure you could, but why would you? I can't pay you."

"To assuage my guilt," he replied. I sat back and stared at him, wondering if he'd been genuinely upset watching me try and end it all. I filed the idea for later consideration and took a welcome sip of coffee. He was watching every move I made. I shivered, the combination of being thoroughly wet, cold, and tired began to have its effect. My hair, previously plastered down, began to dry in an unruly mop. I blew a tendril out of my face, hoping that I hadn't uncovered the ugly scar on my forehead.

"I'll see you home," Andy told me. I could tell by his tone that it wasn't a request. I was puzzled as to why he felt responsible for me. I was nothing to him. I drained the last dregs of latte and stood up.

"That won't be necessary, I can walk," I said.

"It's still pissing down, and getting dark. Indulge me."

I followed him out, my shoes still squelching. "Is that noise you?" He asked, looking down at my feet.

"Yeah," I tried to sound nonchalant. I could feel the familiar blush begin its unstoppable rise up my neck. He flagged a taxi immediately, clearly one of those people who don't have to stand in the rain too long. He held open the door and guided me in.

"Thirty-three Freelands Road please," he said to the cabbie. I was just about to ask him how he knew my address, when I remembered he'd been given all my details by the court.

"Where do you live?" I asked.

"Chislehurst."

I didn't answer. I didn't really know what to say. Making small talk wasn't a forte of mine, especially with a gorgeous man who happened to have saved my life. Instead, I just looked out of the rain-streaked windows as we sped towards my bedsit.

When we pulled up, I opened the door, hopped out and quickly turned. "Goodbye and thank you." He'd been preparing to get out with me, my body language made it quite clear that he wasn't about to be invited in.

"Goodbye Miss Higgs," he said, looking amused.

"Sally. My name's Sally," I corrected him.

As I closed the door, I heard him say, "Till we meet again Sally."

CHAPTER 2

The only great thing about my bedsit was that it was warm. For some fortuitous reason, the radiator in my room was the hottest in the house. As soon as I got in, I peeled off my soggy clothes, carefully hanging up my useless coat, leaving everything else in a heap on the floor for the wash.

My little studio, as the letting agent had called it, was clean and tidy. I didn't have much, but what I had, I took great care of. I wrapped a robe around myself and filled the kettle.

After a cup of tea, followed by a long, hot shower, I felt better. Having faced the demon that was MVDI and learning that they had no real power over me, I almost felt jubilant. The debt would still need to be repaid, but in the meantime, they couldn't make me homeless or throw me in prison.

I picked up the pile of clothes and took them downstairs to the laundry area, a cubbyhole beside the main door, which housed a washing machine and tumble dryer. As soon as I'd got the machine started, I noticed someone outside, pressing one of the buzzers for a bedsit. Pulling the robe tight around me, I padded over to open the door for them.

Andy McCarthy was on the doorstep holding what looked like a bag of takeaway. "Hi Sally. I came to help you sort out all the stuff we talked about earlier," he said brightly. "I brought Chinese too. Have you eaten yet?"

Dumbfounded, I shook my head. Politeness took over as I stood aside to let him in. He'd shed the suit and formal coat and was wearing navy chinos and a leather jacket. He followed me up the stairs to my room.

It's always a little awkward entertaining anyone in a bedsit, especially someone of the opposite sex, as the bed is always there, in the room. Thankfully, the landlord had also provided two armchairs with an Ikea coffee table between them. "Shall I hang your coat?" I asked. He shucked it off and handed it to me. It weighed a ton, being made of thick, luxurious leather. Underneath he was wearing a cable-knit sweater, one of those preppy-type ones. I could tell he had broad shoulders and slim hips. The man really had been blessed. Faced with such a good-looking man, I instinctually pulled at my fringe, checking it was in place, covering my scar.

"Shall we eat first?" Andy asked, pulling cartons out of one of the bags he was holding. He placed another bag containing papers on the floor and set about opening the takeaway boxes, laying them out on the table. "I didn't know what you'd like, so I got some choices," he said. "I've brought some wine too."

"Smells wonderful," I said, before I could think of anything snarky to say. I should've been annoyed at him turning up unannounced, but to be truthful, I was grateful. Not only had he saved my life, he would both help me and feed me. All the poor bloke needed was a white charger and a suit of armour, and I'd have fallen at his feet. I wondered if he expected sex in return. In my own mind, it would've been a fair trade for the help he'd given.

I pulled myself together and grabbed two forks. "I'm fine with chopsticks," he said, opening the plastic-wrapped ones that came with the takeaway. He then proceeded to use them expertly to pick up chow mein and rice, using the lid of the carton as a sort of plate. I chose some beef in black bean sauce, which was delicious, as was the wine he'd brought.

"I didn't realise how hungry I was," I remarked.

"You've had a difficult day. When I get stressed I'm always starving," he replied, before helping himself to some prawn toast.

"I normally can't eat when I'm worried," I confessed. I watched as he leaned over to refill my glass. He didn't seem to be drinking much wine himself. "Are you driving?" I asked.

"Yes. I'd better just stick to one small glass."

I marvelled at his self-control. Not being able to say no to a second, or third, glass was the reason I'd lost my licence. I kept that to myself though. He already knew I was a fuck-up; I didn't need to ram the point home.

With the TV on low in the background, I began to relax. It was the type of evening I'd craved. Having a nice meal and wine, with a good-looking man who seemed comfortable in my company. I wondered if he had a girlfriend. If he did, then she was a lucky girl. I imagined he'd be with someone pretty, with long blonde hair and big boobs. He seemed the type of man who'd get the most popular girls eating out of his hand. I'd always been the skinny, shy one. Due to my lack of funds, I'd not had a haircut in well over a year. I wore leaky, cheap shoes and chose my clothes on the basis of whether or not they helped me to blend in.

I wanted to ask him questions about himself but wasn't sure how to phrase them. It wasn't as though we were friends. I wasn't entirely sure what we were, apart from hopeless fuck-up and the bloke who felt sorry for her. In the end, I decided I needed to make some small talk.

"How long have you been a lawyer?"

He took a sip of his wine. "Nine years. How long have you been a veterinary nurse?"

"I started when I was sixteen really, although I didn't become fully qualified till I was eighteen, so six years."

"Must be a very rewarding job?" He asked.

I smiled, probably for the first time that day. "I love it. I've always loved animals. There are parts of my job that can be sad, but on the whole, it's my dream job." I adored the animals I worked with, nursing them back to health after operations and looking after them when they were feeling poorly. It was probably the only thing I felt I did well. If the truth be told, I related better to animals than humans. "What about you, did you always want to do law?"

"Not really," he said, shocking me, "but it's a good, secure job. My dad was a lawyer, still is actually. It was kind of expected."

"What did you want to be?" I asked. I was curious.

"No idea," he admitted. "Apart from professional footballer, racing car driver, or astronaut, I was a bit clueless. Law seemed ideal. On the whole it's mainly paperwork. It's rare I have to attend court."

"Only when a stupid girl tries to challenge things, eh?"

He smiled, "something like that, yeah."

"Do many people try it?" I asked. I was genuinely interested. I'd read a lot online about people challenging debts.

He shook his head. "Not really. The credit agreements are pretty watertight. Unless it's a really old agreement, there's no chance. Even with the historical ones, you've got to know how to challenge them. I think people talk the talk online, then quietly accept the debt before it goes to court."

"But it all seemed so genuine," I exclaimed. Almost instantly feeling stupid at how easily I'd believed what I'd read online. "I'm such a sucker, aren't I?"

He nodded, his expression wary. He was probably terrified of upsetting me; worried I'd fling myself out of the window if he so much as said a wrong word. I really regretted the train incident. "I'm not generally unstable and suicidal," I told him, "You can tell me how stupid I've been."

"Good to know," he said gruffly. He seemed to be suppressing a smirk. "I thought we could go through all these papers. I did promise I'd help you, and this is all the practical stuff." He pulled some neat files from the bag beside him, and put them on the table. I quickly cleared away the cartons, surreptitiously saving the leftovers in the fridge for the following day. By the time I was finished, he had everything laid out and ready.

"I'm gonna need your last six payslips," he said. I quickly found them and cringing, handed them to him.

He read through them quickly. "This isn't minimum wage."

The words hung between us. I didn't really know what to say. Eventually I found my voice. "Isn't it?" I asked weakly. "My hours were cut two years ago, that's why it's so low."

He frowned, before pulling out his iPhone and doing some calculations. "According to this, you've been being paid the under twenty-one rate. You're twenty four....right?"

I nodded.

"We need to tackle that. Are you only working twenty hours a week now?"

"Paid hours, yes."

"Are you doing unpaid?"

I nodded. I'd known I was being taken advantage of, but I hadn't been able to let the animals suffer. The head of the practice had cut staffing to the bone during the recession. Even as things had improved, and we were busier again, she'd not increased either the staff, or our wages, content that we were breaking our necks to ensure that the work was done.

"I love the animals, I couldn't just leave them just because I wasn't being paid..." I'd been taken advantage of, but had been so scared of losing my job that I'd never complained. "You must think I'm beyond stupid."

He didn't answer straight away, just filled in form after form with my pay details. Eventually he looked up. "That's not my place to say. I do think you've been taken advantage of though."

"Story of my life," I muttered, before standing to fill the kettle. "Is tea OK? I don't have any coffee."

"Fine thanks," he said, sounding distracted. "How much is your rent and rates, electric, water, that kind of thing?"

I knew the numbers by heart. It's what comes of living close to the edge of a salary. I'd spent many evenings poring over the figures, trying to work out ways of making my meagre wages stretch just a little bit further. I reeled them off, answering his questions easily, without having to find papers or past bills. He filled in the forms as he went.

I sat quietly as he totted up all the columns of figures, frowning at the end result. "Are you only spending thirty quid a week on food and clothing?" He asked eventually.

"Something like that, yeah," I admitted.

"How?"

That single word was loaded, like a bullet. It pierced through my bravado, straight through the defensive walls I'd built around myself, and hit me square. I wasn't living like a normal person. I was the twenty-first century equivalent of a peasant.

"I don't know," I whispered, avoiding his eyes. "I'm just... careful."

"How on Earth are you feeding yourself on thirty bloody quid a week? Our takeaway just cost more than that." His voice had raised; his anger on show. I stared at the floor, fighting the urge to apologise for being poor and exploited. "I'm sorry, I didn't mean to shout at you. I don't mean to judge."

"Now do you understand?" I mumbled, referencing my feelings of complete and utter hopelessness earlier that afternoon. I glanced up at him, expecting to see disdain or pity. Instead his lovely face belied a compassion that had been missing in the coffee shop. He knew all the facts, and I hadn't held anything back.

"I'll help you," he said. "First of all, I'll sort MVDI. You'll be paying a token one-pound a month. There'll be no more interest added either. It may well be worth declaring you bankrupt. I'll look into it for you, but I think you're just under the threshold for it to be allowed. Second, I'll send off these forms to get you the benefits that you're entitled to."

"I don't want to be on benefits."

"Tough. You can't live on what you've got. Third, I'll see about your wages. I'll enlist HMRC to do a payroll check, so that they uncover it and force your boss to pay you what's owed. Better than you having to confront them yourself."

I hadn't thought of that. To be truthful, it hadn't occurred to me that the taxman would be bothered that someone was being paid less than minimum wage. "Will they really tell her to pay me more?"

He eyed me strangely. "Yes," he said slowly, as if talking to a child. "It's why it's called minimum wage, it's the law."

"I didn't know."

"Well you do now." He sorted through the papers, clipping piles together. "I need you to read through these and sign them. I've done some stamped, addressed envelopes already. I can drop them in the postbox on my way home."

I did as he asked and watched as he prepared the envelopes, mesmerised by his tongue licking the gum to seal them. I wasn't sure if he realised the effect he was having on me. He was probably used to women staring at his pretty face.

"I'll ring you when I've sorted HMRC," he said. "What's your number?"

I shook my head. "I don't have one, sorry." My elderly pay-as-you-go had given up the ghost a month earlier, probably worn out from all the MVDI calls. They'd been ringing me several times a day, so it'd been a bit of a relief when it broke. I watched as Andy rolled his eyes at yet another example of my sorry state. "You can email me though. I still have my computer." I scribbled my email address down and handed it to him. He shoved it into his pocket and placed a business card down on the coffee table.

"Thank you," I blurted, "for all this. You have no idea how much you've helped."

He stared at me a little strangely. "No problem. It's the least I can do." With that, he stood to leave. I retrieved his jacket from its little peg and handed it to him. "I'll be in touch. Any problems, ring me. My number's on my card."

"Will do."

With that, he was gone. I wondered if I'd ever see him again.

There's a lot to be said for facing one's demons head-on. Since the court case, and subsequent help from the man I'd thought was my nemesis, I'd felt a lightness I hadn't experienced for a very long time. Just knowing that at some point, life could change for the better, made my immediate situation easier to bear. Just that morning, I'd had a letter from Alpha, accepting my offer of payment set at one pound a month. I'd dutifully filled in the direct debit form and sent it straight back, relieved of the burden of fear that they'd suddenly decide they wanted my entire salary. The next few days passed by without event.

A week later, I'd agreed to stay behind at work for an extra couple of hours to care for a particularly poorly spaniel who'd been operated on earlier that morning for a strangulated hernia, which was a serious op. Poor Bessie's life was touch-and-go, and she really needed intensive nursing. I was just nipping to the loo when I saw a suited man at the desk. My stomach leapt, thinking it was Andy, but on closer inspection, I could see that it was just someone who looked a bit like him. As I came back through, I saw the practice manager speaking to him, and heard the words "HMRC inspection."

I scurried back to the recovery room, an involuntary blush covering my cheeks as a result of a guilty conscience. Thankfully, Bessie woke up shortly afterwards, so I was able to concentrate on her, taking my mind off my traitorous behaviour. As I gently cleaned her up, I mused that maybe I'd done the right thing. My colleagues were all working unpaid overtime too, which was unfair, and if they were also being paid less than the law allowed, then my actions would do us all a favour. In the meantime, I had a pen to clean out and some medication to administer.

The suit was still in the office with the practice manager when I left, so there was no way of telling what was going on. I handed Bessie over to my colleague, Maria, who was equally conscientious about caring for our charges, clocked out, and made my way home.

I walked in to find a couple of letters in my pigeonhole. One was from the legal firm confirming that they'd received my direct debit mandate and would be in touch in six months to see if my circumstances had changed. The other was from the benefit office, telling me I was entitled to something called universal credit. I would get almost a hundred pounds a month towards my living expenses. It would be paid into my bank account on the same day as my salary. It wasn't a fortune, but would help an enormous amount. I practically did a dance around my room.

As I ate my beans on toast, I fired up my elderly laptop to email Andy with the good news. As soon as I clicked onto my emails, I saw I'd received one from him already, asking if anyone had turned up at my work that day, followed by a winking smiley. A plume of excitement rose in my belly at the thought of uptight Andy sending such a fun email. I immediately replied to him, sharing the news of my benefit award and the arrival of a tax inspector at the practice. I added in a couple of smileys myself, partly to be friendly and partly to show that I wasn't depressed and liable to fling myself under anything that might squash me.

All evening, I kept one eye on my laptop, hoping he'd reply. By ten, it was abundantly clear that he wouldn't. Disappointed, I closed the computer and set it on the floor. I pulled the duvet around me and nodded off.

The buzzing sound permeated my dream, relentless and insistent. I came to and realised it was my front door buzzer being pressed almost continuously. I pulled my dressing gown over my pyjamas and padded down to the front door. I didn't want to just let whoever it was into the building. "Who is it?" I called out.

"S'Andy, let me in," a voice called back. Gingerly, I opened the door to find a clearly rather drunk Andy, glassy-eyed and swaying slightly.

"What are you doing here?" I asked.

"You should be out celebrating," he slurred, before lurching forward into the foyer. I closed the door quickly; it was freezing out. "I wanted to buy you a drink, to celebrate, but I couldn't phone you," he rambled. "You need to get a phone, little poor girl."

I froze. He actually called me "little poor girl."

"I think you've had too much to drink," I said. "Please tell me you're not driving?"

"Carsathome," he slurred.

"Good, well give me your phone, and I'll sort you a taxi," I said.

"I wanted to see you, to celebrate," he insisted, before lumbering up the stairs towards my room.

"Andy," I hissed, "you can't go up there."

"I came here before. When I saved you," he mumbled before resuming his unsteady climb. Huffing somewhat, I stood behind him, worried that he'd lose his footing and fall down the stairs. A dead lawyer in my building was all I was short of.

The heat in my room seemed to subdue him. He ignored the chairs and sat on the side of my bed. I decided to make us some tea. "So why did you come round?" I pressed. I was secretly quite pleased to see him, having convinced myself that he'd simply done his good deed and would disappear out of my life.

"I went out with the boys. Phil got a new job. You should celebrate too. You need a new job." He was incoherent.

"Is there someone I can call to come and get you?" I asked. He looked up at me with unfocused eyes.

"No," he shook his head violently from side to side. The movement made him topple slightly. I heard a sickening crunch as his foot came down on my laptop.

"Sorry," he looked like a contrite drunk. "I don't know what that was, but I'll fix it."

"I doubt it," I muttered. I turned back to our teas. By the time I'd poured it, Andy had passed out on my bed.

I debated what to do. He was far too heavy for me to lift and was still wearing a jacket. Sighing loudly, I placed the bowl from the sink beside him and assessed how to at least remove his shoes and coat to make him more comfortable.

I stared at him for a while; his face was angelic and serene in sleep. A small dimple on his chin, coupled with his perfectly-square jaw, gave him the appearance of an old-fashioned movie star. He was too beautiful, too successful, and too clever for someone like me. I knew that he felt sorry for me, even had some kind of Sir Galahad complex towards me, but I'd bore him after a while. He'd get frustrated at my fuck-ups, and I had no clue as to whether he actually fancied me or not. I wasn't bad-looking, apart from my scar, which I kept carefully covered. Men had liked me in the past, chased me even. For some reason, I'd always attracted the wrong 'uns, the losers and users. Men had wanted me for just sex, for a shoulder to cry on, or just an emotional prop when the world was punishing them for their own poor choices. Andy was different. He was a professional man, educated and clever. Looking at him sleeping, I wondered what had driven him to get so drunk, or whether it was a regular occurrence.

I began with his shoes, unlacing them carefully and sliding them off. He didn't even stir, so feeling braver, I tackled his jacket, rolling him into the middle of the bed onto his front in order to peel it off his broad shoulders. Even when I had to tug a bit to get the sleeves off, he barely moved. He was most definitely out for the count. He was also sprawled across the middle of my bed, which wasn't large by any standards.

I glanced at my poor laptop, which now had a large dent in the lid. From the crunch it'd made, I suspected that the screen was broken inside. It had been my only means of communication. I'd have to sneakily log into my emails at work, which was against the rules, but until I could save up for a second-hand computer, it was my only choice.

Sighing loudly, I pulled the seat cushions off the two armchairs and made myself a makeshift bed on the floor. I yanked a pillow off my bed and pulled an old throw out of the cupboard. It wasn't terribly comfortable, but better than nothing. At least I wasn't working the next day, so lack of sleep wouldn't be an issue.

"Where am I?"

His voice woke me up. I shifted slightly on my temporary bed; unleashing stiffness from Hell as my poor shoulders objected to the hard floor I'd subjected them to. I struggled up onto my elbows to peek over the side of the bed. Andy's eyes were open and he was looking around. Daylight was streaming in the window, illuminating my little studio.

"You're in my bed, in my flat," I said. My voice made him jump. He turned to look down at me.

"How on Earth did I get here?" He asked.

"You turned up here last night and passed out on my bed. You were as drunk as a skunk."

"Why are you on the floor?"

"Because you passed out sprawled across the middle of my bed."

"Jesus, my head hurts," he complained, flopping back down.

I got up to make us both some tea. It was only eight in the morning. He was probably still a bit drunk from the night before. At least he hadn't puked in my room, unlike my ex. It'd taken weeks to get rid of the revolting smell. I rinsed out our cups from the previous night and made two fresh teas, making sure that they were nice and strong. I wandered back over to the bed where Andy was laying quietly, his arm across his forehead. He sat up to take the mug from me. I perched on the end of the bed to drink mine.

It was all a bit surreal, me in stripy pyjamas, drinking tea with a rather hung over Adonis. I checked that my fringe hadn't scrunched up during the night.

"We didn't? I mean… I wasn't inappropriate was I?" He asked.

I shook my head. "You were way too pissed for any of that. You just rambled on for a bit, trod on my laptop then passed out," I told him. He had the grace to blush, which was adorable.

"I'm sorry. I don't normally drink that much. My younger brother, Phil just got a new job, so a bunch of us went out for a drink. God only knows how I ended up here. I must've been trying to walk home. Dunno where Phil ended up. Can I borrow your loo?"

I tipped my head towards the door to my bathroom. Andy heaved himself off the bed and staggered over. I sipped my tea while I waited, wondering what would happen next. When he returned, he sat back down on the bed and picked up my laptop. "I did this?" He asked. He shook it slightly, unleashing the rattle of a broken screen inside.

"Yeah, you trod on it. It was my only means of communication," I stated. Good manners would have meant me telling him that it was nothing, easily replaced, but I was over being a nice girl.

"I'll replace it," he said, placing it back on the floor. "Was there anything else I broke or damaged?" I shook my head.

"Why did you get so drunk?" I was curious.

"The boys were doing shots, so I joined in. I'm not good at holding my beer." He looked sheepish. "Have you got to work today?"

"No, it's my day off."

"Got anything planned?"

I shook my head. He seemed to forget that I was perma-skint. "I might take a walk up to the library later. I need to take some books back and get new ones."

"I need to go home and get a shower. Maybe I could pick you up and take you for breakfast? I need a full English to shift this hangover."

"OK," I said. I was a little wary, unsure of his motives. He seemed to want to be friends, but I wasn't sure. It was, of course, possible that he thought I needed feeding up and breakfast was part of his plan to make sure I wasn't malnourished.

"Excellent," he said, before striding over to his jacket and pulling his iPhone out of the pocket. He jabbed at the screen and ordered a cab, telling them he was going to Yester Park in Chislehurst. "Give me about an hour," he said, "and I'll come and get you. I know a great place that does organic fry-ups. We'll go there."

With that, he was gone.

I tidied up, puzzled that he wanted to spend the morning with me. Regardless of whether he was only doing it because he felt sorry for me, I was determined to enjoy myself and not play the part of the tragic pauper.

I did my hair carefully, blow-drying it as smooth as I could. I added a touch of makeup and dressed in my favourite black jeans and a loose pink sweater. Shoes were more of a problem. I'd dried out the leaky heels, but they didn't go with jeans or feel right for a Saturday morning breakfast date. In the end I had to settle for a pair of trainers and socks. They might be too casual, but at least my feet would be warm and dry.

I grabbed my jacket and bag when I heard the buzzer go, skipping down the stairs happily. Andy smiled as I opened the door, making my stomach jump. The man had a smile that could corrupt a nun. He was fresh from the shower and had a little more colour in his cheeks. I was also delighted to see that he was also wearing jeans and trainers, coupled with a rugby shirt and his leather jacket. He looked almost edible.

He glanced down at my feet, "I meant to warn you to wear flats. It can get a bit muddy where we're going."

I was intrigued. He led me to a shiny, silver BMW and opened the passenger door for me. I slid into the luxurious soft leather and surveyed the interior. It smelt like a new car, and I could see that Andy liked to keep things neat and tidy. "Is this car new?" I asked when he'd hopped into the driver's seat.

"Fairly new, I bought it about eight months ago," he said absentmindedly as he started the engine.

"It smells new," I commented. He didn't reply, just concentrated on pulling out of Freelands Road, across the traffic heading towards Bromley Town Centre. Once out on the main road, he switched on the radio, which was tuned to Smooth FM, which I felt was rather predictable. He drove carefully but confidently, precise in his movements. "Where are we going?" I asked as we headed down the A21 into Kent.

"There's a little organic café in a country park not far from here. They do the best breakfasts around. We can walk through the woods there too. It's a lovely place."

We drove for about twenty minutes before he pulled into a wooded car park, just off a little lane. "We're a little early yet, it doesn't open till ten. Shall we walk first? I need to clear my head a bit."

"Sure."

We walked along a little path, across an open space, towards the woods. Andy seemed a little quiet, maybe lost in his own thoughts. I hoped he didn't regret asking me. "How's your hangover?" I asked, hoping to break the ice a little."

"A bit better," he said, flashing me his lovely smile. "Fresh air always helps doesn't it?"

"I find spending a day under the duvet works for me," I replied.

"I can't imagine you drunk."

"I've been drunk a few times. Why can't you imagine it?"

"Because you're so reserved," he said, surprising me. "OK, I bet you're one of those girls that gets upset and cries when they've had too much."

"Wrong," I laughed, "I get giggly and chatty and flirt shamelessly."

"Really? Now that I'd like to see," he said.

"Why's that?" I asked. I found him impossible to fathom out. I needed to find out if he was actually interested in me or just felt sorry for me. If I was just a charity case to him, I'd stuff my face at breakfast, then be on my merry way. If he was interested, then I'd be a bit more reserved.

He just shrugged. "I think you'd be fun." He paused, as though he wanted to say more. I waited. "It'd be nice to see you having a good time, loosening up. I suppose I met you on the worst day of your life, so I think of you as being sad and depressed."

I felt quite offended. "I'm not a sad or miserable person at all, and I can assure you that it most certainly wasn't the worst day of my life. I don't think anything will ever top that day." I sounded fiercer than I meant to, but he'd made a lot of assumptions about me. I decided that he was being kind out of pity or charity. I'd eat the bastard out of house and home, then not see him again.

"Tell me about your family," I said to change the subject. I liked hearing about intact families, it was a kind of masochistic pleasure I had.

"It's quite a big family. I've got an older brother then two younger ones. My dad was a lawyer and my mum doesn't work. We all get along pretty well. What about you?"

"My parents died when I was eight. No brothers or sisters. I have an uncle though, who I last saw just after the accident. Think he was scared he'd get lumbered with me."

"I can't imagine not having a family. No wonder you felt all alone that day."

"I'm used to it," I said. As we strolled along, I tried to visualise what it must have been like having three brothers, all the noise and games that they'd have played. Having a mum who was there when you got in from school, possibly with home-baked cookies waiting, was a regular fantasy of mine, as was a dad who wore slippers and told amazing bedtime stories. My own dad had been a rather distant character, who'd worked a lot and got home too late most of the time to read stories. My mum hadn't been the earth-mother type at all, happier to go out to work than stay home and bake. I'd been farmed out to childminders a lot.

I smelt the bacon before I even saw where the café was. It permeated the trees, making my stomach growl in anticipation. It was set in an old walled garden, part of the remains of a formal mansion that had once stood on the site. Andy led us inside, and sat at a small table. He handed me the menu. "I'm having the full English, super-sized. What would you like?"

"I'll have the same thanks," I said, before confirming that I'd also like a latte. I watched him as he went up to the bar to order, noting how a group of women seated at another table all followed him with their eyes. One of them glanced over at me, and then whispered something to the group. Instantly my feelings of inadequacy flooded back. I picked up the menu to read it in its entirety, so I didn't have to look at them.

"Sally!" Andy called out, interrupting my studious appraisal of the menu, "Tomato or beans?"

"Tomato please," I called back, "and white bread for my toast." He smiled and turned back to the server.

"Yes, he's with her," I overheard one of the women say. "You can tell by the way he looks at her."

I allowed a small smile to play across my lips at her remark.

"There you go," Andy said as he plonked a cup of latte in front of me. "Our food won't be long."

"I can't wait, just the smell in here is making my tummy rumble," I admitted.

"Me too. You must need feeding up a bit," he said.

I think as soon as he said it, he regretted his comment. I saw a flash of "Oh, shit" cross his face. "Andy," I said. "Are you only doing this because you feel sorry for me? I'd really like to know."

"Of course not," he looked affronted, "I'll admit that I felt guilty in the train station, and that I'm happy I could help you, but it's not out of pity or anything like that."

"And how does your wife or girlfriend feel about you helping me?" It was a sneaky way of getting the question in, but asking outright if he had a girlfriend seemed a bit awkward.

"I don't have a girlfriend and I certainly don't have a wife. Why did you think I was married?"

"I just didn't expect you to be single I suppose."

"Why?"

"Well you must be around thirty."

"Thirty-one actually."

"Right, and you have a good job, and you've not been hit with the ugly stick..."

"I see. Well in answer to your question, I split up with my long-term girlfriend last year."

"I'm sorry." I wasn't really. Inside I was delighted.

"It's OK, it was a mutual decision."

"Were you together long?"

He nodded. "We met at uni, Cambridge. I was reading law, Charlotte read physics."

I did a quick mental arithmetic. "Ten years then?"

"Yeah-- too long really. My career path is rather slow and steady, while she got snapped up by an international investment bank. She's your typical high flier, travelling 'round the world all the time, gathering promotions and accolades. We wanted different things in life."

I took that to mean that he wanted a girl who wouldn't outshine him. Maybe even one who'd be happy to stay home and bake cookies. I couldn't bake, but would be willing to learn.

"So I'm now single for the first time since I was twenty," he went on. "It's not as bad as I expected. Phil, my little brother is staying with me at the moment while he's having some work done on his house, so I'm not lonely. If anything, I'll be pleased when the messy bugger goes home."

"So you come from Chislehurst?" I asked.

"Yep. None of us moved out of the area. My older brother, Matt, he's married with two kids, and lives over by Kemnal Manor. Rupert lives in Sundridge, and Phil lives on Old Hill. None of us strayed far. We all like Mum's Sunday lunches too much."

We were interrupted by the waitress bringing over two enormous breakfasts. There was enough to set me up for an entire week, the plates loaded up to almost overflowing. "I'll be really impressed if you can eat all that," Andy laughed.

"I might be skinny, but I can pack it away," I joked before digging in.

It was glorious. You could tell by the wonderful flavours that it was organic. Even the eggs had bright yellow yolks, unlike the insipid supermarket ones. I completely cleared my plate.

"So, can I ask what happened to your parents?" We'd ordered more lattes, and it seemed that Andy was going to start his fact-finding.

"We were having a day out....to Margate. A lorry hit our car on the way. My parents were both killed instantly. I was injured but obviously survived."

"So what happened to you after that?"

"I was sent to a children's home. When I had to leave at eighteen, they put me in a hostel, which was full of addicts and schizos, so I found my little bedsit myself and moved out."

"That sounds... horrific," he said, his face a picture of sympathy. I just shrugged.

"It's been and gone now. There's times I wish I felt better-equipped for the way the world is, but at eight years old, I didn't know I could ask to be fostered, or demand my social worker actually keep her appointments with me. When you're in a kid's home, you're invisible unless you misbehave."

"So why didn't you play up?"

I shrugged. "Not my nature I suppose, plus I was scared. I had nowhere to go, and I thought they'd throw me out. I just kept quiet and accepted what was happening." I paused, "I was only eight and an orphan you know." Why I felt I had to justify my lack of assertion, I didn't know. Maybe it was the way Andy looked at me, a mixture of pity and annoyance that made me feel as though I'd brought it all on myself.

"Sal, that's…awful. You'd expect a child who'd gone through all that to be looked after properly."

"I think it was why I'm so scared of this debt. I'm not terribly worldly-wise really. All the stuff your parents teach you as you get older, well I missed out on all that. When I got the bedsit, I didn't even know how to change my address or pay bills. It was a steep learning curve." I drained my cup and placed it back down, noting that Andy hadn't even started his. I wondered if he'd mind me drinking it, as in my mind, lattes should never be wasted. To my disappointment, he took a large gulp.

"Yeah well, you've got me now. I can help you with all the practical stuff," he said quietly.

"Why would you do that?" I asked. I really wanted to pin him down as to why he wanted to help me.

"Because I can." He replied, before finishing his coffee in one big gulp. "Now I seem to recall that I owe you a laptop. Shall we go choose one?"

"You don't have to," I said, my "nice" side getting the better of me. I could've kicked her.

"Don't be daft. I promised I'd replace it, so come on." He stood up and pulled on his jacket. I did the same. To my utter shock, he held his hand out for mine in an unconscious gesture. I slipped my hand into his, and we walked back to the car in companionable silence.

CHAPTER 3

I had a new laptop, one that didn't take five minutes to warm up. It was sleek and pristine, and best of all, it was brand new. In addition, Andy had insisted on getting me a new phone, telling me that he would feel better if I had one for my personal safety. I had a stupid, goofy grin on my face all the way back to my bedsit.

I made us some tea, then set about unwrapping my new purchases. We both lay on our fronts across the bed to set up the laptop, setting up my email and sorting my password. One of my neighbours had unlimited Wi-Fi, which we all chipped in a pound a week for, so I logged into it and got online. We spent the next half hour watching funny video clips, laughing at crazy cats and a hilarious dog-shaming site. We clearly shared a similar sense of humour and had both relaxed. The more time I was spent with Andy, the more I fancied him. He hadn't made any sort of move on me, so I wasn't sure if he felt the same.

"Don't you have to go to the library this afternoon?" He asked after we'd watched another episode of "Simon's Cat" on YouTube.

"No rush," I said, "I get the books for a month, and I've only had them two weeks. I'm off on Monday afternoon, so I can change them then."

"Excellent. So what shall we do this evening then?" He propped himself up on his elbow to look at me. I felt a blush rise up my neck. I knew what I wanted to do.

"Aren't you bored with me yet?" I asked.

He gave me one of his heart-melting smiles, "Not yet. Are you bored with me, then?"

I shook my head. "Nope."

"So, we have the choice; dinner out, or a show. We could go see a film, go up to town. Tell me what you'd like. My only caveat is that it must include alcohol."

I frowned slightly, concerned that he had a drinking problem. "Why's it got to include drink? Do you have a dependency?"

He laughed. "Not at all. I just want to get some wine down you, to see you get giggly and flirty."

"I can be all flirty without the wine," I murmured. I gazed at his beautiful face, willing him to move closer. He shifted a little, seemingly unsure about making a move, so I leaned in too, to give him a little encouragement. Instead, he pulled away rather abruptly.

"I need to go home, I've got some errands to do before tonight. I'll pick you up around eight?"

"Oh, OK," I replied. Even I could hear the disappointment in my voice. I must've completely misread the signals. He sat back down on the edge of the bed.

"Sally, before things go any... further, there's a discussion we need to have." He seemed embarrassed.

"No need. Look, I'm sorry if I embarrassed you. Please forget it." I knew my face was blushing pink with my mortification of having assumed he'd be interested in me. I turned away and collected our cups, moving to the sink to avoid him seeing my face.

"Listen, thanks for everything, but I'd rather get an early night, if you don't mind." I began to wash up.

"No, you've got it all wrong," he protested. "I wasn't rejecting you at all, but there is something I need to tell you before we go any further. I mean, it's probably quite obvious by now that we fancy each other."

"It wasn't obvious to me," I muttered, still refusing to look at him.

"Well it should've been," he snapped. "Do you really think I'd be hanging round you if I wasn't interested?"

"I don't know," I admitted. I turned to face him. "All I know is that you just turned me down."

"No," he said, "I just tried to tell you that there's a discussion we need to have first."

"What sort of discussion? If it's safety, then use a condom, and yes, I'm on the pill."

"No, it's not that sort of discussion," he said, sadness creeping into his voice, "I'll pick you up at eight and tell you over dinner." He picked up his coat and slid it on, before joining me at the sink. To my surprise, he leaned down and kissed me gently, a soft, sweet kiss, only distinguishable from a friendly kiss by virtue of it being on my lips. His hand cupped my jaw in a tender gesture. "Eight o'clock," he repeated. Then he was gone.

My mind raced with possibilities, different scenarios that he might want to discuss. I'd read "Fifty Shades," along with the rest of the world, and my main worry was that he was one of those kind of men. As much as I fancied him and was eager to get naked with him, there was no way I could join in with any kind of BDSM rubbish. Being tied up or whipped just to get a shag wasn't my idea of a good time, and despite being a fuck-up of epic proportions, I wasn't a masochist. It would be a bad decision too far if I was to agree to a setup like that.

My other concern was that he might have a permanent STD, like herpes or something. I knew from experience that I was always the unlucky person who beat the odds on having bad stuff happen. If there was a one in ten chance of catching something, I'd be that one. Again, I made the decision not to risk it.

By the time I started getting myself ready, I'd pretty much talked myself out of seeing him again. I'd decided not to sleep with him, as I was convinced that whatever the "discussion" was, it wouldn't be good. Normal men didn't require a "talk" before they jumped your bones.

What to wear that evening was a problem. I didn't have a cute little black dress, nor did I have a lot of choice in my rather limited wardrobe. In the end, I chose black trousers and a loose, dressy top. I finished it off with my leaky shoes and the smart but useless coat. I prayed it wouldn't rain. Staring at myself in the mirror, I came to the conclusion that I didn't look cheap or peasant-like. I'd twisted my too-long hair up into a knot at my nape, leaving a few tendrils to fall around my face. I watched a YouTube tutorial on smoky eye makeup and had done a pretty decent attempt. I felt groomed and attractive, the loose top stopping me looking too skinny and accentuating my bust, the only bit of curve I possessed. I was even wearing my "best" underwear, the set I kept for when I thought it might be seen. The girl in the mirror was determined to shag Andy McCarthy, no matter what he said.

He arrived bang on time, of course, dressed in a suit and open-necked shirt. My tummy flipped at the sight of him, if his "talk" was so bad he thought I might be put off, he wouldn't have made so much effort, I reasoned. "Sally, you look... wow," he said, smiling widely at me. "We're going to Chapter One, I managed to get a table."

"Fantastic," I replied, delighted. I'd heard all about Chapter One, it was the only restaurant in Bromley that had a Michelin star. It was too expensive for me to visit, or for any of my previous loser boyfriends to take me. I was glad I'd made an effort with my makeup.

Andy had a cab waiting, so we hopped in the back. "You look lovely," he said, before squeezing my hand.

"Thank you," I replied, "so do you."

"I'm not sure whether I need a tie or not, so I brought one just in case. I've not been there for a while."

I realised he was nervous, as he rambled on about dress codes. My heart sank a little, because if he was nervous, it didn't bode well. I realised that all my tough talk about not sleeping with him if he was pervy would fly out the window when faced with his perfect body and movie-star looks. It'd have to be really bad to have me doing big legs out of his life.

Chapter One was an impressive place from all angles. It sat like an enormous detached house in the centre of Locksbottom Village, even becoming a local landmark. We pulled into the car park outside the covered portico. The staff even opened the car doors for us, before showing us into the lobby and handing us over to the staff in there.

I felt embarrassed handing my cheap, thin coat to the attendant, but she didn't react at all. Andy was pleased that his tie wouldn't be necessary. We were shown through to a fairly private table at the back of the restaurant, which was plainer than I expected. "Would you like an aperitif?" The impeccably-attired maitre d' asked.

"I'll wait for the wine thanks," I told him. I needed to keep a clear head and rarely realised I'd had too much to drink until it was too late. He handed Andy a wine list and gave us both menus to peruse.

I nearly had heart failure when I opened mine. I had no idea what any of it was. It was written in a foreign language, all *volute* this and *jus* that. Andy must have sensed my discomfort.

"Would you like me to order for you?"

"Please," I said, relieved at not having to try and pronounce anything. For the first time ever, I regretted sitting at the back and not paying attention in French classes at school.

"You can choose from beef, chicken, fish, lobster, or veal," he said.

"Beef please."

"I'll surprise you with your starter, shall I? Is there anything you don't eat?"

I shook my head. I'd never eaten anywhere like that before, so had no clue what the food would be like. Whatever he ordered, I'd eat, even if I hated it. I'd seen the prices. "Red or white?" He asked, reading the wine list.

"I don't mind. I like both. Whatever goes better with our food." I was so out of my depth in there that I didn't want to make even the smallest decision. I normally bought the one ninety nine specials out of the supermarket.

I sat back and watched Andy order. Just the way he pronounced the words so confidently was a huge turn-on. He even knew about wine, asking the wine waiter about the estate the wine was from. Pulling my eyes away from Andy, I glanced around the room. It was mainly tables of twos and fours. The women expensively-dressed and glamorous but relaxed, chatting happily without the worries of the world on their shoulders. These were life's winners in their natural environment. I felt like an interloper, intruding into their world to gawp.

"Penny for them?" Andy's voice penetrated my thoughts. "You're a million miles away."

"Sorry," I smiled at him, "just people watching."

"Do you do that a lot?"

I nodded, wary of the question.

"What do you see when you're watching all these people?" He seemed genuinely interested. I decided honesty would be the best policy.

"These are life's winners. These women in here... they're not worrying about stuff. They all have nice clothes, nice hair. They're happy I guess."

"Everyone has problems," he replied. "Money doesn't solve all life's challenges. These women in here, they'd look at you, with your youth and natural beauty and be envious because you have something they can't ever buy. They can afford a nice dress and a good hairdresser, but they can't buy youth."

He'd pointed out something I'd missed. I was the youngest woman in the room. "Most of the girls your age are either hanging around in a grotty bar right now, hoping some 'Kyle the gas fitter' will buy them a drink, or they're sitting indoors miserable and lonely because they've no-one to babysit." He was scathing, which surprised me.

"You sound snobby. Aren't you forgetting that I'm one of the poorest members of the working class?"

"You're missing my point. Compared to the women in here and the 'normal' girls your own age, what you have is priceless. You just don't have lots of money right now. What you do have, however, is youth without crassness, and a job that you love. That's more than ninety-nine percent of the population."

"Is this the talk we're going to have? Where you tell me how lucky I am? Or is this the lead-up to the bit where you tell me you want to tie me up and whip me?" I went for the jugular. He began to laugh.

"Is that what you thought? Oh, heavens no. I'm not into anything like that. Are you then?"

I shook my head. "I thought that was what you wanted to tell me. I almost didn't come tonight."

He flashed his movie star smile. "That's quite funny. I can't believe you think I'm the type to whip people though. Can't think of anything worse."

I relaxed a little. I was about to ask him to get to the point, when both the wine waiter and our starters interrupted us. A large plate was placed in front of me with a grand flourish. A single, albeit large, ravioli parcel sat in the centre of the plate, looking incredibly lonely. It was accompanied by a thimbleful of sauce, which the waiter poured on carefully, with great reverence.

"It's a lobster ravioli," Andy explained before taking a test sip of the wine, declaring it "fine thanks." I fought the urge to laugh; the pomp and circumstance around what was still just a single ravioli struck me as quite funny.

I will admit that it tasted wonderful, the flavours intense and rich. I stretched it out to three mouthfuls, savouring each one carefully. I could've eaten a whole plateful quite easily. I wondered if the main course would be as skimpy. I'd need to stop for some chips on the way home if it was.

Andy sipped his wine. "I suppose you want to know why I needed to talk to you." I nodded. "In some ways, admitting to being a dominant or a pervert would be easier than what I need to tell you." I watched as he blushed, his awkwardness and embarrassment on show. I leaned in closer for privacy. "You're the first woman since Charlotte," he said. I was surprised but puzzled.

"So you've had a bit of a dry spell. Why is that such an issue?"

"The last few years we were together, we *didn't*. I mean, *I couldn't*."

I caught on. "Have you seen a doctor?"

He nodded. "I had some tests. They said it was psychological. I just..." He struggled for the words. "I needed to tell you first, because if it doesn't happen, I don't want you thinking it's you, because it's not. I don't know if it will happen or not." His eyes were downcast. It had clearly been a difficult thing to admit. My heart went out to him.

"I have a problem too," I confided, "I have scars, from the accident. I'd worry that the scars would put you off."

"Why would scars put me off?" He sounded incredulous. I shrugged.

"Some people are funny about things like that I guess. I have a really bad one on my right leg, one on my stomach, and skin graft scars on my bum."

"I'd be so busy staring at your tits I doubt if I'd even notice," he said, a wicked smile playing across his lips.

Our main course arrived, interrupting the conversation. As the waiter fussed around, pouring the *jus*, I thought about what he'd told me. When we were alone again, I took a deep breath. "When you say it didn't work, does it work OK when you're alone?" It was the most tactful way I could think of to ask if he could still have a wank. If it was floppy all the time, then there was obviously more going on than he was letting on.

I watched a blush creep up his neck, which I thought was super-cute. "Yes, it works just fine. The problem seemed to be when I tried to... erm... *insert it*."

I snorted, narrowly avoiding spitting my wine over the table. "It's not funny," he said, annoyed at me.

"Its your choice of words that's funny, that's all," I said, arranging my features into neutrality. "How come you haven't tried it out since?"

"Because it's awkward. Nerve-wracking, you know." He concentrated on his food, avoiding my eyes.

"Isn't a bit of awkwardness better than years of celibacy?" I was curious.

"I don't know," he confessed. "All I know is that I tried everything, all the pills, pumps, and stuff. None of it worked for me. Charlotte thought it was her. I suppose she couldn't face a celibate life, or at least one without kids. Since then I've been... avoiding it. Until you that is."

"You think you might be OK with me?"

"I don't know, but I'd like to try. I just wanted to warn you, you know, beforehand. I know you're a little... fragile, and I don't want to hurt you any more than you've already been."

"I appreciate your honesty." I didn't really know what else to say.

He leaned forward. "Earlier, when you were people watching, would you have watched us two, thinking we'd have been having the conversation we've just had?" I shook my head, understanding dawning. "Exactly. Everybody has problems. The only problem you have is lack of money."

"I've got more problems than that," I argued. "I'm in hopeless debt, I live in a bedsit and I lost my driving licence." I slipped it in at the end, sort of hoping he wouldn't notice.

"All temporary problems," he dismissed.

"So is yours," I purred in what I hoped was my most seductive voice. He glanced up at me and smiled. "Would it be better if we didn't try actual sex at first?" I asked. "Get comfortable with each other in other ways before we, you know, shag?."

"Maybe, I don't know. Let's play it by ear."

We resumed eating. My meal was lovely, but I was too preoccupied by Andy's revelation to fully appreciate it. Half of me was relieved that he hadn't revealed anything terrible, the other half was disappointed that he wasn't the supreme alpha male I'd expected him to be. In some ways, it made him more real, less of a remote Adonis. I figured the "Mr Grey" types really only did exist in novels.

"Are you disappointed?" He interrupted my train of thought.

"I don't know," I admitted. "I'm surprised, mainly because you seem so confident and so very masculine. I'm pleased that you're not a perv though."

"So you think I'm masculine?" He beamed at me.

"Extremely masculine," I clarified. It seemed to please him. Despite his revelation, I still fancied the pants off him. I longed for him to kiss me, feel his hands on me. It hadn't put me off him, if anything it had become a challenge.

CHAPTER 4

We went back to my place. I was quite eager to see Andy's house, but he explained that his brother Phil would be there, and he'd feel quite inhibited. The moment we walked through the door, my nerves began to kick in. If he were impotent with me, my already-fragile ego would take another battering.

He closed the door behind us, then stalked over, never breaking eye contact. I shivered with anticipation as he grasped my shoulders, pulling me into him. He leaned down to kiss me, softly at first, almost chastely. His lips felt incredibly soft pressed against mine. I relaxed into his hold, just as his tongue met mine for the very first time.

As our tongues gently explored, his hands roamed over my back, into my hair and finally came to rest at my nape. His touch felt confident, almost soothing. I could let this man lead me without fearing him. There was nothing malevolent about him whatsoever; all I sensed was his reverence. He really wanted me. His mouth pushed harder against mine, devouring my lips in a show of barely-restrained passion. It was difficult to believe that he was a man with sexual hang-ups as he pressed kisses up my neck, tasting me.

I threw my head back to give him better access to
my neck, revelling in the feelings of nerve endings
igniting as his lips caressed the sensitive skin. My entire
body was responding to him in a way I'd never
experienced before. I felt my nipples harden and my clit
begin to pulse. He began to push my jacket off my
shoulders. I tensed, knowing he wouldn't stop at just my
outerwear. "What's the matter?" He murmured softly,
obviously aware of my reticence.

"Before we go any further, would you do something
for me?" I asked.

"Sure." He opened his eyes to gaze down at me.
"What would you like me to do?"

"Can you turn the light off before we undress? I
don't want you to see my scars."

I wished I had a beautiful body to present to him,
one that was alluring and perfect. I'd always been
ashamed of my scars and kept them covered as much as
possible. The one on my tummy was a jagged, stretched
mess, a particularly unfortunate one, as I had nice,
perky boobs and a flat stomach. In another life, I'd have
had a bikini model's figure. In this life, I had to put up
with hideous imperfections.

"I'm not worried about them," he said softly, "but if
it makes you feel better..." I watched as he shed his coat
and flicked the switch. The room plunged into darkness,
punctuated only by the glimmer of the streetlights
below, seeping round the edges of the ill-fitting blinds. I
relaxed a little. I preferred sex in the dark, my body
hidden from view. I could concentrate on how he felt,
how he tasted, without pesky self-consciousness getting
in the way.

The Debt

His hands were back on me, roaming over my torso, feeling their way around my body. I pulled the dressy top off over my head and flung it on the chair, desperate to feel him touch my bare skin. I worked on the buttons of his shirt while he kissed me. We were both getting hungrier for each other; our breathing was ragged as I slipped his shirt off his shoulders and ran my hands over his pecs.

I could feel his chest hair. I longed to see it, to see him naked, but that meant exposing myself. It was vital that we were both relaxed, at least for the first time. Taking a deep breath, I unclipped my bra and let it fall to the ground.

His hands immediately wrapped round my breasts, feeling them, kneading them gently. He groaned then dipped down to suck on my nipples, which were standing up proudly, begging for attention. As he flicked each in turn with his tongue, I felt the sensation travel straight to my groin. My clit was pulsating so hard it almost hurt. I prayed to God that he'd be able to give me some relief from the tension building within me.

"I knew once I started kissing you that I wouldn't be able to stop," he murmured, before switching back to my mouth. I felt his hands move to the waistband of my trousers. He fumbled slightly before popping the button and sliding them down my legs, along with my thong.

Not to be outdone, I made short work of opening his trousers. I could feel his erection pressing against the waistband of his Calvins. I ran my hand over the outline of it, making him groan. At that point, we both kicked off our shoes and remaining clothes, both impatient to get to the other.

I grasped his dick as he bent down to kiss me again, pressing his chest to mine. His skin felt warm and wonderfully smooth, like satin wrapped around wood. I jumped with surprise as his finger probed my soaked pussy, sliding back and forth over the slippery folds. My own arousal intensified tenfold, and I was beginning to ache to be filled. His cock was straining in my hand, leaking pre-cum, so I knew he was as turned on as I was. I prayed that it would stay hard enough to at least bring me off.

He guided me onto the bed, where he carried on kissing my body, alternating with licks and nips. His thumb found my clit and began circling. The ache inside grew stronger until I couldn't ignore it any longer. "Andy, please," I gasped.

"Please what?" He said softly.

"Fuck me, please," I begged. I felt the bed shift.

I held my breath as he pressed into me, praying and hoping that it would work.

It felt as hard as steel.

"Oh Jesus," he gasped, as it slid in, right to the hilt, hitting that sweet spot inside. He began to move, cautiously at first, then bolder as he realised it wasn't going soft anytime soon. I reached between us to carry on rubbing my clit. He raised himself up on his arms to allow me easy access.

Damn, it felt good.

He began to fuck me at a punishing pace, filling me totally. I felt a soul-shattering orgasm begin to brew. "Oh God, I'm coming," I called out, lost in the sensations overtaking my body. I was vaguely aware of his breathing becoming ragged before I fell into my climax.

"I can feel it," he gasped, as my insides pulled upwards. "I'm coming too." He pressed in deep and let out a growl as he came. I felt it pulsate inside me.

We stayed like that for a few minutes. I could feel his heart hammering in his chest as we both got our breath back. Eventually, I broke the silence. "Wow... That was incredible."

He nuzzled my neck. "Sally, you have no idea just how incredible that was for me."

We made love three times that night, interspersed with little interludes of talking and finding out about each other. I discovered that he didn't like sushi; he found out that I was terrified of spiders. He also confessed that he'd thought he'd never have sex again. "Nothing wrong with you," I said, giving his dick a little squeeze. If anything, he seemed quite insatiable, which he put down to the excitement of actually being potent again. He'd told me about how horrified he'd been when he'd struggled with impotence, how it would refuse to co-operate, and the terrible arguments and blame that would follow. He'd resigned himself to solo sex until he'd met me.

"Somehow I knew you'd be different," he'd said, before tweaking my nipple playfully. Then he jumped me. Again.

I think we finally dozed off just before the sun came up, snuggled together in my lumpy little bed.

I woke up to a naked Andy making us cups of tea. As I struggled up onto my elbows, I got the first full view of this perfect specimen of manhood. He was muscular, with broad shoulders and slender hips. His bum was rounded and peachy and when he turned around to smile at me, I gulped. His dick was thick and meaty.

Although I'd felt it when we'd made love, the darkness hadn't done it justice. "God you're sexy." The words were out of my mouth before my brain engaged.

"Good morning to you too," he said, smiling warmly, "and I happen to think that you're dead sexy too, so we're even." He brought our teas over and placed them on the bedside table. I instinctively checked my fringe and pulled the covers up higher. He perched on the edge of the bed. "Last night... It was incredible." He began, "It's as though I never had the problem." He kissed me softly and chastely on the lips, avoiding the horrors of morning breath.

"Do you regret telling me?" I asked. He shook his head.

"Not at all. It was important to me that I was honest with you. If I'd kept quiet, it would've added to the pressure, and given that it was a psychological issue, might have made it flop." He smiled at me and stroked my face affectionately. I flinched as he touched my hair, pushing it back from my face, the scar on my forehead in full view.

"Is this one of the scars from your accident?" He asked quietly, staring at it. I felt tears prick the corners of my eyes as the full horror was revealed. I nodded, the lump in my throat preventing me from speaking. In daylight, my defects would put him off, I was certain of it. He traced the line of the scar with his finger, then bent down and kissed it. "You're still beautiful. I don't know what you were worried about," he said finally, "although you are doing a passable impersonation of a panda right now."

I'd forgotten about the smoky eye makeup. In the heat of passion, it'd been the last thing on my mind. I licked my fingers and ran them under my eyes. Judging by the amount stuck to my fingers, I must've looked quite comical. He looked amused as he sipped his tea. "My scars are horrible. I wish they weren't there," I admitted.

"If you hadn't been constantly tugging at your fringe, I'd never have even noticed it. It's very faint. Can I see the others?" He didn't wait for permission. He set his cup down and peeled back the covers, exposing first my breasts, then my tummy. I cringed. "You really have the most magnificent tits," he said. "They felt amazing last night— really perky and full. I love big boobs." He ran his hand over my stomach, over my scar. "Your waist is so tiny."

"The scar is vile though," I pointed out as he stroked it.

"Not really, it's only a scar. The way you spoke about it, I imagined it would be much worse."

I started to relax a little. If he didn't scream when he saw the mess left of my right leg, then I'd be able to walk around naked in front of him. I pulled the cover down a little further and slipped my leg out. "This is the worst one," I told him. My leg had been trapped by a piece of the lorry. It had been touch-and-go whether it should be amputated or not. It was only still there due to a kind nurse who'd stood up for me and convinced the surgeon to try and save it. As it was, I had scars criss-crossing it. The muscles were lumpy and uneven, and due to the extensive damage, shaving was tricky, so hairs showed here and there. In short, it wasn't pretty, but it was better than the alternative and I didn't even have a limp.

"That must've hurt," he said eventually.

"It did," I replied. He didn't seem horrified, just curious. "I overheard the surgeon telling my nurse that he wanted to amputate it; said it would be quicker and easier than trying to fix it. I was too scared to sleep after that. I was convinced I'd wake up with no leg, that they'd do it without telling me. That was worse than the pain from the damage, the fear of losing it and the total loss of control over the situation."

"You were eight when this happened?"

I nodded. "My nurse convinced him to try and save my leg. After that, even if it hurt, I never let on. I thought if I complained, they'd cut it off to shut me up."

He leaned down to plant a kiss on a particularly lumpy bit of my thigh. "I'm sorry that happened to you, and I'm sad you had to face it alone. When Rupert was about eight, he was in hospital with a burst appendix. Cried like a girl whenever Mum tried to leave, so she stayed there with him. Dad had to take the week off work to look after the rest of us, which we thought was great. The four of us went feral, living off pizza and building a tree-fort in the garden. Mum went nuts when she found out none of us had changed our clothes all week." He smiled fondly at the memory.

"Sounds like you had a great childhood," I said.

"Yeah. With three brothers, all close in age, there was never a shortage of playmates." He was stroking my leg absentmindedly as he spoke, his hands rhythmic and soothing. "Rupes was immensely proud of his scar, used to show it off all the time, told people he'd got it in the Gulf War, stupid idiot. If he'd have had yours, he'd have been delighted and probably told people he'd got them fighting a dragon or something."

I laughed, "I never thought of doing that."

I jumped as his hand slid up my leg to the apex of my thighs. My breath hitched as he began probing gently, pleasuring me. He watched my reactions intently as he pushed first one finger, then two, inside me. I arched off the bed. The man had a magic touch. "You get aroused so easily," he mused as my legs fell open rather shamelessly.

"It's you," I gasped, "I don't normally."

"We didn't use a condom last night," he murmured, "I meant to but..." He trailed off.

"I meant to as well, but you were on a roll, and I didn't want to interrupt. I'm on the pill, so you don't need to worry."

He flashed me what I'll call his naughty smile and dove down between my legs to give me lush, long licks. I squirmed in delight, relishing every sensation. Somehow Andy had made me relax. His easy acceptance of my flaws made sex even more pleasurable, if that was possible.

He managed to wring another orgasm out of me, the stud-muffin.

I stretched lazily as he made another tea. "Can you get some coffee in?" He asked. "I normally drink fresh coffee in the mornings."

"I'll see what I can do," I replied, my mind racing with panic over how I'd somehow come up with a coffee maker. I decided to check out the local charity shops for a cafetière. He really had no idea just what being skint actually meant on a practical level.

"I'm going to have to go soon," he said, pulling a sad face, "I really don't want to, but I promised Mum I'd be there for lunch. I need to run some errands too, get myself ready for work tomorrow."

I felt a pang of disappointment that he'd be leaving, although I wasn't entirely sure why. I decided not to let it show. "I need to get this place cleared up and some laundry done," I told him.

He left, after giving me a lush, deep kiss and a promise that he'd call. I felt strangely flat and lonely the moment the door closed behind him. It was almost as though the whole weekend had been a dream, and I'd finally woken up. Only the presence of the new phone and laptop reassured me that it really had all happened, and it hadn't just been a wishful figment of my imagination.

I stripped the bed and put all the laundry in the machine to wash. Back upstairs, I began my cleaning routine, carefully washing down all the surfaces and buffing them till they gleamed. It was one of those mindless tasks I enjoyed enormously, as it gave me time to think. I wondered what Andy's house was like, whether it'd be all expensive, masculine fittings, or messy and cobbled together from mismatched hand-me-downs, as I believed most men weren't into interior design.

A favourite fantasy of mine was mentally furnishing my imaginary house. I lapped up all the interior decorating shows on the telly and pretty much knew what I'd choose if I ever had the chance. My dream was to own one of the pretty little cottages in Bromley North, a two up, two down with a little front and rear garden. I'd have hanging baskets full of flowers by the front door and make the back garden into a courtyard with a water feature.

I was interrupted by my new phone chirping. I knew it had to be Andy, as he was the only person who knew the number. Smiling, I opened the text.

"Take your payslips/P60 and contract of employment into work tomorrow ;)"

I quickly replied, "Will do," and sorted out the relevant documents, slipping them into my handbag. I wondered if the suited taxman was one of Andy's brothers, and they were discussing my case over lunch.

I was still smiling when I went to bed that evening, on my freshly-laundered and pressed sheets.

CHAPTER 5

I strode into work at half-eight the next morning,
ready to catch up on some tasks before my shift started
at nine-thirty. The owner of the practice, our head vet,
was already in, her presence announced by her
gleaming new Mercedes in the car park. She was
standing in reception talking to the Suit. "Morning," I
said cheerily.

"Good morning Sally," said Ms Gadd. The Suit
echoed her. I smiled brightly and set about signing in to
the system. "Oh, you don't need to do that, the
computer's down," Ms Gadd announced. I frowned and
clicked on Start. It sprang to life.

"It's fine now," I said, before clicking onto the little
icon to clock myself in. I glanced up to see her glaring
at me and making a throat slitting motion behind the
Suit's back.

"Did you just clock in?" He enquired.

"Yes," I replied, puzzled.

"Do you clock in and out every day?"

I nodded. "Of course."

Ms Gadd chimed in, "she may be clocked in, but you
don't actually start work for another hour, do you
Sally?"

I thought of her gleaming Mercedes sitting outside. I owed her nothing. "Well, patients don't arrive till half-nine, but rooms have to be sorted and checked, our overnight patients fed and checked, and you asked me to do some stocktaking before I started work today, so strictly speaking, I either start work at nine thirty and none of those jobs get done, or I come in at half-eight, as you requested on Friday, and complete the tasks you asked me to do, which are part of my job description."

She glared at me, livid at my response, which, I suspected, rather dropped her in it. "Ms Gadd, I'll ask you again, do you have staff timekeeping records?" The Suit interrupted her. She nodded, her face pale and pinched with fury. I escaped into the stock room and left them to it. Later, when I was checking the treatment rooms, I could hear Ms Gadd's raised voice coming from the office.

The morning flew past; Mondays were always busy. As soon as morning surgery was finished, Ms Gadd came to find me. "Mr McCarthy has asked to speak to you. I'm not certain what he wants. Just don't tell him about any overtime, otherwise you'll end up with a huge tax bill." She leaned in closer and lowered her voice, "You should've been paying tax on that overtime. They'll crucify you if you mention it. You could end up going to prison for tax evasion."

"I haven't been paid any overtime," I pointed out.

"They'll think it was paid cash-in-hand," she said. I went cold. If they thought I'd been paid cash, I'd end up in even more trouble. It would be my word against hers.

I panicked. "I just need to go to the loo first," I said, grabbing my handbag. I called Andy from the toilet. Thankfully, he answered straight away.

"She's got me over a barrel," I said without preamble, "said they'd think I've been accepting cash-in-hand, and that I'd end up with a huge tax bill."

"Calm down," he replied. "If she wants to admit to paying you cash, then she's admitting fiddling cash out of her business. It'd be her in trouble, not you. A quick investigation would easily show that you haven't been living beyond what's been paid legitimately. Keep calm, don't let her rattle you and just tell Rupert the truth."

"I thought it might be your brother," I said, "you look alike. Listen, I gotta go."

"OK. Tell the truth."

I hurried out into the office. Rupert was seated behind Ms Gadd's desk, flicking through papers. "Hello, Sally isn't it? I'm Rupert McCarthy. I gather you're a friend of my brother's?"

"I am," I replied, "I figured out that you were related. You look alike."

"He thinks he's the good-looking one, so thank you." He flashed me a smile. "Please take a seat. Now, I'm here to check out this allegation of your boss paying below minimum wage. Did you bring the documents he asked you to?"

I handed over my payslips, P60, and contract. Rupert pulled out a little camera and photographed them. "I've got a list of questions I need to ask. Some of them are intrusive and some are a little obvious, but I have to ask them and record your answers, is that OK?" He was business-like but kindly. I doubt if Ms Gadd shared my opinion of him. I nodded. He pressed a button on his little voice recorder.

"Are you Sally Higgs of 33 Freelands Road in Bromley, Kent?"

"Yes I am."

The questions were easy at first, mostly concerned with my length of service, job description, and qualifications. Eventually they became more difficult. "Do you work unpaid or paid overtime?"

"Unpaid."

"Are there records kept of your overtime?"

"I have to clock in and out, so yes."

"Is there time during your work hours where there is no work for you to do?"

"Never. We're understaffed, so always busy."

"Do you get breaks? Lunch hours?"

"No. The animals need feeding and their cages cleaned during the times there's no active surgery. Plus, of course any operations are scheduled for then, which only Maria and I are qualified to assist in."

"Are you paid cash, cheque, or bank transfer?"

"Bank transfer, monthly."

"Have you ever had your pay topped up with cash?"

I looked him in the eye, "No, never."

"Have you ever received gifts from your employer or benefits in lieu of wages?"

"No, never."

And so it went on. It was pretty damning. I hoped that the others would tell the truth as well. Ms Gadd didn't deserve anyone lying for her; she clearly wasn't going short herself, judging by her expensive car and frequent holidays.

"What will happen next is that we will work out what monies are owed to you under the minimum wage laws. Your employer will have 28 days to pay you. If they don't pay, we will prosecute them on your behalf."

My tummy flipped. "So I'd get it all?"

He nodded. "We work out the net amount for them to pay you, so there can be no arguments. She's in trouble, not you," he said, smiling kindly.

"Thank you," I said.

"Not a problem. It's my job to make sure businesses are acting within the law. When Andrew told me about you, it gave me an excuse to come back out into the field, as it were. I'm normally stuck behind a desk all day."

I wondered what else Andy had told him.

Maria was called into the office as I left. I knew she'd been angry about the cut in hours and pay. I just hoped that she too would tell the truth and not let Ms Gadd frighten her into silence. I grabbed my coat and prepared to clock out.

"Bye Sally," Ms Gadd called out behind me, all friendly for a change, probably hoping I'd covered up her wrongdoing.

I skipped into Bromley to change my library books, finding a copy of a book I'd been waiting for. I was in an even better mood when I found a cafetière in the Oxfam shop for fifty pence. It was a sort of sick-coloured yellow plastic, but it looked nearly new and had all the parts intact. Pleased with my purchase, I popped into the supermarket to get a packet of ground coffee. Sadly, when you're on a tight food budget, even the cheapest coffee puts a serious dent in it. I had to forgo my weekly bottle of wine in order to buy it.

"Hey sexy, what you up to tonight?"

I grinned stupidly at Andy's text. I found a bench, set my bags at my feet, and tapped out my reply. "Nothing much yet ;) Wanna come over? I bought a cafetière..."

"Well done. I'll bring a takeaway. See you about seven."

Back home, I unpacked my purchases and carefully washed out my new coffee maker. I made sure my room was tidy before taking a long, thorough shower in my tiny bathroom. As the hot water poured over me, I mused at how happy I felt compared to that terrible day in court. The debt still weighed heavily on me, but at least I felt as though I had a future that didn't consist of beans on toast every night for the next ten years. Since meeting Andy, I'd been eating better than I had in years. He certainly didn't seem to stint on food.

Not for the first time, I wondered how much he earned. I knew lawyers were well-paid, but beyond that, I didn't have much clue. He didn't ever talk about work, so I didn't really know too much about it. I resolved to Google it on my new laptop.

Andy arrived exactly on time, bearing a curry. He greeted me with a deep, lush kiss, before handing me the bag while he hung up his coat. I laid all the little foil trays on the coffee table in between us, so we could pick at the whole selection. "Can you cook?" I asked. I'd only ever seen him eat out.

He shook his head. "I'm not great. I can manage simple stuff. Rupert's pretty good. He's quite into cooking, but the rest of us are useless. Mum always did everything, so I suppose we never really learnt." He paused, "I spoke to Rupes earlier, he said you have a solid case. The other nurse has been underpaid too. He'll be speaking to the others during the week to find out if their situation is similar."

"I only know about Maria and myself," I admitted. "What else have you told Rupert?"

A silence stretched between us. Eventually he spoke; "Everything."

"Why?" It was a question born more of curiosity than anger that he'd revealed my story.

"Because he's my brother. We don't keep secrets like that. I had to ask him to investigate your work. He doesn't normally do that sort of thing, but if he'd just put it into the system, it could've taken years to sort out."

"He knows how we met?" Andy nodded warily. "Does he know I tried to kill myself?" Another nod. "Oh great. Does he know we're sleeping together?"

"Not as such, but I'm sure he's got a good idea. Phil did mention I stayed out all night Saturday."

"So Rupert knows you're having a fling with a girl you shafted in court over a debt, who then tried to top herself and is too stupid to realise she's been taken the piss out of at work?" My voice rose with indignation. All daydreams about being accepted into Andy's big family flew out of the window. They'd think I was some sort of loser gold-digger.

"Nobody's judging you," he said quietly. "I've told him the circumstances. Rupert's a nice guy deep down and just wants to help."

I wasn't sure quite what to say. On the one hand, I was angry that Andy had broadcast my mistakes, but on the other, I didn't want to fall out with him. I wrestled with the concept of whether or not that made me a gold-digger. "It's embarrassing," was all I said in the end.

"Don't be embarrassed. Rupes is family. I can tell you plenty of embarrassing things that he's done."

"Such as?" I asked, pleased to be changing the subject.

"Well, he wet the bed till he was ten."

"That's embarrassing. You shouldn't be telling people," I admonished. He just grinned.

"It doesn't matter though. I doubt if he does it now. Well, I wouldn't like him in my bed when he's drunk, just in case."

I laughed. The thought of a drunken taxman wetting the bed tickled me for some reason. "How come he became a taxman?"

"He wasn't academic enough for law. My profession is all about detail and memory. Matt, the eldest, he wanted to do it, but it wasn't for him. He went into dentistry instead. He's doing well, got his own practice. Rupes joined the civil service after uni; he had to switch his course from law to history, but even then, he only scraped a 2:1. Phil is the brightest out of all of us and works in the city. I'm the only one who followed in Dad's footsteps."

"Sounds like you've all done well. Your parents must be very proud of you."

"They have all the cheesy graduation photos on the mantelpiece, which is embarrassing. I was experimenting with growing a beard in mine, so it's particularly awful."

"What degree did you get?" I was being nosy.

"I got a first in law," he said quietly, as though he was shy about his achievement.

"So you're clever in every way," I declared, which made him smile.

"Not in everything. There's still a lot I need to learn about lots of things."

"Such as?" I asked.

"You." He paused. "I need to find out more about you. I know you've had a tough life, but it's made you wary and closed off."

"What do you want to know?"

"Let's start with why you don't have a boyfriend?"

I sat back in the chair and pulled up my legs. "I've had boyfriends in the past, losers mainly. Nobody long-term or longer than a few months. As soon as they started leeching off me, I dumped them. Not going out much does make it harder to meet people, and I guess I'm not good at friendships. I used to go out with a group of girls, but when I just couldn't afford it, I sort of drifted away from them." It was better than telling him that I'd always been the one driving them and had been ditched once I'd lost my licence. They'd all been glamorous, spending fortunes on new outfits and expensive hairdos. I'd been a bit mousey in comparison.

"How did you get into debt in the first place?"

It was a tricky question. I thought for a moment how best to word my answer. "I tried to start a side-line business, to top up my pay. My friends all used to go and get their nails done, so they encouraged me to learn how to do it. I thought I could start a mobile business, you know, evenings and weekends. I did a load of research and found what was apparently the 'best' company." I did air quotes with my fingers around the word "best." "I paid nearly fifteen hundred quid for my course, then another fifteen hundred for the kit. Almost as soon as I started, my car went wrong, which cost a thousand. I then discovered that none of my friends thought they'd have to pay for their nails. They seemed to think I was doing it as a favour. The final straw came when my fancy-pants nail lamp blew up and the company wouldn't replace it. I ended up buying another new one about a week before I lost my licence. I flogged the lot on eBay in the end for two hundred quid. By that time, I was five grand in debt. The rest was late fees, interest and charges."

I could see the compassion and concern in his expression. "Did you think I'd splashed out on clothes and holidays?"

He shook his head. "I didn't really give it much thought to be honest. As the lawyer for the plaintiff, I'm only concerned with getting repayment. I suppose I never actually asked that question before." He fell silent for a moment.

"How did you lose your licence?"

"My drink was spiked. I was drinking Fanta, and some fella thought it'd be funny to slip some vodka in each one. Probably thought if he got me a bit pissed, he'd get lucky. Instead, I got stopped, breathalysed and found to be seriously over the limit. I got a two-year ban." It was a lie, but better than admitting I'd lost track of how many glasses of wine I'd had.

"Is your middle name lucky?"

I laughed, "It is a bit of a tale of woe. I'll admit I'm a bit of an unlucky person. You must think I'm a right Calamity Jane."

"Yeah, it does sound like you've had a run of it. You need someone to take care of you."

I stared at him, dumbstruck. He blushed slightly. A heavy silence hung between us for a moment, mine because he'd stated my secret desire. I wanted a capable man, someone I could rely on and look up to. I wanted to be cherished, loved even. It was something I'd never really had, and I knew it existed. I wondered if Andy needed to play the part of being the strong one, whether the emasculation he'd experienced with his super-successful ex had caused his impotence. If that were the case, then the two of us would fit together perfectly.

"Yes, I suppose I do," I replied. I busied myself clearing our plates and putting the leftovers in the fridge. Andy always seemed to buy enough to last me an extra day, whether by accident or design, I wasn't sure.

I felt him standing behind me as I rinsed our plates. His hot breath caressed my neck, sending tingles down my spine. Any sort of close proximity to him made my body respond. It was an unconscious reaction. As soon as his lips touched my nape, I softened into him, pressing up against his firm body, fitting mine to his and feeling his warmth.

His hands snaked around my waist, pulling me in tighter, as his lips worked their way around my jaw. He gently twisted me round to face him and pressed his lips to mine, in a kiss that began soft and chaste, before it deepened to an erotic devouring. My hands instinctively wrapped around his shoulders, feeling his strong body. He pulled away for a moment, "You are so beautiful; you know that don't you?" He murmured, before resuming the kiss. I didn't answer. I was too caught up in the moment, in him and in the way he made me feel.

Our lovemaking that night was frenetic. Clothes were ripped off, adventurous positions tried out, and a bed leg broken. Andy had to stack my library books under the corner to hold it up, before we could resume. We even kept the light on, which for me, made it incredibly erotic. I could gaze into his beautiful blue eyes as my orgasm tore through me, expressing my gratitude at his prowess.

As I snuggled into his chest, the hairs tickling my face, I marvelled at my change of fortune and thanked whoever was in charge for sending him into my life.

CHAPTER 6

I skipped into work the next morning, after another passionate session and a shared shower. Andy even dropped me off on his way home, as he didn't have to be in till a little later than I. I frowned at the sight of Ms Gadd's car in the car park. She didn't normally get in till the start of surgery at half-nine. I had a long list of jobs to get done before the patients started arriving at eight for pre-operation checks.

She was standing behind the desk as I walked in. She was a tall, slightly forbidding woman. Her expensively highlighted hair was cut into a sleek bob, ironed into flat submission. She was also the most humourless person I'd ever come across. "I'd like to speak to you Sally," she barked as I walked to the desk.

"Morning Ms Gadd," I replied, rather sarcastic at her lack of greeting. People skills weren't her forte. She ignored me and strode into the office. I followed her rather meekly. She had that effect on me.

She glared at me for a moment. "So you're the traitor trying to bankrupt me?" She began. I went cold, a prickle of fear ran up my spine.

"I what?" Was all I could splutter. It felt like I was in big trouble.

"Mr McCarthy, the tax inspector, is a friend of yours, sent in by you?" She was livid; I could see it on her face. I tried to hang on to my self-control and not run screaming from the room. I could feel myself begin to shake.

"I don't know…" I began, but she cut me off.

"I have proof." She took her iPhone off the desk and prodded it, before thrusting it in my face. I could clearly see myself seated behind her desk, the back of Rupert's head visible. I hadn't noticed her phone there. I heard myself answering his questions.

I cringed.

She prodded it to switch it off. "You are a lying, thieving, little troublemaker. You made all that up about not being paid."

By that time, I was shaking uncontrollably, my entire body engulfed in mini-convulsions at the confrontation. "You should have paid what the law said," I found myself saying, albeit in a small voice. "I didn't go to them, they came to me."

"You expect me to believe a word that comes out of your lying little mouth? He clearly says you're a friend of his brother. You know what this is? Conspiracy to blackmail, that's what. You might think you can extort money out of me, but you broke data protection telling your boyfriend about my private business. You could go to prison for that." She was yelling right into my face. Instinctively, I stepped backwards, only to find myself trapped by a filing cabinet. She looked as though she was going to slap me, her face contorted in fury. I lifted my arm across my face, thinking she was about to strike.

"Oh, you're sorry now, you lying little toe-rag! Well, I won't give you any excuse to sue," she spat, backing off slightly, "but you can fuck right off out of my surgery. We have no use for liars, blackmailers, or thieves. Consider yourself sacked for gross misconduct."

Her words had the desired effect. I'd flinched when she'd sworn at me and cowered as she'd dismissed me. I knew I should've shouted back, told her the truth: that she'd been the one to break the law, not me, but I was too shocked and traumatised. I let out a huge sob and fled, pushing past the receptionist on my way out.

I sucked in lungfuls of bitterly cold air through my sobs, my body and emotions out of control. I was shaking from head to toe and unable to think straight. I sat down on someone's garden wall across the road and sobbed. It felt like my day in court all over again, only this time I still had the debt plus I'd lost the job that I loved. I fumbled for my phone. I needed Andy to save me. Again.

My hands shook so much that I struggled to press the speed dial key. Eventually I managed to prod it and waited for it to ring. He answered straightaway, "Hi babe, what's up?" His gentle voice caused another wave of sobs to rack through me, and I could barely get the words out.

"She... She sacked... me."

"She did what?" He sounded horrified. "She can't do that. You were acting within the law."

"Gross misconduct," I managed to say, "for talking to you... about my wages." Another wave of sobs hit, preventing me from hearing what he said. I think he was swearing. "I don't know what to do," I wailed. This had always been my worst fear. I could get through anything... except losing my job. I wished I had just kept quiet, either that or managed to get it right at

Bromley Station. At least I'd have died a gainfully-employed veterinary nurse. As it was, I felt lost, a serial loser. In a tiny corner of my mind, I even blamed Andy for making me speak up, for causing it all.

"Try and keep calm," he said. "I'm coming to get you. Can you tell me where you are?" I could hear panic in his voice. He was probably worried I'd go back to Bromley South.

"I'm outside the surgery," I managed to say. I was hyperventilating a bit as uncontrollable sobs shook me, making it hard to breathe.

"Stay there. I think Rupert's nearby. I'll call him to pick you up and take you home. I'll be as quick as I can."

"Why are you bothering? I asked. "I'm just a lost cause." I wanted to be alone with my humiliation. I even regretted calling him, although it had been my first reaction.

"Sally, let's not go there," he warned. He sounded exasperated, probably due to my never-ending calamities. "Just sit tight and wait for Rupert. I'll get off the train and come straight back."

"There's no need," I said. "I can walk home."

I don't think he heard me, as his phone went dead. I foraged around in my handbag for a tissue to stem the flow of tears and snot. The street seemed eerily quiet, especially for rush hour, but I saw Bessie's owner lead her in for her pre-op checks. I fought the urge to go and wish her luck. I prayed that Maria wouldn't get sacked as well. Bessie needed a good nurse looking after her.

An Audi screeched around the corner, like it was being chased. The driver slammed on the brakes to bring it to a halt beside me. I peered in and saw Rupert, looking grim-faced. "You OK?" He said.

I nodded and ran round to the passenger side. I hopped into the car and shut the door behind me. Rupert took one look at my tear-streaked face and said; "I'm sorry she did this to you."

Cue more tears.

I cried all the way back to my bedsit. I felt a bit sorry for Rupert, having to put up with me sobbing in his car. Eventually he spoke. "How did she know what you told me?"

"She recorded us," I managed to say.

"So did I," he said, "and you did nothing wrong. I bet Andy has a field day with this."

"What do you mean?"

"He's a lawyer, and a good one too. Loves a bit of litigation. He'll rip her apart."

"For what?" I asked.

"Oh, where do I start? Unfair dismissal, minimum wage violations, breach of contract, and they're only the ones I can think of, and I'm no lawyer. Andy's an aggressive little shit and bloody good at his job. That's why he's done so well."

We pulled up outside my flat. I thought Rupert would just drop me off, but he jumped out of the car and followed me in. "I'm fine, I don't want to take up any more of your time," I said, sniffing. I desperately wanted to be on my own for a while and have a good howl.

"It's OK. I can get to Ms Gadd anytime. Andy asked me to stay until he got here. Cheeky bastard told me to put the kettle on. Thinks I'm his tea boy." I sat down on my bed and watched as Rupert filled the kettle and switched it on. "What might be best is if I stay here, and you can tell us both what happened in there. Save you telling the story twice. I'll probably launch a full tax investigation as well as the current payroll one. That'll make her life a misery for a while, especially if Andy unleashes the hounds of Hell who work in his litigation department." He paused and looked at me with his clear, compassionate eyes, "We'll do worse to her than she's done to you."

More tears rolled down my face. I swiped them away with my now-soggy tissue. Rupert disappeared into the bathroom, re-appearing with a large wedge of loo roll, which he handed to me before busying himself with the tea. I dried my eyes before watching him expertly move around the little kitchenette in the corner of my room. He resembled Andy, possibly not as good-looking, and his body was heavier set, more prone to run to fat in middle age. Andy was leaner and more muscular. He placed three teas on the coffee table and plonked himself down in the armchair.

"He'll get fed up with all my fuck-ups," I blurted out. "Seems every time he sees me I've got a fresh crisis."

"Oh, I don't know, I think he quite likes being a knight in shining armour for a change. It must beat being treated like a imbecilic puppy."

"Charlotte?" I asked. He nodded and pulled a pained face.

"'The Horror Bitch,' we used to call her, behind Andy's back of course. She was the bossiest, coldest, and most condescending woman I've ever met. God knows how Andy put up with her for as long as he did. Even our dad was scared of her."

I smiled, albeit a wan one.

"Mum breathed a sigh of relief when they broke up. I think she's hoping for a gang of nice daughters-in-law. She gets on brilliantly with Mel, Matt's missis, so it was a shame she couldn't warm to the Horror Bitch." He sipped his tea.

"Does she like your girlfriend?"

"I've not taken her home yet, not been with her long enough. Mum's pretty easy going; it was only Charlotte she struggled with. She adores Phil's girl, although I'm not sure that Phil always feels the same way."

I wanted to ask how long was deemed "long enough" before meeting the family, but kept quiet, not wanting to sound pushy. I took a swig of my tea, the hot liquid soothing my rather sore throat. "What happens now in regards to the wage investigation?" I asked him.

"It carries on as normal. If she doesn't pay it, it will be passed to the industrial tribunal to add onto any damages. I'll also make sure she receives the maximum penalty fine possible."

"She won't pay up," I said despondently. "I've seen her screw people over plenty of times." I'd actually seen her inflate bills, not pay final wages, and massively inflate pet insurance claims. I should've known it'd be my turn one day.

"Andy can use the high court bailiffs. They'll get the money out of anyone, plus of course, she drives a nice, expensive car. It might take a while, but they'll get it."

We were interrupted by the front door buzzer. I went down to let Andy in. Seeing his concerned face started me off again, and I sobbed as he gathered me into his strong arms and gently stroked my hair. "I'm sorry this happened to you," he murmured, before pulling me into a tight hug.

After releasing me, he followed me upstairs. He sat in the armchair opposite Rupert and picked up his tea. "So tell me what happened in there. I need every detail. I'm gonna record it if that's OK?"

I nodded my assent before telling them in minute detail the story of that morning's events. Both of them asked questions as we went, making sure they had every piece of information they could possibly need. Eventually, we finished and they both seemed satisfied that I'd relayed everything. Andy switched off the recording app on his phone. Rupert made another tea. Rather stupidly, I calculated how many tea bags I had left.

"You look in another world," said Andy, "What are you thinking about?"

"How to afford more tea bags," I blurted without thinking. "I paid my rent for the month yesterday, and the bills are up to date, but I've only got fifty pounds left until I get another job."

"You'll have to go and sign on," he told me, "then your rent will be paid and you'll get job seeker's allowance."

I glanced over to see Rupert staring at him, his jaw dropped open in shock. "I don't know how to sign on. I'll just look for another job," I said quietly. I was sure I heard Rupert mutter something like "insensitive git."

"You can apply online," he said, oblivious to both my refusal and Rupert's look of horror at his suggestion.

"How much is your rent?" Rupert asked.

"Three-fifty a month, but it includes the heating and electric bills," I replied. Rupert threw Andy a look that I didn't understand before plonking his drink in front of him.

"That's not a lot," Rupert commented.

"It is when you haven't got it," I pointed out. "Anyway, I need to get a job, I can't live on fresh air. I'll get online and start applying straight away."

"You'll still be paid at the end of this month though?" Andy said.

I laughed, "I doubt it. She's never paid final pay to my knowledge. Fobs people off until they get fed up and go away."

"She sounds like a total shyster," Andy said. "Isn't there vet registration that you can complain to, you know, like dentists have?" I shook my head. Miss Gadd had been a law unto herself and had gotten away with it for such a long time that she probably didn't even realise it was illegal.

Rupert drained his cup, "Wish me luck, I'm going into battle..."

"Let's hope you get out in one piece," I said. "And thank you, you know, for today."

"No probs," he replied in his good-natured way. "I'll speak to you later," he told Andy, who nodded his goodbye, and with that, he went.

"He's nice, kind," I said to Andy once we'd heard the door slam.

"He's a bit of a prat at times, but his heart's in the right place," he agreed. "Listen, will you be OK on your own? Only I'd like to get into work and make a start on this. The sooner we can get papers served, the better."

"Yeah, I'll be OK," I reassured him. I glanced at the clock; it was almost half-ten. I hoped he wouldn't get into trouble for being late.

As soon as he'd gone, I buried my face in my pillow and howled out the disappointment and despair. Even with Andy in my life, I felt lost— hopeless even. He hadn't understood my poverty at all and been dismissive of my admittance that I had just fifty quid to my name. I was only a month away from being on the streets, which was a terrifying thought.

With sore, puffy eyes, I logged onto the Social Security website and read up on how to apply for benefits. I dutifully filled out all the forms, which took over an hour and finally pressed "submit," breathing a sigh of relief at actually having done something practical about my situation.

Two seconds later, an email appeared in my inbox from the DSS to tell me how much I was entitled to. I opened it quickly and scanned through it, until I got to the bit where it said:

"Your entitlement to out-of-work benefits is: £0"

I felt sick. With shaking hands, I dialled the helpline number. After waiting half an hour to speak to someone, eventually I got an officious Scottish woman. I explained my situation, spent another half an hour going through all my details again, only to be told I didn't qualify. In her words, I hadn't paid enough in to the system.

"But my hours were cut, and I was paid below minimum wage, which is being investigated," I wailed.

"You should have taken another part time job then," was her reply.

"Am I not entitled to anything at all? How am I supposed to eat? I was getting tax credits." I asked.

"Your doctor can refer you to a food bank if needs be, but the computer says you're not entitled to any benefits at all. They've been subject to all the cuts you see. Hardly anyone qualifies, usually only people with dependant children under five, or asylum seekers. Out-of-work benefits are different from in-work ones."

I could tell from her tone that she was scathing about the system she had to administer. "You can appeal this decision by writing to your local benefit office, but I can tell you that only one percent of appeals are successful and given that you were sacked, even if it's wrongful dismissal, they'll say no to you. Best try and get another job then," she said kindly.

Mindful of running up a phone bill, I gave up. I texted Andy to tell him I'd tried to apply for benefits, but wasn't entitled due to being both underpaid and sacked. He didn't reply.

Despondent, I Googled "veterinary nurse jobs, Bromley." To my surprise, a few popped up. I read through them all and applied for two. One was at a large surgery in Bromley South. They needed someone ASAP with surgical experience. I'd only been qualified to assist with operations for a year, but I figured it might be enough to get me in the door.

The second one I applied for was quite interesting. It was a private individual looking for a full-time caregiver for his or her two dogs, both of which were German Shepherds. I pondered for a while over the application form, which was long and complex. Some of the questions were a little strange, things like; "Why do you want to look after animals?"

I'd replied that I not only loved animals, but I respected them too and was committed to making sure their lives were as happy and healthy as possible. I didn't know if that was the right thing to say, but it was the truth. I pressed "send" and went back to perusing other job ads.

CHAPTER 7

Andy arrived quite late that evening, bearing a takeaway and a bag of shopping, which thankfully included both tea bags and a bottle of wine, which he opened expertly. I told him about the call to the benefit office and how unfair the system was. He seemed preoccupied, lost in his thoughts.

"Penny for them?" I asked when I caught him staring into space.

He smiled, "Nothing much, just planning a strategy."

"Are you getting sick of having to help me all the time?" I asked. It had been preying on my mind. I would've bet he regretted buying me that phone already.

"Of course not. I feel sad for you, naturally, but all of it can be sorted out."

"I meant to ask, how do I top my phone up? I must be nearly out of credit with that long call today." I needed the phone more than ever, what with applying for jobs. There was no way I could let it run out. When we'd bought it, Andy hadn't let me see how much it was, sending me out of the shop while he dealt with it.

"Oh, it's OK, I put it onto my contract. You don't have to pay for calls or texts." As soon as he said it, another bit of stress fell away. It was another problem I wouldn't have to deal with. "Just don't hammer it, OK?"

"I wouldn't do that," I told him, annoyed at the suggestion. "You see how frugally I live, why would you think I'd change?" He just shrugged.

"So what shall we do this evening?" He asked, changing the subject.

"TV, film, or wild sex?" I offered. I was good at creating a distraction too. He smiled and shot me a look that could scorch the sheets. Without warning, he scooped me up off the chair and dropped me onto the bed, before leaning over me, pinning me with his arms and kissing me fiercely. He seemed as needy as I was, albeit for different reasons. He was my lifeline at that moment; I truly couldn't afford to lose him.

I showed my appreciation with a long, thorough blowjob, spending a long time alternately licking and sucking his wide, beautiful penis. He let out little moans occasionally, showing me the moves he liked the best. He seemed to love getting his balls licked with long, lush strokes of my tongue. I could feel his cock straining as I licked him, so heavily engorged I could barely move it from where it lay across his belly. It was leaking pre-cum, which I greedily sucked off the tip.

"Sal, I'm coming! Oh God, I'm coming," he called out. I didn't miss a beat, taking every drop into my mouth, swallowing it all as it pumped out. I needed to become his everything, just as he was to me, and that meant showing him what I could do for him in exchange for everything he was doing for me. It may have been a little calculating, but I never meant it in a bad way. I just wanted to keep him, to make him my man.

I crawled up his body as he lay recovering; pressing tiny kisses on his smooth skin as I went, until I'd reached his face where I softly placed my lips on his. Instinctively, he wrapped his arms around me, pulling me on top of him. His tongue found mine and treated it to long, slow licks, before we came up for air. let out little moans occasionally, instinctively, he wrapped his arms around me, pulling me on top of him. His tongue found mine, and treated it to long, slow, licks before we came up for air. "That was amazing," he whispered, "I never wanted it to end."

"Neither did I," I told him.

With that, he flipped me over in a sudden, but smooth, movement, as though I weighed nothing. He peeled my soaked thong down my legs, seemingly not noticing my scars. I fully expected him to plunge his cock into me, as his erection was back at full strength. Instead, he pinned my legs open with his elbows, and dived down to pleasure me with long, soft licks, flicking my clit with the tip of his tongue. One hand held me open, while he slid two fingers of the other inside me, which bumped repeatedly over my g-spot as he gently pumped back and forth. I felt my orgasm begin to brew.

He must have felt it too, as he stopped abruptly. As I whimpered in annoyance, he reared up and slammed his iron hard cock into me. I cried out with the intensity. "You OK?" he asked, concerned.

"I'm good," I muttered, willing him to move. I rocked my hips to show I was ready for action. He fucked me at a punishing pace, slamming himself into me hard. I worried that the remaining bed legs would give out as he pounded me relentlessly, pushing me into one of those orgasms that shake your entire body as it rips through your nerve endings.

He came the moment after I did; he'd clearly been holding himself back to satisfy me first. My body was still convulsing around his when I felt him stiffen and then let go. He slumped onto me, slicked with sweat. I pushed his damp hair back from his face and was rewarded with one of his film star smiles. The man was so very beautiful that he took my breath away.

"You," he said, running his nose along mine, "are so damn sexy, I just can't get enough of you."

I swallowed the disappointment that he hadn't made a more loving declaration. "So are you," I replied, not wanting to push him and maybe scare him off.

We snuggled together to watch the news on my tiny TV, our arms and legs entwined as we lay in companionable silence. I was still concerned that something was bothering him, but wary of prying and possibly being a nuisance, I kept quiet. Eventually, he spoke, asking if I'd looked for a new job, in a nonchalant sort of way. He was probably worried I'd be penniless and dependent on him forever.

"Yes, I applied for two jobs this afternoon," I said. I felt his body relax. "I'm just waiting to hear back."

"That's good. I'll keep my fingers crossed for you." He seemed a little uncomfortable, as though he wanted to say something.

"Spit it out," I said.

"It's not important," he replied. I stayed silent, just turning my head to stare at him in the dim glow of the TV. "Alright, I was thinking I should go home to sleep. I've got an early start in the morning. I'm appearing in court over in Kingston and need to be there by half-nine."

"You've not done anything wrong have you?" The words came out without thinking. Thankfully, he just laughed.

"Of course not, it's another case for MVDI. We get all the cases requiring litigation."

"Oh, I see." As much as I understood it was just his job, I couldn't help but feel sad for another poor soul who was about to go through the same as I had.

After he'd left, I pondered our relationship. All of Andy's actions towards me indicated that he felt something for me. I was certain he wasn't just seeing me due to guilt or a sense that he needed to continue saving me, yet he seemed to be hiding me away, not sharing anything of his life. He was making no moves to show me where he lived or where he liked to socialise. I knew he fancied me and regarded us as sexually compatible, yet I didn't know if he actually *liked* me or not. Eventually, I fell asleep in a fitful doze.

I awoke to a sense of unease, the full impact of not having a job to go to finally hitting me like a sledgehammer. All my morning routines felt aimless, even getting dressed, as thanks to Andy, I didn't even need to go shopping. I decided on a duvet day, so pulled the covers back over me and opened my laptop as I sipped my tea.

Checking my emails, I saw straightaway that both jobs had replied. I opened the first one and read through all the spiel from the surgery. My tummy flipped as I saw that they wanted me to attend a first interview. It sank again when I looked at the date; it wasn't for another two weeks. In the spiel, it had said that there would be three separate interviews, followed by a trial week. It could take a month or more to get back to working again.

Despondent, I clicked on the next one, which was from the ad for the private animal caregiver.

From: marcusbrookes@pryce.uk
To: sallyhiggs@bahoo.com
Your application for the position of full-time animal caregiver
21st January 2015 21:48

Dear Miss Higgs

Thank you for your completed application form. I would like to invite you to attend an interview on Wednesday 21st January at 6 p.m. I realise this is very short notice, so if you cannot make it, please let me know, so that we can find a mutually acceptable time.

The interview will be held at Lakeswood, Keston Common Road, Keston, BR8 4RY. The initial interview will be with me, then a further interview with Mr Pryce, who would be your potential employer.

Please bring your certificates, plus copies of your passport and another form of ID. I look forward to meeting you.

Kind regards
Marcus Brookes
Household manager

I re-read it at least three times, my sense of panic growing with each moment. An interview that evening was just so quick; I wouldn't have time to prepare. I'd need to look smart. My mind went blank as to what I should wear. I didn't even know how to get there, so I'd need to research buses. I quickly pushed my laptop away and jumped out of bed. Looking in my wardrobe, I scanned through all the cheap tat until I found my sensible grey trousers. I could team them with a plain black top and my useless coat. I'd just have to put up with the cold.

I used Google Maps to find the postcode and discovered it was a large house, set in its own grounds just situated between the A21, where Andy had taken me to Chapter One, and the road that led down towards Westerham. I would need to get two buses, which would be a pain, but it was far better than the alternative; plus it seemed as though they were in a hurry to find someone.

With a renewed sense of purpose, I made another tea and checked through the rest of my emails. The usual selling ones and spam ones hid a note from Ms Gadd, apologising for her outburst the previous day and offering to meet with me to "find a way forward." I guessed that she'd been given a hard time by Rupert the previous day, although I doubted that Andy had served any papers at that point. She probably felt it was safer to keep me on her side. I didn't feel up to responding to it. I knew full well that both Andy and Rupert would be appalled if I even entered into dialogue with her, let alone if I went back to work there. I'd just have to take my chances at this interview.

I texted Andy to tell him I had an interview at six, so I wouldn't be home till late, and he'd replied by wishing me luck. Then he sent another text a few minutes later to say he'd use the opportunity to work late that evening, so he would see me the following evening. It felt like a slap of rejection, but I dismissed that idea, giving myself a firm talking to about becoming needy and clingy. Andy clearly had an important job and couldn't be running after me seven nights a week. I spent the day cleaning my room and getting ready for the interview, trying hard to ignore the anxiety rising in my belly.

I'd only been for a couple of interviews in my life. One was for a Saturday job while I was at school. It had been an informal affair, being in a greeting card shop. The other interview had been in the surgery. I'd been a bundle of nerves for that one, literally shaking from head to toe as I'd sat in front of Ms Gadd and lied about my made-up hobbies. I hadn't told her that I'd been in care, simply listing my address as 34 Dunston Way, omitting the name of the children's home.

I left with plenty of time to spare, in case I got lost or buses were delayed. I made sure I had enough cash on me for bus fares and checked that I had all the documents Marcus had requested. I'd memorised the map and also done a little drawing, which was stuffed into my handbag. I wasn't leaving anything to chance. Being organised did little to calm my nerves on the bus ride over to Keston. I was unfamiliar with the area and it seemed quite dark, with few streetlights and what looked like huge houses with vast, unlit front gardens. I was relying on the bus driver to help me with where to get off. I sneaked a look at him concentrating on his driving and wondered if he'd forgotten me.

Eventually he pulled up in a lay-by on a dark country road. "The lady who wanted to get off at

Lakeswood?" he called out. "It's your stop." I rose out
of my seat. "Just over there," he said, pointing at a pair
of enormous iron gates.

"Thank you," I said; grateful for his help, I'd never
have found it on my own in the dark. I hopped off the
bus and walked slowly towards the gates. I checked the
time. I was ten minutes early. I pondered whether or not
I should just go in, or walk around outside for a little
while longer. Frozen to the bone in my useless coat, I
made the decision to press the button to go in.

"Pryce residence," said a cheerful voice from the
intercom. It sounded out of place floating out of the
speaker beside the forbidding, lavish gates that guarded
the property.

"Sally Higgs to see Mr Brookes," I said, feeling a
little self-conscious about speaking into a pillar.

"Super," said the voice, "I'll open the small side gate
beside the large ones, just give it a push and it'll open.
Come all the way to the top of the drive and I'll come
and find you." I heard a loud buzzing sound coming
from a smaller, but no less ornate gate on the other side
of the pillar. Gingerly I pushed it, expecting it to be
heavy, but it swung open easily, then clanged shut
behind me, making me jump.

My eyes soon got used to the darkness of the
driveway and it was a fairly clear night. The moon
illuminated trees running on either side of me as I made
my way up to the house at a fairly fast pace, glad that
I'd not prevaricated outside and half-froze to death. As I
followed the curve of the drive, the house loomed into
view. It was an enormous place, although I wasn't sure
what era it belonged to. It was lit by up-lighters as well
as from the windows. The end of the drive was a

circular area, lit by old-fashioned lampposts. It was stunning. I wondered who on Earth could afford to live in such a vast house.

The man who stood waiting for me was not what I expected, being youngish and quite hip. He was shivering in just shirtsleeves and skinny jeans. "Mr Brookes?" I asked.

"Marcus, please," he replied, "and you must be Sally? Delighted to meet you." He held his hand out to shake mine. "Now please, lets get into the warm, it must be below freezing out here." He led me into a large hallway, where we were greeted by two large German Shepherd dogs. They came over and sniffed me before the smaller one gave my hand a small lick. "This is Roxy. Seems as though she likes you already, her brother is Bruno."

"I love dogs," I told him. I'd always had an affinity with them, probably because they only ever craved being part of a pack, rather like myself. I kept quiet and followed him and the dogs down the hallway, staring at the artwork on the walls. It was a tasteful, neutral sort of space, a bit like one of those achingly-expensive London apartments you see in magazines. The walls were a perfect shade of taupe to go with the pristine and shiny pale cream tiles on the floor, which had been polished to an almost mirror finish.

"Did you find it OK?" Marcus interrupted my gawping.

"Yes thanks, no problem at all."

"How did you get here?" he asked, "I saw you came on foot."

"I took the bus," I said, cringing slightly at how lame it sounded, surrounded as I was by extreme opulence.

He ushered me into a large office and indicated that I should be seated.

"Can I take your coat?"

I shrugged off the useless coat and enjoyed the warmth emanating from a modern pebble-filled fireplace to the side of the desk. I wondered if the whole house was as perfect as the bit I'd seen. "Tea or coffee? I'm having a latte if you'd like one?"

"That would be lovely, thank you," I said, pleased that I didn't have to figure out if it was bad manners or not to accept a drink. Marcus seemed to have a nice way about him that put me at ease. The two dogs lay down in front of the fire and watched the proceedings through sleepy eyes. I watched as Marcus picked up a phone and pressed a button, before asking the person at the other end to bring our drinks. I was impressed.

"Are there many household staff here?" I asked.

"Around eight of us usually, but only myself and Gerry, the chef, live in, the rest come in to do their shifts. A house like this takes a lot of upkeep." He smiled brightly at me. "So Sally, you're a qualified veterinary nurse?"

I pulled my certificates out of my bag and slid them across the desk. "I'm fully qualified in all aspects of animal care and surgery management up to NVQ level three," I said proudly. He flicked through them, reading the more relevant ones.

Our coffees arrived, announced by a small knock on the door. A large, rather scruffy man in chef's whites came in bearing stylish white cups and equally-striking accoutrements on a black slate tray, which he slid onto the desk. "Thanks Gerry," Marcus said, flashing a wide smile. "Sally, this is Gerry, chef extraordinaire. Gerry,

Sally, potential babysitter for your two favourite doggies."

"Bloody things," Gerry said, rolling his eyes at them. "If you can keep those two under control, then you're a better trainer than the last one."

"They're fully trained, Gerry, it's just you they don't behave for," Marcus said, grinning at him. He turned to me, "Don't worry, we're not looking for a trainer."

"Bloody thieving creatures need one," said Gerry as he disappeared through the door. Marcus handed me my latte.

"So what exactly are you looking for?" I asked. I was beyond curious. It seemed such a strange set up.

"We are looking for a caregiver, a sort of nanny for the dogs if you like. Mr Pryce works long hours and can't always look after them as well as he'd like. He wants someone whose sole function is to supervise them, walk them, and care for their well-being."

"I see. Do either of them have any health issues?"

"No."

"So why a nurse?"

"I needed to find an animal lover, a true animal lover, so who better than a veterinary nurse?" I nodded, understanding immediately what he meant. Nobody went into nursing if they weren't devoted to animals. It was a vocation, a calling. "So Sally, tell me, why are you applying for this job? Your CV says you worked at Bromley Animal Care for a long time."

His question threw me. I should've practiced a good answer as to why I was unemployed and looking for work. I hadn't even realised I'd be asked. I decided on honesty being the best policy. "We had a minimum wage inspection at the practice and they found out I'd

been underpaid. I refused to lie about it, so my
employer sacked me." I watched as my words sank in,
and his lips pursed in disapproval. I wondered if I'd
blown my chances.

"That's shocking," he said. "How on Earth did they
think they'd get away with it? I hope you take it to
tribunal. Employers like that deserve to get done."

"I'm not one to make a fuss," I said. "I enjoyed my
job and didn't want to lose it, but by lying for her, I
would've got into trouble with the taxman."

"You absolutely did the right thing," he said. "You'll
be pleased to know that we do things by the book here.
Mr Pryce is a very prominent businessman, and as such,
wouldn't dream of treating his household staff like
serfs. The pay for this position isn't great; it's only
twenty thousand a year, but you get free
accommodation, as it's a live-in position."

I nearly fell off my chair. Twenty grand a year
sounded like a fortune, especially if I didn't need to pay
rent. The job sounded a breeze as well; taking care of
two dogs wouldn't be particularly hard work, even if
they were a bit spoilt and naughty. I'd dealt with much
worse at the surgery.

Marcus asked a lot of questions about my career and
my attitudes to animal care. He was extremely detailed
and precise with an almost forensic way of getting the
information he required. His cheery demeanour
concealed an intelligent man who was clearly very good
at his job, despite his appearance being that of an
excessively-groomed hipster. His hair was short, but
perfectly cut, with a trendy little quiff at the front. His
clothes were expensive, possibly designer and suited his
slender, almost wiry frame. He looked as though he

could have been a media type or a trendy designer, so I wondered how he'd come to be a glorified housekeeper to a businessman, pondering the possibility that he might be Mr Pryce's gay partner. I got a homosexual vibe from him.

"So you'd be available to start straightaway?" His question shook me back to the present.

I nodded, "Yes, I'd be able to start whenever you'd like."

"Have you any questions for me?" Marcus asked.

"Have the dogs had a nanny before?" I wanted to know if this was a new position, or whether I was stepping into someone else's shoes.

"Yes they have." He pulled a bit of a face.

"What happened?"

"Mr Pryce's girlfriend and Sonia, the previous nanny... had a disagreement," he said. I could tell he wanted to say more so I stayed quiet. "Shari, that's the current girlfriend... she's quite a handful." He paused. "It's why we're on such low staffing levels right now."

"I see," I said in a non-committal way.

"Aaron, Mr Pryce," he corrected himself, "has been working ridiculously long hours lately, so hasn't been privy to some of her... excesses."

"I'm sure she can't be that bad," I said cheerfully. Compared to the icy and sociopathic Ms Gadd, Shari would be a walk in the park. Being a mousy little thing often protected me from the ire of spoilt princess types, they didn't tend to find me a threat, so usually left me alone. Marcus just smiled thinly.

"So what happens next?" I asked. I was keen to progress to the next stage in the process.

"You'll need to meet Mr Pryce," he said, "He has the final say. Let me check his diary and see when he can fit you in." He opened a drawer and pulled out a tablet. I watched as he swiped at it a few times. "Hmm, he's quite tied up over the next few days. Are you available at ten on Saturday morning?"

"Yes, that's absolutely fine," I said. As soon as I'd said it, both dog's ears pricked up, and they went on alert. A moment later, I heard a door slam and footsteps click up the hall. "This might be him," Marcus said, "Stay there, I'll go and check." He got up and left the office, followed by the dogs, who seemed eager to see whomever it was. I could hear voices coming from the hallway, but they were too muffled to make out what was being said.

I drained my cup and looked around. Marcus's office was decorated in pale grey with charcoal furnishings, giving it a sleek, polished look that reflected his overall demeanour. Everything was achingly tasteful, even the polished silver ornaments next to the fireplace and the blown-glass uplighter on the walls. It was as if the inhabitants of the house had never owned a bit of cheap tat in their lives.

I jumped as the door swung open. Marcus strode in, followed by possibly the most imposing man I'd ever set eyes on. He was tall, slender and could only be described as dark. He was English, but his hair and stubble were deep ebony and between them, gave him a forbidding appearance. His eyes were dark blue, lined with long, dark lashes. He was dressed in a navy suit and white shirt, without a tie, as if he'd taken it off during the journey home. He smiled at me in a friendly way. My mouth immediately went dry. He held his hand out for me to shake. I took it rather hesitantly, expecting electric shocks to run up my arm. His hand was extraordinarily soft, but that was about it.

"Miss Higgs, it's very nice to meet you. Marcus was just filling me in about you," he said, "I'm Aaron Pryce. Roxy and Bruno are my little ones."

"Delighted to meet you," I replied. I wondered if I'd still need to come back on Saturday or whether it would count as a second interview. He perched on the edge of the desk, which made him loom over me.

"Marcus tells me you're very well-qualified. Have you ever pet-nannied before?"

"Well, we sometime took boarders at the surgery while people were on holiday. We had large kennels there. I often took care of the dogs who were staying with us." I'd walked them too, during my unpaid time, while Ms Gadd charged the owners extortionate amounts, I thought to myself.

"And you're available to move in and start straightaway?"

"Yes."

The two dogs were sitting on either side of his legs, both gazing up at him in total adoration. I watched as he addressed them, his voice softer and warmer; "Roxy, Bruno, have you given Miss Higgs a check-over?" He smiled as Roxy leaned over to sniff my hand and give me another little lick. Bruno was more suspicious, checking me out quite thoroughly before granting me the lick of approval.

"Where's their favourite place to walk?" I asked.

"There are several acres of grounds, mainly woodland. Aaron prefers them walked here as it's more secure," said Marcus. I'd been so mesmerised by Aaron

Pryce that I'd forgotten that he was still there. "I can
provide you with a full care file. It lists out their food,
our policies on discipline, that sort of thing. I had to
prepare it for their last nanny."

"That would be great. Changes often confuse and
upset dogs, so it would be best to try and keep their
world as normal as possible." As soon as I said it, Aaron
smiled broadly.

"That's what I like to hear. Marcus said that you
don't drive? Might be an issue for any vet trips that are
needed."

I blushed. "I'll be getting my licence back in a few
months. My drink was spiked…" I tailed off, wondering
if it would blow it for me. The job had felt within
grasping distance up until that point.

"I suppose one of the groundsmen could drive her if
needs be for a few months," Marcus mused. I could've
kissed him. He was clearly rooting for me.

Aaron stood up, towering over me, "OK, move her in
Saturday, run through the job spec and start her on
Monday." He gazed down on me for a moment. "Does
that suit?"

"Oh yes. Thank you, Mr Pryce," I said, cringing
slightly at how gushy I sounded. With that, he left, the
two dogs following along behind, tails wagging madly.

"OK," said Marcus, "Scrub that Saturday interview,
we'll concentrate on getting you moved in. I'll show
you the flat." He opened another drawer and pulled out
a set of keys. "It's quite a nice place, even though it's
above the garage."

I followed him back through the lavish hallway and
out of the front door. We walked across the driveway to
a set of garages. They looked to me as if they were

larger than most people's houses. Down the side of the first one was a front door, he unlocked it and stepped inside to switch on a light.

Directly in front of me was a staircase, fully enclosed. I followed him up, barely listening to his description of the estate. At the top of the stairs, he flicked on another light, and I saw the "flat" for the first time. It was fantastic.

It was a vast room, spanning about three of the double garages, and divided into areas while retaining its open plan look. The kitchen area was fitted with shaker-style cabinets, housing cupboards, a washing machine, and to my excitement, what appeared to be a dishwasher. The hob was set into the black worktop with the oven housed below. It was a million times better than the two cupboards and sink with a portable ring and grill affair I had in my bedsit.

The living area had a large grey corner sofa, a glass coffee table and a TV. It was separated from the sleeping area by a pair of black screens. The bed was a large double and the wardrobe was built-in on the far wall. It had the feel of a New York loft, not that I'd ever seen one outside of a magazine. A small bathroom had been partitioned off, just beyond the sleeping area. It wasn't large, but was nicely fitted with a nice bath and shower combo, loo, and sink.

"I'll get the heating put on for you on Saturday morning. Sonia did tell me that this place warms up fairly quickly. Do you like it?" He sounded a little nervous.

"It's gorgeous," I breathed, trying to take it all in. "Do I have to pay rent for it?"

"No. It's why the salary is quite low. Heating and electric are included. You'll come under the household council tax too, which saves a fair bit."

"Fantastic. What time on Saturday should I get here?" A million things were whizzing through my mind, primarily how I'd get my stuff over there with only fifty quid to last me until the end of the month.

"I don't know, ten-ish? If you like I could send one of the groundsmen over with a van, if you don't have a car?"

"That'd be really helpful," I said. I could've kissed him.

"OK, that's settled then. Well, welcome to the household Miss Higgs. I'm sure you'll be very happy here."

CHAPTER 8

The next couple of days were a whirlwind of packing up, changing addresses and slinging out old tut that didn't have a place in my sleek new pad. Andy was delighted for me, although I hadn't told him too much about my new employment. If he could be secretive, then so could I. He came round on the Friday evening, bearing a takeaway and a bottle of wine. "All organised?" he asked cheerfully, clearly in a good mood. He surveyed the stack of boxes in the corner of the room.

"Just the bedding to bag up in the morning, and I'm ready to go," I said proudly. "The landlord is OK with me leaving tomorrow, as I've paid the rent up to the end of the month. I doubt I'll get the deposit back given the damage we've done to the bed." Having taken my library books back, I'd had to try and do a makeshift mending job with some string and a bit of duct tape I'd found in the utility room.

"Good," he said, smiling warmly, before capturing me around my waist and pulling me into a kiss. I kissed him back with fervour, weaving my fingers into his hair, anchoring him to me. Eventually he pulled away.

"Food'll get cold," he said. I took the hint and started laying it out on the coffee table. It smelt divine. As we ate, I asked him about his day. "Normal really. Oh, by the way, I served papers on your old boss. She has fourteen days to respond."

"That probably ruined her weekend," I commented.

"That's why I always serve on a Friday afternoon, the later the better. They have all weekend to stew and panic before they can get a lawyer on a Monday morning."

I gasped. "That's really mean." he just grinned.

"That's the idea. So what time are you moving tomorrow?"

"Ten. A van's coming to get me."

"Good. I'd struggle to get all this in the car," he waved at my pile of boxes. "By the way, have you checked out these new employers?"

"Yeah, Googled them," I said dismissively. I'd actually pored over every article about him on the first six pages of Google. Aaron Pryce was a high achiever, from a single-parent family who sent him to private school, then on to Oxford. He'd made his first million by the tender age of twenty-two and had an estimated fortune of over a hundred million. He was just thirty-one, the same age as Andy. I hadn't shared any of this information, as I thought it might put Andy's nose out of joint. I'd been deliberately evasive when he'd questioned me, just telling him I'd be working for a couple in Keston, which technically I was, given that Mr Pryce had a girlfriend. It didn't hurt to be a bit sensitive to Andy's ego.

I was pleased that Andy stayed the night, although I was a touch disgruntled that he was evasive when I asked about his house. "I'll take you round there soon, maybe when Phil's moved out," he said, before distracting me with his beautiful body, again.

I sent him home the next morning before the van arrived. He didn't seem to mind. In fact, I thought he seemed to be relieved that he wouldn't be roped in to helping. We arranged to meet for dinner that evening in a little pub in Keston, which apparently served amazing food. With a quick kiss goodbye, he was gone.

After bagging up my bedding, I did a final clean of the room, and took the rubbish down to the recycling area downstairs. As I was sorting the paper from the plastic, a van pulled up outside. A rather grizzled-looking man got out. "I'm looking for a Miss Sally Higgs," he said in a gruff voice.

"That's me," I told him, "are you from Mr Pryce's place?" I held my hand out to shake his, which turned out to be rather grimy and calloused.

"Call me Jed," he said, sounding much friendlier. "I can't wait to get those bloody dogs off hand. If they're not stealing out of the kitchen, they're crapping in the formal gardens or getting themselves lost in the woods. Little sods need a permanent nanny."

"I'll make sure they stay out of your gardens," I promised. I led him upstairs and pointed at the pile of boxes. "Sorry, there's quite a bit of stuff to move."

"Not as much as I expected," he said, picking up two as if they were weightless. With the two of us loading up, it didn't take long. I gave the bedsit one last, long look, and locked the door. After dropping the key in to the landlord, Jed drove us over to Lakeswood. In the daylight, I got a better sense of where it was, and saw where I'd be meeting Andy that evening.

"Has anyone given you the code for the gate yet? Jed asked. I shook my head. "I'll see if Marcus is around and remind him. We each have our own code, so they can see who goes in and out. It's a security thing," he told me.

"Security is important then?" I asked.

Jed nodded. "Very important. Mr Pryce is very aware that he's a target. He takes no chances, especially where the dogs are concerned. He'll have done a full background check on you before you were even asked to interview. Don't be fooled by the laid-back Marcus either, he's as sharp as a tack, and nothing gets past him."

"I see," I said. I didn't really. "So what does Marcus actually do?"

"Everything. He takes care of the property, the staff, and supplies. He organises decorators, builders, and repairs. He's very good at his job."

"The house is beautiful," I said. "Well, the bit I've seen of it."

"All down to Marcus. Mr Pryce is barely there really. I hardly ever see him because I work during daylight and he's up in the city doing his deals. Gerry, the chef, says he hardly ever gets home before eight in the evening, and even then that's if he doesn't have an evening function to attend. Gerry spends most of his time cooking for the staff, moaning that we only ever want eggs and chips. He's a bit wasted really. He does all that fancy cuisine stuff."

We pulled up outside the garage. "Nice little flat this one," said Jed, hopping out of the van. "Marcus gave me the key to give to you." He pulled a key out of his pocket, attached to a little fob that simply said "Garage 1 Flat." I took it and unlocked the front door. Picking up a box to take with me, I skipped up the stairs, delighted that the heating had been switched on as promised.

I dumped the first box on the bed and looked around. It appeared to have been cleaned since I'd seen it a few days earlier. The surfaces shone with polish, and it smelt clean and fresh. I wandered over to the window and saw that I overlooked the gardens, which were manicured and rather formal. "That's the rose garden," said Jed, making me jump. "I made that one from scratch. It was just bare lawn seven years ago."

"Is that how long you've been here?" I asked. He nodded. "So he bought this place when he was just twenty-four?"

"I gather it was a single, rather lucrative deal that paid for it. Well, that's the legend anyway. I've no idea whether it's true or not. Now, where shall I put these boxes?"

"In the middle is fine, thank you," I said.

"The bins are round the far side of the last garage. Just flatten down your boxes and stack them there when you're done. If you need anything, the house phone is by the telly. The kitchen is round the back of the house if you need milk or anything."

"Thanks, I should be fine," I said, smiling at him. "By the way, am I allowed to have friends round in my free time?"

"Yes, of course. As long as you accompany them at all times. Well, that's the rule I've always had to follow. It's pretty laid back as long as security rules are followed." He went off to get the rest of the boxes. I spotted an envelope on the coffee table with my name on. I ripped it open.

Dear Sally,

I hope you settle in OK, please don't hesitate to call the house by pressing 3 on your phone if there's anything you need. Your security code for the entire estate is 4657. Use the large keypad for the main gate, the smaller keypad below it for the pedestrian one. Keypads are at all access points into the main house.

Your hours will be 8 a.m. till 6 p.m., Monday to Friday. Occasional weekend and evening babysitting will sometimes be needed. I've enclosed the care plan devised for Roxy and Bruno. It details feeds, timings, and key points from their training. I hope it's enough for you to go on.

I'll meet with you at 9 a.m. on Monday to sort out your contract and payroll. Please come straight to my office.

Kind regards,
Marcus Brookes

I memorised the code, reciting it in my head until I was sure I'd remember it, then I put the sheaf of papers down and got on with helping Jed unload the van. I spent a rather lovely afternoon unpacking my things and putting them away carefully so as not to spoil the New-York-loft-look of the studio. Compared to my bedsit, it felt as though I had acres of room and a positive glut of cupboard space.

My new kitchen was far nicer than I'd had before, with a built-in washer/dryer and a proper hob and oven. The utensils provided were basic but would do me fine. I unpacked my meagre grocery supplies, putting everything away in cupboards. Only the kettle would be allowed on the worktop. I preferred to keep things neat.

I cursed when I discovered that my duvet wasn't really the right size for the bed, only stretching to the very edges. With my first month's wages, I vowed to purchase a decent king-size bedding set and two more pillows. My small duvet cover stood out in the gorgeous room as being cheap and wrong. A pale grey set would've looked amazing.

Ignoring the nasty duvet for a moment, I sat down on the bed and surveyed my new digs, hugging myself with excitement. I was interrupted by the noise of a car pulling up outside. Peeking out of the window, I watched Aaron and a blonde step out of a sleek black sports car. He pulled a load of those stiff cardboard bags that you get from designer shops out of the boot and followed the blonde into the house. Instantly, I felt the nag of envy. She seemed so confident, so certain that he was hers. She wouldn't be hidden from his family or treated like a hopeless cause. I longed for that self-confidence.

I didn't want to leave the flat to meet Andy that evening. I'd have preferred to just sit and enjoy my new place, but I dutifully got myself ready, wondering if he'd notice that I wore the same outfit on every date. I walked down the dark driveway to the gates, praying that my code would work. I had to use my phone to illuminate the keypad in the dark, but it all worked fine and I was able to step outside into the real world again.

It was a cold, crisp night, with clear skies and a biting wind. I hurried along to find the pub, which was only a few hundred yards away. It was a relief to step into the warm, beery-smelling room, filled with the chatter of groups of people having their Saturday evening out. I scanned the room, spotting Andy straightaway, parked in front of a roaring open fire. He smiled and stood when he saw me making my way over. "How'd it go today?" he asked, before kissing me on the cheek.

"Great thanks. It didn't take long. I was all unpacked by three."

"Good."

A slightly awkward moment stretched between us. I busied myself unwrapping my scarf and taking off my coat. Andy disappeared to the bar to get more drinks. I sat on the sofa to enjoy the fire. A few minutes later, he was back, bearing a glass of wine for me and a pint of beer for himself. "They do 'Old Fox' bitter in here," he said enthusiastically, taking a long sip.

"Are you driving?" I asked, frowning slightly. He shook his head.

"Got a cab. I need a drink after the week I've had. He stared into the fire, seemingly lost in his thoughts. "That case I had to litigate for," he paused. I stayed quiet. "It was a young fella, trying the same tack as you did."

"Probably read the same website," I said.

"Yeah, well, I demolished him, just as I did you. He looked shocked, as though I'd punched him in the gut."

"I know that feeling," I interjected.

"I used to enjoy winning," he said quietly. "All I could think of was him harming himself. I followed him out of the court, just in case. What I saw..." he trailed off.

"What?" I pressed.

"He had a wife and a baby. They were waiting outside for him. He was as white as a sheet, and she cried when he told her." He stroked my face softly. "I feel like the biggest bastard who ever walked the planet."

"If it wasn't you, then someone else who takes on those cases would do the job," I reminded him. "The thing I've learnt about debt is that there is no escape. It walks with you everywhere you go. You carry it around like a backpack. It weighs you down at every moment of your life. It's like my scars; always there, always making me feel inferior."

"Why?" he sounded incredulous.

"Because every time I have something nice, I feel guilty. Instead of sitting here enjoying this lovely glass of wine, I should be having plain water and giving the money to MVDI."

"But I bought it for you, and MVDI owes me money, not the other way round."

"I wouldn't expect you to understand," I muttered.

"I don't understand why you think living on gruel would help," he said. "Anyway, I've sorted MVDI for you. It's only a pound a month remember?"

I rolled my eyes. "It's still there. It hasn't gone away. It still occupies my thoughts and I still panic about paying it back."

"Sir, madam, your table's ready," said the landlord, effectively ending the conversation. We followed him out to the dining area at the back of the pub. He handed us a menu each, which was thankfully written in English and consisted of mainly British classics and upmarket nursery food.

"If you listen to that stupid voice in your head and pick the cheapest pasta dish, I'll be bloody cross," he said sternly. "You're having either the filet steak or the sea bass. Take your pick." He had a particularly stubborn curl to his lip that told me he wasn't prepared to argue. I sighed, annoyed that he just didn't understand.

"I'll have the steak please," I muttered, snapping the menu shut.

"Good girl," he said approvingly, a self-satisfied smirk on his face.

"Could you be any more patronising if you tried?" I huffed. He looked hurt.

"I wasn't trying to be patronising. I was trying to be nice, to look after you. I didn't see you being huffy when you needed me," he reminded me, his face impassive. He had a terrific poker face when it suited him.

"I know. I'm sorry," I said, chastened. I'd leant on him repeatedly, and then blamed him for feeling he had to take charge of me. I resolved to be a bit less helpless in the future. My apology seemed to relax him, and he beamed a glorious smile.

"Shall I order?"

"Please. Can I have another of whatever that wine was too?"

I sat back and watched as he motioned for the waitress. He treated her to a full-on dazzling smile. I saw her blush pink and get flustered as she wrote down our order. I marvelled at the ease with which he travelled through life with his self-confidence and beautiful face. Idly, I wondered if any of it would rub off on me.

"Penny for them?" he asked. The waitress had scuttled off to get our drinks.

"Just musing," I said, noncommittal. He stayed silent, a tactic he used to get me to talk. I sighed. "I just wish I hadn't been so needy around you. I'm forever going to be the stupid girl who needs saving from herself."

"Really? I don't see it that way at all. I'll admit I had to save you at Bromley South, but some of that was my doing. I was brutal in that courtroom; I know that. I've not had to save you since though." He seemed puzzled, not really understanding what I was on about.

"The wage issue, benefits, getting the sack. If you give me a bit longer I can give you a list."

"I didn't save you from any of that. You got this job on your own. All the rest of the stuff would've happened anyway, regardless of me. Can I also remind you that you saved me from a life of celibacy, so I think we're even." He paused, "Anyway, why're you in such a bad mood? You just got a new job, a new flat, and you're about to get a filet steak."

"I love my new flat," I said. "It's the best place I've ever lived. It's got a dishwasher and everything, not that I think I'll use it much. I need to get some bigger bedding though, mine doesn't fit."

"I see."

"And it's got a decent-sized telly too, and a proper oven. I can learn to bake."

"So would you have rather sat in your flat tonight and practised making cakes?" his eyes were dancing with mirth. "So you're pissed that I made you come out and eat steak rather than let you have a go at cooking it in your fancy new kitchen?" he was trying his best to keep a straight face. I didn't reply, not wanting to admit that the smug bugger was indeed correct. I was saved by the arrival of our drinks, carried by the rather giggly, flirty waitress. I glared at her.

Andy took a sip of his beer. "There'll be plenty of time for you to practice your cooking. I'm just pleased that things are improving for you. I saw Rupert earlier. He's going to be giving your old boss some bad news next week. Apparently you're due backdated pay of just over ten thousand pounds. If she doesn't pay it within twenty-eight days, he'll be issuing fines and interest."

I reeled with the news. "Do you know how much Maria is due?" I really hoped her pay would be backdated too. He shook his head.

"I didn't ask."

"I'll be able to pay a chunk of my debt," I said. What I really wanted was to be able to go shopping, buy some warm clothes and have a small contingency fund, but with him being the lawyer for MVDI, I figured every penny would need to go to them. I wondered if he'd be telling them I had a better-paying job. I did a quick calculation, with the unpaid wages, plus my new rent-free salary, I'd probably be able to clear the debt in a year. I began to cheer up a bit.

"Where did you live when your parents were alive?" Andy asked out of the blue.

"Bromley South, why?"

"I just wondered what happened to their house and stuff."

I shook my head, "It was probably only rented. My uncle took care of it all I think. He gave me a few trinkets that belonged to Mum, but they were only costume stuff. I don't think my parents were rich."

"What about the insurance? There must have been a payout?"

"I don't think there was, well, I was never told about it. I don't even know whose fault it was; whether Dad hit the lorry or the lorry hit us. I was kind of unconscious through most of it; I can't even remember the actual crash." It was one of those things I didn't want to forage through my memory for. Even talking about it made me fidgety and uncomfortable. "If there was a payout, either the home got it or my uncle. I told you before I was forgotten. Plus, I was only eight." It seemed he was pressing home just another example of what a loser I'd been my whole life, that at age eight, alone and terrified, I'd not been able to take charge, negotiate a payout and supervise the disposal of my parent's belongings. At the time I'd been more concerned with making sure they hadn't chopped bits off me.

"I'll look into it. It's been bothering me," he said.

"It's been and gone. There's no point looking back, let's face it, if there had been anything, my uncle would've spent it."

"Possibly. I'm more convinced it would've been placed in a trust, but the home forgot to tell you."

Our food's arrival interrupted us. The steak smelt amazing and was served with fat, homemade chips. I picked one up and tasted it, instantly I was transported back to my childhood. I recalled sitting at the kitchen table, eating chips with fish fingers and peas, my mum singing along to the radio as she stood at the stove stirring whatever she was making for their dinner. I felt my eyes welling up.

Andy was watching me with his knife and fork poised to cut through his steak. "Are you OK?" He asked gently. I nodded.

"Flashback," I whispered, unable to say more than that.

"OK, let's change the subject," he replied, catching on straightaway. "Tell me about your new charges. What sort of dogs are they?"

I relaxed immediately. "Two German Shepherds, both as spoilt as you like. The house manager gave me their care notes today. They're actually fed steak, can you believe it?" I'd been a little disapproving when I'd read it, not because I didn't agree with a raw meat diet for dogs, but because it seemed so extravagant. They'd have been just as happy with meaty bones from the butcher. "They're walked twice a day in the woods, fed morning and night, and I'll be responsible for making sure they're clean and healthy. Doesn't seem too onerous."

"Sounds a doddle, unless they're particularly naughty. My mum has a little Maltese terrier who seems to rule the house with an iron paw. Mum always says that Lola's more work than all us boys were, put together. The bloody thing'll only eat Marks' roast chicken and is at the hairdressers more than Mum is."

I smiled. "Terriers can be quite a handful. I've not been bitten many times at work, but on those rare occasions, it was always a nippy little terrier. The bigger dogs always seemed more careful of their bite. The two German Shepherds, Roxy and Bruno seem friendly enough."

We chatted easily through the rest of our dinner, both having got over our earlier funk. Andy outlined the lawsuit he was bringing against the surgery on my behalf. He was taking them to an industrial tribunal for unfair dismissal, unpaid wages, breach of contract, and

The Debt

dismissal due to failure to pay the minimum wage. He told me that reducing my hours had been unlawful as there'd been no consultation beforehand. "I'm going for the jugular," he said. "Rupert's put in the unpaid wage and minimum wage amount, but even if she pays that to avoid all the fines he can impose, it still leaves the other issues on the table."

"If I won, what would I get?" I asked.

"Depends on a lot of factors. Unfair dismissal can be up to seventy-odd grand, but the average compensation is a year's salary. In your case, that's around ten thousand. The dismissal due to minimum wage breach and the breach of contract is probably worth a few thousand each. If she's clever, she'll settle out of court to avoid costs and fines. I'd suggest settling for around fifteen thousand on top of the amount Rupert's set."

I gaped at him. If he could win it, my debt would be paid and I'd have plenty left over. "That would be amazing," I told him. The prospect of being debt-free, living in a posh flat and having spare cash to spend on nice clothes was tantalisingly close.

"It could take several months," he warned. "The law works slowly." His words deflated me. In reality, nothing would change for the foreseeable future. I still had just £45 to see me through to my first payday.

Andy was extremely impressed with my new flat, commenting on how much better it was than the bedsit. He seemed to spend a long time staring out of the window at the main house, which was again fully illuminated. "It's a beautiful house," was all he said, before turning back to me and kissing me hard, his hands roaming my body.

We kept the little reading light above the bed switched on as we made love; its gentle light casting shadows around the room as our bodies joined with an erotic tenderness. Andy had proved to be a kind and gentle lover, touching my body with a reverence I'd never experienced with anybody else. He never just "fucked," he always made love.

We fit together perfectly, his hard, masculine body felt perfect against my soft, slender flesh. He liked to get closer than close, always holding me to him, as though he wanted to be inside me in every possible way. We made love for hours that night, delighting in the knowledge that nobody could hear us, either loudly performing our sexual gymnastics, or when we sat drinking tea and talking into the small hours.

Andy talked a lot about the man he'd seen in court, I could tell it really bothered him. "How many cases do you have to attend court for?" I asked. We were sitting up in bed, and it was one in the morning.

"To be honest, as I said before, yours was a fluke, I don't normally do the court attendances."

"So why did you do that one?"

He sighed loudly. "I needed to know if it would affect me again." I stayed silent and sipped my tea, silently urging him on. "Years ago, when I was starting out, I did a lot of those cases. I'd get a buzz out of winning. I knew those contracts inside out and off by heart, so could easily defend the card companies. After seeing what I did to you, I just felt as though I didn't have the stomach for it anymore. It's why I attended the Dixon case rather than send one of the lawyers. I needed to know.."

He seemed in turmoil, wrestling with his conscience. "Those contracts you sign when you take out a credit card, they cover every base. The whole system is rigged against the customer. They know they put temptation in everyone's pocket, and then they rely on compound interest to really leech as much as possible. Seeing its effect with my own eyes, what its done to you, what its done to that family, I just don't know if I want to renew my contract with MVDI, with any of them."

"Do you work for other card companies as well?"

He nodded warily, "All of them. Alpha is the "go to" law firm for enforcement. We're retained by the top eighteen credit card issuers." He picked at a bit of fluff on the duvet cover, avoiding my eyes.

"It's a job. If you didn't do it, someone else would," I told him. "Turning it down wouldn't make it disappear, so you may as well carry on if it's lucrative work. I don't blame you for my debt. I blame myself for being stupid, and the card company for being sneaky with the interest and charges. It's not like it's you getting the interest, is it?"

He shook his head and smiled. "I'd be a very rich man indeed if I was. I do make money out of it all though."

I knew he was referring to the three thousand pounds his firm had added to my debt. "Well, if you buy me enough meals out, I'll have it back in kind, won't I?" I joked, bumping him with my shoulder. I ran my hands over his pecs, twining my fingers in the soft curls of his chest hair. He lay back on the bed, his own hands threaded through my hair. I traced each nipple in turn with my tongue, marvelling at how silky his skin was.

As I kissed my way down his treasure trail, his breath hitched and all talk was forgotten.

We slept in late the next morning, luxuriating in the space the new bed provided. I woke first, my legs entwined with his. I gazed at his beautiful face for a while, trying to just soak in every detail of the moment, of feeling his warmth and presence. I struggled with the sense of him being just too beautiful for me, too clever and successful to want an ordinary mortal such as I. With those doubts always in my mind, I concentrated on living in the moment while I was with him, creating memories to look back on fondly when he'd left me for someone better suited.

I pushed the thought aside as he opened his eyes, catching me in the act of admiring him. I was rewarded with a movie star smile. "Good morning beautiful."

"It's almost good afternoon," I said, nodding at the clock on the wall. It was half-eleven. I hadn't slept in that late for a long time.

"Bloody Hell is that the time? I need to be at my parents' in an hour. I was hoping to get some errands done first." He rubbed his eyes. I slid out of bed and filled the kettle.

"What errands? Anything I can help with?" I asked. He shook his head.

"I was gonna go into Bromley and get my hair cut. It's not important, I can do it tomorrow up near work."

"Where is it you work?" I asked.

"Near Cannon Street," he said, "there's a barber nearby."

He practically gulped down his coffee and pulled on his clothes. "How do I get out of the gate?" He asked.

"I'll need to come with you. I think the rule is that visitors have to be accompanied at all times." He rolled his eyes. I pulled on a track suit and trainers and grabbed my key, while he phoned for a taxi. He seemed to be in a dreadful rush to get out.

It was a dull, slightly misty winter's day outside. The wind whipped through my track suit jacket, freezing me to the core. We set off down the driveway to meet Andy's cab just outside the gates. We'd gotten no more than twenty yards down when I spotted Mr Pryce's car coming the other way. He slowed to a halt beside us and slid his window down. I thought he'd say hello to me.

"McCarthy! What are you doing on my estate?" I glanced at Andy, who was stone-faced and clearly not happy to see him. Mr Pryce seemed surprised too.

"I didn't know it was your place, Pryce. Who'd you rip off for this one then?"

I was horrified. Andy had just insulted my new boss, and I hadn't even started work. I kicked his ankle.

"Nobody at all. Don't tell me you're still sore about losing the captaincy of the cricket team to me? It was years ago McCarthy, it's time to get over it. Let your grudge go." He grinned wickedly at Andy's unsmiling face.

"Fuck all to do with the cricket team and you know it." He turned to me, "why didn't you tell me you'd be working for this shyster?"

"I take it you know each other then?" I said, which was stupidly obvious. Inside, I was panicking that either Aaron would kick me out, which would leave me homeless and jobless, or Andy would insist that I leave, which would have the same end result.

"We went to the same school," Andy muttered sulkily.

"And McCarthy here never forgave me for stealing captaincy of the cricket team from right under his nose, did you?" Aaron said, seeming to enjoy winding Andy up.

"I'm long over that," Andy snapped. "You seem to have forgotten about the Dutroix case, or is it that you'd prefer to forget losing that one in court?"

"Small change," Aaron said, waving his hand dismissively. "You hardly won it. Barely got thruppence out of me. Now a good lawyer could have taken me for much, much more." He grinned at Andy, showing a neat set of very white teeth.

"Given how much of a liar you are, I doubt it," spat Andy, ignoring my now-frantic ankle kicking.

"Now I find out that your lady friend works for me, on top of me owning Lakeswood."

"Leave my girlfriend out of this," Andy said. I blinked at him. It wasn't the nicest of ways he could have reassured me that I was more than just a fuck-buddy, but hearing him call me his girlfriend for the first time gave me a slightly goofy smile. I looked down at my feet, trying to hide my face from Aaron.

"How fortuitous, your girlfriend is an employee. You can check up all you like; you won't find anything."

"She knows nothing about any of this," Andy muttered, probably catching on that I might well get the sack. "I had no idea she was working for you, or that you had Lakeswood. It's a surprise for me too."

"You'd be amazed at what I can snatch from under your nose, McLoser," said Aaron, grinning widely before waving. "See you around," he called out as he drove off down the drive to the garage.

"What on Earth?" I began.

He held up his hand to stop me. "We went to school together. He's always been a flash git, as jealous as hell. He hated me at school, and when I was the opposing lawyer in a business deal he was involved in, it just cemented our view of each other. Now, I need to get my taxi."

We walked in silence for a while. "I'll go to that other interview in two weeks," I said quietly.

"I'm not saying you shouldn't work here. I'm sure he's a perfectly OK employer." He was gruff and obviously displeased.

"I don't exactly have a lot of options right now," I reminded him. "I'd struggle to get another bedsit given my credit rating. I don't have another job, and I've got forty-five pounds to my name." A stupid tear made its way down my cheek. I felt a very genuine fear of homelessness. Without the job, I'd be on the streets, which at the end of January was a terrifying prospect. He didn't answer.

I could see his taxi waiting on the road outside. I let him out of the pedestrian gate, pausing only to receive a rather sulky peck goodbye. "I'll call you," he said as he got into the cab.

With the glow of the previous night well and truly snuffed out, I trudged back up the drive to the flat, fully expecting to get my marching orders. Instead a rather contrite-looking Aaron Pryce was waiting for me.

CHAPTER 9

"I came to apologise," he said as I walked up to my door. "I shouldn't have teased Drew like that, at least not in front of you." I pulled out my key and turned the lock.

"I didn't know you knew each other. I didn't tell him your name when I got the job." The door opened. I was desperate to get inside and was shivering almost uncontrollably at that point. Aaron followed me in and up the stairs.

"I should explain, besides, I have some questions." He parked himself on the sofa.

"Would you like some tea? Or a coffee?" I asked, being polite.

"Tea please, builder's strength, two sugars."

I busied myself making our drinks. "Settled in alright?" He asked, looking around. The flat probably appeared empty still as I'd put everything away.

"Yes thanks." I brought our drinks over and put them on the coffee table. Aaron didn't seem as "posh" as Andy, with a softer, more South London accent and a more relaxed demeanour. I sat down opposite and watched his tall, lean frame sort of sprawl across the sofa.

"Are you going to kick me out?" I asked nervously.

His brow furrowed. "No, of course not. Why would I do that?"

"Because I'm seeing somebody you seem to have a bit of history with," I answered.

"It's not really any of my business who you go out with," he pointed out. "If anything, I find it quite funny. I'm the bane of that bloke's life, but he's got to walk into my place to see you."

"Not really, I can meet him elsewhere," I pointed out. "Why don't you like him?" I was curious. Andy had always seemed one of those affable, decent sorts of people. I hadn't expected him to have an enemy.

"We were at school together. I was the scholarship kid, while he came from money. I was envious, and he was an entitled little snob who liked to rub my nose in it."

"He's not like that now," I pointed out.

"Really? So how come he's got a girlfriend who's got an active County Court Judgement and has had to take a live-in position? That intrigues me."

"How did you know about the CCJ?" I gasped. Instantly the shame hit, and I felt my cheeks burn.

"Marcus does checks on employees. He'd be remiss if he hadn't picked it up. So, tell me, have you been seeing Drew long?"

"A few weeks," I said sulkily. I wanted him to go, to leave me to wallow alone in my embarrassment. "Does anyone else know? You know, about my debt?"

He shook his head. "Things like that are confidential. It won't be broadcast around the household. Marcus is extremely discreet. Does Drew know about it?"

I nodded.

"I see. He hasn't paid it for you?"

"No... Why should he?"

"Because you'd be happier without it. I paid off all of Shari's debts when I started seeing her. It made her happier, more relaxed. It's a drop in the ocean to him, he's got plenty of money."

"Some girls get all the luck," I thought. I scrubbed my hands over my face, making sure I didn't dislodge my fringe. "I wouldn't expect Andy to pay it. It's not his debt, nor would I ask him." The whole turn of the conversation was making me uncomfortable. Actually, Aaron Pryce himself made me edgy. He was just too cocky, too confident, and way too sexy for his own good. I stared at his hands wrapped around the mug. His long, slender fingers inexplicably made my tummy do that squeezing thing.

"He should have offered. I can see how embarrassed you are about it. Debt can be a terrible burden. It's an easy fix and would've cheered you up no end." His index finger tapped against the mug, giving an indication of his impatience. "Drew's loaded. It'd mean nothing to him; mind you, he was always a bit tight."

"Andy's not mean in any way," I told him, annoyed by his remark. "He treats me to some lovely meals out, never asks me to pay, besides, it's not really anything to do with you and your issues with him." I was more forceful than I meant to be, but his assertion that Andy was tight felt grossly unfair. Aaron simply smiled, clearly pleased he'd got his point across, no doubt banking on having placed a seed of doubt in my mind.

"Twice I've screwed him over," he said, "once at school, when I managed to lock him in a broom cupboard before an important match. Him being absent cost him the captaincy. He hated me for that."

"The second?" I asked, trying not to look amused at his first disclosure, even though I thought it was quite funny.

"I outbid him for this house, then had my lawyer exchange on it before Drew had a chance to come back with a better offer."

I gasped, "Andy bid for this house?"

He nodded, grinning widely in a smug, self-satisfied way. "He didn't know it was me. Well, he does now. He thought he got his own back a few years ago in an insider dealing case. He was representing the investors who were on the wrong side of the deal. Poor bugger was overjoyed to have beaten me, but the amount he won for them was nominal. I was just happy in the knowledge I had Lakeswood."

I reeled with the information. "So at twenty-four years old, Andy could've bought this house?"

He nodded warily. "He joined the family firm at twenty-two, so that his dad could semi-retire. It's one of the biggest law firms in the UK; they're all loaded. I heard on the grapevine he bought Yester Manor, but I've never been there. Is it nice?"

I shrugged, "No idea."

His eyes widened. "You've not seen it?" I shook my head, too despondent to say anything. Aaron drew in a breath. "I'd better go, my mum's coming to stay for a couple of days. She'll be here soon, so I'd better be there to meet her."

"Sure, well, thanks for the explanation," I muttered. I followed him down to the door. He just gave me his sphinx-like smile as he said goodbye.

When he'd gone, I made another drink and sat down to think about his revelations. He'd painted Andy in a light I'd never even thought of before, but Andy's constant deflection regarding where he lived and other aspects of his life began to make sense. He either expected me to be a gold digger, or he'd decided that I wasn't proper girlfriend material and was determined to have me as a no-strings fuck-buddy, hence why he was being secretive. I went over and over the problem in my mind, driving myself nuts. I decided to get some fresh air and explore the gardens in daylight, mainly to take my mind off things.

Gardens are never fantastic in winter, but although the formal gardens were a bit bare, the hedging which separated the space into rooms gave it an undeniable structure. Idly, I wondered if it was Jed or Marcus who was the talent behind it. Aaron hadn't struck me as being a garden-lover. As soon as I stepped out of the formal area and across the lawn into the woods, I felt my body relax. The smells and sounds of the forest always had that effect. I felt my hands loosen and my shoulders drop. I smiled at the idea that from the following day, I'd be paid to walk there twice a day. I really had landed on my feet.

I plotted out a decent walk for the dogs, so that I'd take them around the whole perimeter. I reasoned that they'd need plenty of exercise, being so large. With daylight failing, I headed back to the flat.

Andy had tried to call, I'd left my phone indoors, but I could see from the display that he'd phoned about quarter past three. I debated whether or not to call him back, but wracked with indecision, decided to have a hot bath instead.

My problem was that I had feelings for him; every time I pictured his beautiful face, my heart lurched.

Every time he touched me, my body responded to his. Knowing I was being treated like a dirty secret or a short-term lover made me want to guard myself from him. If I fell any further in love, I'd be torn to pieces when he moved on to someone more suitable. As I lay in the bath, luxuriating in the sensation after years of only showers, I stared at my accursed scars and allowed a few, fat tears to fall.

I didn't call him, and he didn't try again that evening. I needed to avoid him while in the midst of a pity party. I steeled myself to keep things casual and not allow myself to fall too deep. I would constantly remind myself that I wasn't the girl for him. Instead, I spent the evening researching raw meat diets for dogs. If the pups would be spoilt, I'd at least make sure they were healthy and spoilt.

My first day went quite well. I arrived in the kitchen at quarter to eight to find Bruno and Roxy waiting patiently. Gerry showed me where their meat was kept and watched as I added an egg and a grated carrot to their bowls, which they loved. "Who's been looking after them?" I asked while the pair were wolfing down their breakfast. Gerry had kindly made me a latte, which I was enjoying.

"I've been feeding them and either Jed or Marcus has been walking them. Marcus doesn't really enjoy the outdoors, so they've only been getting five minutes round the garden. It's not enough for them really. Would you like some breakfast?"

I shook my head. "I'm gonna take them out for an hour, then I'm meeting with Marcus to sort out paperwork."

The dogs loved the woods, and they bounded around happily, sniffing trees, checking out fox holes and finding sticks. They were clearly quite well-trained, as their recall was good and they could both fetch when I threw bits of branch for them. I cleaned them off in the boot room and watched as they settled into their beds for a nap, both a bit worn out.

Marcus was in his office, working on his computer when I arrived. He smiled widely, especially when he realised I was carrying two lattes, one of which was his. "Settled in OK?" he enquired.

"Great thanks. The dogs have already been out and are fast asleep. They're really well-behaved," I told him. He pulled a face.

"Are they? Little sods always seem to run away whenever I've walked them. I ended up having to keep them on the lead. I don't have time to go chasing round the gardens looking for them."

"So what tasks would you like me to do when they're asleep?" I asked. I knew they'd be asleep for at least a couple of hours.

He shrugged, "Just make sure their bedding's clean, they're clean, claws kept short, that kind of thing. As long as they're fed, walked and looked after, your time is your own."

"I see," I said, unsure if he realised just how much well-walked dogs slept. We spent the next ten minutes signing my contract of employment and sorting out my pay details.

"Aaron mentioned that you needed some suitable bedding. We have plenty in the laundry store if you'd like to choose some," Marcus ventured. I wondered what else Aaron had told him about his visit to my flat.

"That'd be great, if it's not too much trouble."

"None at all. Come on, I'll show you where it is and help you carry it back." I followed him out of the room and back out into the hall. He led me up the magnificent staircase, and then down a wide corridor, which was decorated in identical colours to the downstairs. All the doors seemed the same, but Marcus opened one about halfway down that proved to be a storeroom filled with shelves of various linens and duvets.

"The bed in your room is a kingsize, so you want to choose one from this shelf," he said, gesturing to the third shelf up. "I'd suggest the pale grey with a charcoal tweed runner." He pulled out a dove grey set.

"It's lovely," I breathed, "but it's only for me, I don't need anything posh."

"It's only cotton," he said, seemingly a bit affronted. "Your home should always be a visual feast. It's good for the soul to be surrounded by beautiful things. Aaron said that your bedding was too small and was pink. It jarred with the rest of the space."

I momentarily panicked, concerned that Marcus thought that Aaron had been in my room for less innocent reasons. "He wasn't there to look at my bed," I squawked. "He was there to explain why he was a bit argumentative with my fella."

"Yeah, he told me he bumped into Drew McCarthy, revealing that he was actually the one who beat Drew to Lakeswood. I'd have loved to have been a fly on the wall for that one." Marcus grinned a bit too widely at the thought.

"You know him too?" I asked.

"Oh yes. I went to Eltham College too. Everyone knew the McCarthys. I thought Drew was gonna end up with that stuck-up bitch. She made Shari seem like a sweet, thoughtful angel."

"I gather nobody liked Charlotte. Well, I've only met Rupert, but he called her the Horror Bitch," I confided. "Why doesn't anyone like Shari?"

He leaned in to whisper conspiratorially, "Because she's as common as muck, but sticks her nose in the air. She's away for a few days because Aaron's mum came to stay and can't get along with her. Says she's only with Aaron because of his money. I'd agree, but Aaron can't see it."

"So why don't you like Andy?" I wanted Marcus's take on it.

"I didn't dislike Drew, I just thought he was a bit of a snob. You had to be one of the rich kids to be in his crowd. Aaron and I weren't, so we were excluded. My parents scraped to send me there, and Aaron was there on a scholarship, so we couldn't join in with all the school trips and parties. It set some of us apart." He paused. "Aaron got his own back though. Success is always the best revenge."

"What about you?" I asked. "How did you come to manage his estate?"

Marcus pulled the bedding set off the shelf and started loading it into my arms. "I did interior design at college, but to be honest, I didn't have the drive to set up a practice or anything like that. I was drifting a little aimlessly really. When Aaron bought this place, he needed someone to do it up and run it. He's too useless to figure out how to decorate or organise anything, so he asked me to do it, plus it leaves me plenty of free time for my other interests."

"The house is perfect. You're very talented," I said. He smiled widely before pulling an enormous duvet off the shelf.

"Thank you. Now, shall we go sort out this bed of yours?"

The two of us made short work of changing my bed. Marcus had shown me how to dress the end of the duvet with the tweed blanket, making sure that the oversized buttons sat on the outside and in a straight line. It looked really classy, like something from an interiors magazine. It would also save me having to buy a set from my paycheck, so I was doubly delighted. I think Marcus was pleased to see me so happy, blowing me a kiss before wandering off back to his office to sort out a curtain order that he said was overdue.

I went back to the kitchen to check on the dogs. An older lady was seated at the kitchen island peeling sprouts while talking ten to the dozen at Gerry. They both stopped when I walked in. "Maggie, this is Sally, the dog nanny," said Gerry. "This is Maggie, Aaron's Mum." I held out my hand.

"Delighted to meet you," I told her. She quickly wiped hers on her skirt before shaking mine.

"Lovely to meet you too dear. I'm so pleased that the babies are being properly looked after again. Gerry told me you're an expert in how to feed them."

"I'm a veterinary nurse," I told her, "so I've studied animal nutrition."

"Super," she exclaimed, "I just hope you can cope with living with all these men. Gerry here's a darling, but Marcus is a bit of a fusspot. Keeps sending cleaners in to make my bed and stuff, as if I can't make my own bed. Been doing it for sixty-odd years."

"But do you get the cushions straight?" Gerry interjected. Maggie laughed.

"Probably not, but life's too short to straighten cushions." She turned to me, "If you're going out on a walk this afternoon, I might join you. I quite enjoy a stroll round the woods. It'd have to be after *Bargain Hunt* though, I do like to watch that."

I liked her immediately. She was a little out of place in the silent and intimidating house, being rather loud, a little common and very smiley. I discovered that she'd moved down to Sussex after retiring from her sales position at Marks and Spencer, only visiting Aaron for a couple of days each month "for a mini-break." I was interrupted by Roxy waking up and padding into the kitchen to nuzzle Maggie. Bruno followed soon after, yawning widely.

"I think some teeth cleaning, claw clipping and a good bath is next on the agenda," I announced. I led them back into the boot room where their supplies were kept. They clearly weren't used to having their teeth cleaned, both of them wriggled and squirmed a little when I touched their mouths.

Clipping their claws was easy in comparison, and long overdue by the length of them. I quickly swept up the clippings and switched on their shower. Immediately, both tried to hide, scratching at the door to escape. "You're getting washed whatever you say," I told them. Bruno let out a bark of protest. "No arguments," I said firmly.

By the time I'd gotten them both washed, I was almost as wet as them. Bruno had objected so much, that I'd had to put a collar and lead on him to gain enough control to get him in the dog bath. They'd both delighted in shaking off in front of me, soaking both myself and the entire room in the process.

Once bathed, the pair of them were extremely pleased with themselves, bouncing around the room as I attempted to clean it up. "So you've decided to play now?" I said to Roxy as she chased every movement of the mop, making it almost impossible to wipe the floor. By the time I'd gotten the room back to some sort of semblance of normality, both dogs were almost dry, while I was still soaked and a little ragged. I let them back into the kitchen.

"Don't you look lovely," Maggie exclaimed, confusing me for a moment until I realised she was talking to the dogs. "All shiny and sparkly." She caught sight of me in the doorway and began to laugh. "Oh Sally, did they give you the runaround? You look like you need a cup of tea." She began filling the kettle before I could answer. "After Sonia left, nobody would bathe them; they play up too much. I think the gardener hosed them down outside once, which they hated." She wittered on while making a pot of tea. I couldn't get a word in edgeways. "That's a nasty scar there on your forehead. How'd you get that?" She asked, peering at my face. I froze, before pulling my fringe back down, cursing myself for forgetting to check it.

"I was in a car crash when I was a child," I muttered.

"Poor thing," she said, her voice full of sympathy. "Same thing happened to Aaron. It's how we lost his dad. Thankfully Aaron survived, although his left arm is a bit scarred up. He suffered terrible nightmares for years. Did you have those too?"

Stunned at her revelation, I just nodded.

"Took him years to get over," she said. "Mind you, he was only six, children are so sensitive at that age. How old were you?"

"I was eight."

She tutted loudly and concentrated on pouring our teas. Gerry wandered back in, so she fussed around, getting another cup for him and making his drink exactly how he liked it. She then turned her attention to Roxy, who was on the cadge for biscuits, laying her muzzle across Maggie's hip. Our conversation was forgotten.

Maggie joined me for the dog's afternoon walk, first showing me around the gardens, describing in great detail the planting plans Marcus had drawn up and how wonderful it all looked when everything came out. We then meandered through the woods, talking about the dogs, the house, and all sorts of random subjects. I liked her enormously. She was one of those people who could chat about anything, and she clearly had a compassion and empathy I'd rarely experienced. I even confided about losing my parents, to which she'd grasped my hand and said "you poor girl."

The dogs were exhausted by the time we returned, so I gave them their evening feed, washed their paws, and put them to bed. Maggie was preparing a roast for Aaron as a special treat, so Gerry had the evening off. I left her to it and went back to the flat for a hot bath.

I'd left my phone in the flat, thinking I wouldn't be allowed it while working. I checked it while my bath was running, to see I had three missed calls from Andy. I called him straight back.

"Hiya, what're you doing tonight?"

"Nothing much," I replied, "I'm just about to get into a hot bath. I've been soaked once and frozen twice today."

"Oh dear. Well, I can come over with a curry if you like."

"Why don't I come over to you?" I thought I'd try it.

"Don't be daft. Save yourself a taxi fare, plus it'd mean you'd have to get dressed. It's easier if I come over to you. What's the code for the gate?"

"I don't think I'm allowed to give it out. Ring me when you're on your way and I'll walk down and let you in."

"OK." He sounded annoyed. "You really need to ask if I can just be let in. It's not like he doesn't know me."

"I'll ask Marcus," I promised, although I figured they wouldn't want him in the estate unaccompanied. They might know him, but neither of them liked him.

Andy was quite perky that evening, asking about my first day, the dogs and the woods. I chatted happily, telling him about Aaron's mother and how nice she was.

"We used to tease him about her, because she worked in a shop," he said, shifting in his chair. He stared at the floor. "Kids are cruel."

"At least he had a mum," I pointed out. "So when am I gonna meet yours?"

"Soon. This curry's a bit hot. Do you want another poppadom?"

"Don't change the subject."

"Well don't put pressure on me then. Why do you want to meet my parents so much?"

"Because," I paused. "Am I just a fuck-buddy?" I wanted to know.

"Course not."

"Then why are you treating me like one?"

"I wasn't aware that I was."

I stayed silent. He wasn't a stupid man, and it was becoming pretty obvious that he was ashamed of me. The only doubt clouding my mind was that he'd introduced me to Rupert. Wary of making another bad decision, I decided to drop the subject.

"Marcus said he knew you from school too."

He seemed surprised. "Marcus Brookes?"

I nodded.

"He's the house manager here. Runs everything."

"Well, he always trailed around after Aaron like a lovesick puppy. Everywhere Pryce was, Brookes would be two steps behind. He's a sneaky little shit too. Wonder why he settled for being just an errand boy though."

"I think he's a bit more than that. He did all the interiors and designed the gardens. I suppose a place this big needs a lot of people taking care of it, which means someone managing it all."

"So Marcus is Aaron's wife then?" Andy sniggered a little nastily. "Marcus came out when we were in sixth form. I just didn't realise Prycey was that way too."

It answered my question about Marcus. "I don't think Aaron is. He's got a girlfriend. I've not met her yet, but I saw her the other day, she's very glamorous."

He didn't answer. I watched as he swallowed the last piece of nan bread. A few moments later, he was stroking my face, whispering seductive words into my ear. "I really want to peel you out of that track suit and make wild, passionate love to you on your pretty, new bed." My belly squeezed.

I shoved all my misgivings to the back of my mind as Andy made good his promise, sliding open the zipper of my top, revealing that I was naked underneath. He made a guttural noise as his large hands enveloped my breasts, softly kneading them, and then flicking his thumbs over my nipples repeatedly. I groaned at the sensation, arching my back to increase the pressure.

"I think you need to be satisfied first," he said, smiling at me. He lifted me off the chair and dropped me onto the bed, before dragging my yoga pants down my legs. He stroked his hand slowly up my good leg. "You have such lovely skin," he murmured. He kissed his way up the inside of my thigh, before treating my clit to some long, slow licks. I was desperate to feel him inside me.

"Please," I begged. I was trying hard not to come.

"Please, what?" He murmured against my skin, before flicking my clit with his tongue.

"Oh God, please fuck me. Icantholdonmuchlonger." The words came out a jumbled mess. I felt him fumbling with his buttons, wriggling his trousers down just enough to release his erection. He slammed into me, pushing me up the bed.

He reared up onto his knees, pulling my hips forward, before licking his thumb and continuing to rub my clit while he slid in and out. It felt amazing. I gave myself over to it completely, losing myself in his rhythmic ministrations.

My orgasm exploded. Most orgasms flutter into existence, or race through the body. This one blew me apart. I practically convulsed with pleasure as he kept up his careful rhythm. "Hmm, think we've found something you like," he said softly, seeming amused by my helpless reaction. I opened my eyes to see him gazing at me in rapt fascination.

Then he let go. His sculptured lips parted and let out a cry. I watched as his beautiful face screwed up, as if in pain, and then relax into a serene expression of pure bliss. He was as in the moment as I. Whatever else we had going on, we were at that moment just one entity.

He leaned down to kiss me, his tongue stroking mine in post-lovemaking happiness. All my doubts and worries were far from my mind as I just revelled in the afterglow. "Can I stay the night?" He murmured, "I've missed sleeping next to you, and now you've got a massive bed and a fancy new duvet, we should christen it."

I smiled and snuggled into him, nuzzling his chest. "I'd like that."

CHAPTER 10

My first week sped by without incident. The two dogs were a delight and seemed to have taken to me, my flat still felt like the lap of luxury and Andy had visited every other evening. The only issue I had was a very real lack of cash. I was getting by thanks to Andy's generous provision of takeaways, and Gerry slipping me the odd sandwich during the day. I'd had no word from the surgery and wasn't really expecting to get my final pay. It meant I just had to grit my teeth and wait for my first payday. I planned to get a warm coat with my first month's wages, maybe some warm boots too. I was walking a lot every day and regardless of how many layers I put on, I could really feel the biting wind. On one of the coldest days, it felt as though I wore almost every item in my wardrobe at the same time. Even Gerry had laughed as I'd waddled into the kitchen resembling the Michelin Man.

"Don't laugh, have you felt how cold it is out there?" I said while fastening the coats onto the dogs. They had better coats than I did.

"I'd rather not. I'm happy in my nice warm kitchen, thanks. Still, in two day's time I'll be basking in the sun, sipping a cocktail. I can't wait." Gerry was off to Egypt for a fortnight and was annoying everyone by gloating about it. His girlfriend was also a chef, working long hours, so they were both looking forward to spending some time together.

"So who looks after Aaron while you're away?" I asked.

"Shari's back tonight. I suppose she will. No doubt I'll have to deep clean the kitchen when I get back. Last time I went away, the place was a pigsty. It took me a day to get it shipshape again. I don't think she knows how to wipe a surface."

"I'll try and keep it clean for you," I promised. I was quite intrigued to meet Shari after hearing so much. Maggie had been scathing, telling me she was nothing but a gold-digger who was, in her opinion, not making her beloved son happy. Having listened to all the others gossiping, I'd actually felt quite sorry for her. Nobody had a good word to say, even Jed, who was quite mild-mannered.

She arrived that afternoon in a flashy Porsche, parking it on the skew outside the front door, which blocked the route to the garages. I was preparing the dog's evening meal in the kitchen when I heard her arrive.

"Park the car Marcus; there's a good boy," she barked in a strident tone. I cringed on Marcus's behalf, as did Gerry. "My case is in the boot. It needs bringing in." I heard her heels tapping on the stone floor as she approached the kitchen. I noticed both dogs tense and move behind me.

She was glamorous, in a hard-faced way. Her curtain of icy blonde hair fell in a perfect shape around her unsmiling face. She strode into the kitchen, and straight past me, as though I was invisible, which was disconcerting. "Hi, I'm Sally," I said, smiling at her. The bitch blanked me.

"I'll have a pot of tea and a small tuna salad Gerry," she ordered in an imperious voice. "I'll eat in the drawing room." With that, she swept back out, back past me, without even acknowledging my existence.

"Charming," I said once she'd gone.

"Count your blessings, at least she wasn't nasty to you," Gerry said as he hastily assembled her food. I went back to sorting out dinner for Roxy and Bruno, who were at least appreciative of my efforts. The fact that neither of them had greeted her hadn't passed me by. They went nuts when Aaron walked in, and even I got an excited welcome. If anything, they'd been scared of her.

The next morning, I walked into bedlam. The dogs were hiding in the utility room as Shari gave Marcus a loud and very public dressing-down in the hallway. "Our room was actually cold last night, not the right temperature at all. You forgot to stock the bathroom with my special shampoo, and the flowers in the drawing room look half-dead. It's not good enough Marcus— you're getting sloppy."

I heard him murmur something in reply, but I couldn't hear what was said. "I don't care who hears," she told him, her voice getting louder. "I'm too busy to look after the house by myself. I've got to be at my yoga class at nine, then I'm meeting Sonia for coffee, so I can't supervise the florist, besides, what else exactly are you paid for?"

Gerry stood holding a tray loaded with Shari's breakfast. "Wish me luck," he muttered before heading out to interrupt Marcus' dressing-down.

"What the fuck is that?" I heard her shout. "I said raspberry jam, not strawberry. Can't anyone get anything right in this house?"

He reappeared, red patches on his cheeks as he went to the larder to exchange the jam. "Fucking bitch," he grumbled. I escaped with the dogs, the three of us relieved to get away.

I kept them out longer than usual, mainly because they were so jumpy and skittish that it took over an hour just to calm them down and get their tails wagging again. Roxy in particular seemed glued to my side, trying to stay close. I wondered if she'd ever actually hurt them, or they just felt unsure because of her bad temper.

I didn't take them back until gone eleven, even though I knew she'd be out. The afternoon was spent doing ears, teeth, and paws, followed by a thorough bath. She wouldn't have an excuse to be horrid to them. I even wondered if I should take them up to my flat to keep them out of her way. She wasn't remotely interested in them, so wouldn't notice if they weren't there. I decided to let Marcus know, just in case anyone got worried. I knocked on the door of his office bearing a latte. "Come in," he called out.

He smiled when he realised it was me. I put his coffee on his desk. "I'm gonna take the dogs up to my flat for a bit. Roxy seems a little..."

"Tense?" He interjected. I nodded. "Can I come too?"

I laughed, unsure if he was joking or not. "If you like. Won't anyone get cross if you sneak off?"

"Probably, but the way I feel right now, I wish I could just walk out and never come back. She's beyond the pale at times."

The four of us, Marcus, myself, and the two dogs decamped to my flat. I switched the TV on and watched as the pair settled themselves down in front of it. "So they like *Escape to the Country*?" Marcus said, smiling at their rapt fascination.

"Most dogs like a bit of TV. It must get boring just sitting. They're having two very long walks every day, so they need a bit of chill time to rest."

"Aaron thinks you've worked wonders with them. He said how much calmer they are since you started." Hearing it from the horse's mouth, so to speak, was very gratifying. I beamed a smile.

"They're great dogs, but being young, they need a lot of exercise and stimulation, otherwise they will get bored and destructive. I've made their diet a bit more balanced too, which'll help."

He settled himself on the sofa. "So has she been vile to you yet? I take it you heard it all this morning?"

"I've kept out of her way, and so far she's not acknowledged my existence. Long may it last," I paused, "Has she always been like that? You know, difficult?"

Marcus nodded. "She's never been nice, but once Aaron paid off all her bills and bought her a new car, she got insufferable. Personally, I think she's gotten too comfortable, too quickly. I've seen it all before. They start acting like the lady of the manor, then get all upset when Aaron ditches them. He's easy-going, but he's no fool."

"I don't even understand why she's so bad tempered," I mused, "I mean, it's not like she's got a hard life is it?"

"It's because she's so *bizeee*," said Marcus, mimicking her South London accent. I laughed, so he carried on: "*It's so stressful, fitting in all the Pilates classes, coffee dates, and fings. I hardly get time to get a propah manicure, and my waxing girl has to accommodate me on the rare occasions I can squeeze in a visit. It's so hard when everyone in the world wants to have lunch wiv me.*" He was outrageously camp, getting Shari's mannerisms down to a "T." "*It's Shari, not Sharon, and I'll scratch out your eyes if you say different.*"

I was giggling so much that the dogs looked up from their telly program. "Has Aaron ever seen your impression of her?"

He nodded, a mischievous smile on his face. "He thinks it's hysterical."

"So why is he with her?" I was curious.

"God knows. She must be good in bed or something." He was scathing.

"Maybe it's because she's available?" I volunteered. "It's not as though she's got a career to worry about is it? She can just be at his beck and call."

"You've probably hit the nail on the head," admitted Marcus. "Aaron doesn't get attached to women. The moment they make his life awkward, he tends to ditch them. She'll be as nice as pie when he's around, wait and see."

We headed back to the main house around teatime. Thankfully, Shari was nowhere to be seen, so Marcus went to his office to do some paperwork, and I set about making the dog's evening meal. "Where did you two slope off to?" Gerry asked, his nose bothering him. "One of the cleaners was looking for Marcus."

"Just in my flat. We had to sort out the dog's worming regime," I said, arranging my features to appear innocent.

"Always thought he batted for the home team," Gerry grunted, before sloping off to peer into the oven at whatever it was he was cooking.

"It was nothing like that. We were just keeping our heads down," I said. "Besides, I'm seeing someone." Gerry just nodded, as he was busy basting a chicken. It smelt delicious. My tummy rumbled appreciatively. Andy would be over at seven, probably bearing Chinese. I wished I could afford to just go shopping and cook something plain for us, rather than living on takeaways. I wondered how to broach the subject.

Andy seemed quiet when he arrived, preoccupied by something. I dished up our food and switched the telly over to the news, which he liked to watch. "I heard back from Ms Gadd today," he said. "She's not backing down gracefully, so I applied to the court for a hearing date. I should hear back within a week or so."

"I knew she wouldn't just roll over. I bet she gives Rupert the runaround too. I can't see me getting that back pay anytime soon." I wrestled with the idea of telling him how close to the wire I was, but chickened out.

"I did something else... I need to talk to you about it." I glanced up. His lovely face was troubled, a frown perfectly pitched between his eyebrows. He picked up the remote and turned the sound down.

"Go on," I said. Inside I was panicking in case he'd made me bankrupt. Instantly, the eight-year-old girl who had been terrified her leg would be amputated in her sleep reared her little head. I didn't want to be bankrupt, but I also didn't want to be in debt.

"I checked out your accident."

"Oh." I felt strangely deflated. I wondered if he thought I'd made it all up. "It did genuinely happen," I said.

"Yes, I know," he said abruptly. "I never doubted for a moment that it happened. I checked out the insurance and court records."

"And?"

"Your uncle defrauded you." He stared at his food, embarrassed no doubt that he uncovered further evidence of my loser tendencies.

"I did tell you I never got anything. He's probably spent it by now."

Andy ignored me and continued. "There was an insurance payout of seventy thousand pounds, plus the proceeds of your parents' house, which was fifty thousand after the mortgage was paid off. The money was placed in trust for you, with your uncle having full control till you were twenty-one."

"This is where you tell me he spent it all at the bookies, isn't it?"

He shook his head. "Not quite. He did take it all, cleared out the account, but used it for a deposit on a property. The money hasn't disappeared, he's living in it."

"I see."

"I have a complete paper trail. I can prove without doubt that he misappropriated your fund."

I felt a little nauseous. "That means making him sell his home though."

"Not necessarily, he could just remortgage. I've worked out what it would be worth had he not helped himself. A judge would even award you an equity share of the property if he was daft enough to let it go to court." He fiddled with his chopsticks; embarrassed no doubt that loserdom ran in my family.

"I have one living relative, and he stole from me while I was laying in the hospital?" I wanted to cry at the injustice of it all.

"It all happened after that, when you were in care."

"I suppose he figured I'd never find out about it. I mean, I never knew about the money in the first place, nobody ever told me."

"I think there were a lot of failings from the people who were meant to be caring for you," he said softly. My eyes met his. I expected him to be judgemental, disapproving of the fact I'd not taken care of myself during my time in care, but he was full of compassion. "If you agree, then I can pursue this."

"What will it cost me?" I knew his expertise was expensive. If my uncle didn't pay up, I really didn't want to risk being in deeper debt.

"Nothing. I'm not gonna charge you," he sounded offended. "Why do you always think I'm gonna try and make money out of you?"

I shrugged. I wanted to remind him he'd already added three thousand quid to my debt and had wanted it to be more. I kept my mouth shut, not wanting to upset him.

"You're gonna be quite well off by the time I've gotten all these people to pay up," he said.

I tensed. "That's all well and good, but it won't happen for God knows how long. I'm counting down the days till my first payday right now, so forgive me for not getting excited." I knew I was being a brat, but he was so hopelessly unaware that I was constantly cold, had no decent winter footwear, and was down to my last thirty quid.

"I thought your rent here was included?" he mumbled.

"I'm not talking about that," I huffed. "Do you think your coffee, milk, and wine is provided by the pixies? Don't you think I use toothpaste, deodorant, and tampons?"

"I've never really thought about it," he admitted. Anger and disappointment flooded through me.

"I'm walking through the woods twice a day in leaky trainers and rotating the two pairs of warm socks that I possess because I don't have winter boots," I paused. "Are your only expenses your household bills?"

"Well, no," he admitted. "How come you don't have boots?"

I lost my temper, "BECAUSE I'VE BEEN POOR FOR FUCKING FOREVER!" I yelled. Tears dripped down my face. Andy blinked, shocked by my outburst. I'd well and truly lost control, and the now-familiar shame flooded through me. "I'm sorry," I whispered, "I just thought you understood."

"I'm trying to," he said, "but I can only help if you tell me when you're in trouble. We'll go get you some new boots on Saturday."

"I don't want your charity," I snapped. I didn't know what I wanted. I hadn't meant to let out how desperate I was for fear of being accused of gold-digging, but on the other hand, I was tired of being cold and wet. What I really wanted was for the poor bloke to be psychic, I thought. I sighed, tired of being so damn pathetic all the time. "You just seem to think 'poor' is something that happens overnight, and goes away the moment you want it to. It's like those 'cook family meals for a fiver' shows. They assume people have a store cupboard of spices, herbs, and groceries. When you're poor for a long time, stuff wears out and can't be replaced just like the alleged 'store cupboard of food,' you use it up and it's gone forever."

"I'm sorry. I guess I can be a little thoughtless," he admitted. "The offer's still open for Saturday though." He stared at his plate. "I can't bear the thought of you being cold or wet."

"It's been a way of life for a long time now," I said. "Anyway, changing the subject, what do we do about my uncle?" I didn't want to ask why he cared about my cold, wet feet, but was too ashamed to take me home. I had an inkling that argument would be the end of us, and that wasn't what I wanted.

I think he was relieved to pull out some documents he'd prepared and go through them with me. It was basically giving him consent to take recovery action against my uncle for the money he'd taken. Reading through it all, Andy had clearly done his homework, finding all the land registry stuff. Uncle Jim had bought a rather nice house in Downe using my hundred and twenty grand, plus a hundred thousand pound mortgage from the Halifax. Andy had found that a similar house had recently sold for six hundred thousand.

"Now, I worked out that if the money had been left alone, the interest accrued would have taken it to around two hundred thousand. Given that it was 'invested' in property on your behalf, the amount we could go for comes to approximately three hundred and sixty thousand. I think we should hit him with that first, then if needs be, come down a bit. What do you think?"

I just nodded, my mind reeling with the revelation that not only had I been forgotten and neglected, but stolen from too. I really was one of life's losers. I duly signed the papers he placed in front of me, giving him permission to sue on my behalf. "I'd like to look into the home too," he said quietly. "I think there was a failure there too. It may be more difficult and drawn out, but I think you need some answers as to why you didn't get the services you were entitled to." He placed more forms in front of me. I signed them without even reading them. It felt ungrateful, even though in some respects they'd failed me. I still owed them for putting a roof over my head.

"It's my way of taking care of you," he said gruffly. "It's the only way I know how."

"I know," I said softly. "It's just..." I trailed off, unsure how to phrase the next bit.

"It's just what?" He snapped. "Will you just spit it out? You seem to think I'm some sort of mind reader, which I'm not. I'm just sick of making you cry all the time." I was taken aback by his outburst and decided not to say any more.

"It's fine. Listen, I'm exhausted, so I think I need an early night, if you don't mind."

"Have it your way," he barked, grabbing his coat. "I'll see you Friday night. Hopefully you'll be in a better mood by then."

The Debt

He slammed the door hard on his way out. I sank back in my chair to process all the information. I knew he was doing what he thought best for me, taking on my uncle and the home, but in place of all that, I'd have preferred his honesty about himself. I hadn't let on that I knew he'd bid for Lakeswood, or that Aaron had told me he was a wealthy man. His point-blank refusal to share anything about his life showed me he was ashamed of me. He'd clearly decided I wouldn't fit into his family or social circle, making me feel like he was only ever interested in sex.

Sex and business, I thought wryly. His determination to have me suing everyone who ever did me wrong probably salved his conscience, plus it meant he wouldn't have to offer to pay my debt himself, knowing I'd have money in the pipeline.

I decided to be clever; to put up a wall between my heart and his, but keep him onside until the debt was paid. I wouldn't allow myself to fantasise about happily-ever-afters, or choosing soft furnishings together. I'd keep him happy, but continue to believe that a man who would really love me was still out there, waiting to be found. If I repeated it over and over enough times, I'd come to believe it, and save myself the inevitable heartbreak that would come from loving Andy McCarthy.

I wandered into the kitchen the next morning to find Shari presiding over a scene that could only be described as carnage. With Gerry away, it had obviously fallen to her to provide breakfast. The normally orderly kitchen stank of burnt eggs and was a mess of crumbs, spilled coffee grounds, and eggshells. The dogs were hiding in the utility room.

"Morning," I said brightly.

"Glad you're here. This kitchen needs clearing up. Stupid cooker burnt the first lot of eggs." She pointed to a blackened saucepan.

"OK. I'll do it once I've fed the dogs," I said. She seemed a bit frazzled and cross, and I didn't want to make her worse by arguing that it wasn't my job. The cleaners would be in at half-nine, and would tackle it.

"No, you'll do it now," she said, her flinty stare daring me to disobey. "The dogs can wait."

I set about filling the sink with hot soapy water to try and soak off the burnt eggs while I wiped down the surfaces. Without another word, she picked up the tray she'd prepared and walked out. The dogs both peeped around the door, checking she'd gone before coming out to greet me. I quickly finished clearing up her mess, and then set about grating some carrot to go in with their breakfast steak, while the burnt pan was soaking. I'd just finished mixing up their food when she came back in with the tray. Glancing at the sink, she said; "I thought I told you to clean that before sorting the dogs?"

"It's all burnt on, it needs some time in the water," I said sulkily, noting with strange satisfaction that most of the breakfast she'd prepared had been left on the tray.

"When you're told to do something, then just fucking do it," she hissed, before stomping out, leaving the tray for me to clear up as well. I just shrugged and carried on dishing up Bruno and Roxy's breakfast before getting on with chiselling the saucepan.

I heard voices in the hall, it sounded like Aaron and Marcus laughing about something. As I scrubbed away with the scourer, I heard Shari's shrill voice ring out,

"I'll drop you at the station darling." The front door slammed.

Marcus came in, no doubt missing his morning latte. He stopped when he saw me scrubbing the pan. "What on Earth are you doing?"

"Shari instructed me to clear up her mess from this morning," I said. "Only she burnt this so much it's like tar at the bottom. I tried to tell her it needed soaking, but she insisted I scrub it out."

"Take no notice," he said. "Wanna know a secret?" He leaned in conspiratorially.

"Go on," I whispered.

"Aaron just asked me to call his secretary and get her to pick him up some pastries. Shari's food was inedible." We both sniggered. "How on Earth can she ruin toast? The woman's as thick as two short ones. Not a redeeming feature to be found."

"She had to have two goes at scrambled eggs," I pointed out. "Listen, shall I make us both a latte while you go and make that call?"

Marcus smiled appreciatively. "You're a doll." I immediately abandoned my pot-scraping and set about making our drinks. He trotted off to call Aaron's PA. A few minutes later he was back. He perched at the island and blew the steam off his coffee.

"I need to ask you something." I said. Marcus glanced up. "Andy asked me if I could give him the gate code to save me having to go meet him. I said I'd ask, but I understand if it's a no."

He shook his head. "I know one hundred percent that Aaron wouldn't want him having free access. There's too much bad blood. Drew had to call me on the intercom last night to let him out."

"That's OK, I understand. I expected a no, but I promised him I'd ask."

"How's it going with you and him?" Marcus asked. I just shrugged. "So what does that mean?" He pressed.

"It means I don't know. It's pretty casual."

"But he stays over? So it can't be that casual. How come you don't stay over at his place?"

"I don't really know. I don't even know where he lives, or much about him really." Marcus's eyes bored through me, "I've met his brother Rupert though, so it's not like I'm a secret or anything."

"I see," he said, non-committal.

"He's helping me get back the money owed by my old boss," I ventured.

"Will it pay off that CCJ I found on your file by any chance?" He asked. I nodded. "So his firm will get paid twice. Hmm, leopards never change their spots do they?"

"What do you mean?"

Marcus sighed, as though he was talking to a child. "His firm bought the debt from MVDI for about ten percent of the face value. He'll also claim against your old boss, or her insurers, for costs when he wins. He gets paid for legal fees, plus gets full whammy off of you when you use your compensation to pay the debt. He's no fool is Drew, and he always was a greedy bastard."

My head spun. The information Marcus had given me made complete sense. I felt sick at the thought of Andy exploiting me, seeing firsthand how much I was suffering and yet never letting on that I actually owed the money to him. I stood up, desperate for some time alone just to think and process all the information. "I need to take the dogs out," I announced, before pulling on my useless coat and leading the dogs outside.

They knew I was preoccupied as we walked round. They stayed close, as dogs do when a person is upset, and gave my hands occasional licks as we wandered through the paths. It was one of those bright, crisp winter's days, with blue skies overhead to give the illusion of a happy summer's day. The wind was bitingly cold though, even in the relative shelter of the woods.

I thought back to the start of my relationship with Andy, how lucky I'd felt, how he'd reassured me that he'd help me. In truth, I'd been played. He'd turned out no different than the last lowlife boyfriend who nicked a tenner out of my purse to buy weed. Andy was just playing on a bigger scale.

I was glad I wasn't seeing him that evening, it would give me time to figure out what to do without the distraction of his beautiful face and tempting body. I wondered if I should have it out with him, tell him what I knew, but dismissed that idea, knowing he'd figure out I'd been talking to Marcus. There was enough animosity between them all as it was.

One of the cleaners was at the sink attacking the saucepan with a knife when I got back, muttering swear words under her breath. I smiled as I led the dogs into utility room for their teeth, claws, and ear check. They were becoming easier and more trusting of me by the day, although Bruno licked all the beef-flavoured toothpaste off the brush before I could get any on his teeth, necessitating another application. I was making good headway with the plaque deposits on their teeth, so was making it a regular routine. Roxy's were getting quite pearly.

I made a list of items the dogs would require and went down to Marcus's office. He was talking to someone on the phone, immediately ending the call when i walked in. "Am I interrupting?" I asked.

"Not at all. What's the problem?"

I smiled, "No problem, I just did a list of the things that the dogs need. Do I give it to you?" I handed it to him.

He read through it quickly. "Easy enough, I'll get these ordered straightaway. Is anything urgent?" I shook my head.

There was a little convenience shop half a mile from the gates. I tried to avoid it as much as possible as it was expensive, but with the nearest supermarket a four-pound bus ride away, I'd had to suck it up. I stuck my card into the cashpoint, despondently noting that I was down to just fifteen pounds due to some reckless purchases earlier in the week. I'd spent five pounds just on one bottle of wine. It was still another ten days till I'd be paid. I ended up buying just the cheapest store-brand teabags, milk, and a bag of pasta, noting with sadness that even the dogs ate better than I did. As it was, another fiver was eaten up.

CHAPTER 11

I didn't answer the phone when Andy called that evening, not trusting myself to keep quiet about his behaviour. My plain pasta had been a miserable affair, the tasteless spirals reminding me of my poverty. I'd had a luxurious bath to cheer myself up, before slipping into the kind of pyjamas I'd never allow a man to see. I was about to get into bed to watch telly when the house phone started ringing. Its unfamiliar, shrill tone made me jump. I wondered what was wrong, as it never rang. I picked it up. "You need to get here immediately, Bruno's shit all over the hallway." My heart sank hearing Shari's whiny tone.

"Ok, I'll be thirty seconds." I put down the receiver and pulled on my trainers, before grabbing my key and racing over to the main house.

Shari had her jumper pulled up over her nose when I stepped into the hall. "It stinks, it needs clearing up," she said, her voice muffled by the jumper. She pointed to a line of diarrhoea which had been trailed the entire length of the hall. Both Bruno and Roxy were pacing, both looking downcast, they clearly had stomach aches.

"I need to get them outside first," I said, "They don't look well. What have they eaten?" I glared at her. They'd been fine when I'd left them a few hours earlier.

"I gave them Aaron's dinner, that's all," she said. "He decided to go out at the last minute."

"What was it?" I barked, watching the dogs.

"Oh, only some curry I'd made, nothing much. Now clear this up, I can't deal with this smell."

"You gave curry to two dogs on a raw food diet?" I demanded, aghast. "They'll be in shocking pain."

"Fuck the dirty little shits, just do as you're told and clean this up before it damages the stone."

"I need to get them outside first," I said, standing my ground. Shari stalked up to me, her eyes blazing with anger.

"If you don't do what you're told and clean this up immediately, I'll rub your fucking face in it, then have you slung out so fast your feet won't even step in it." She was leaning in, about six inches from my face. I flinched. She pointed to a roll of kitchen paper she'd gotten out. Meekly, I took it and knelt down to start scraping the slimy faeces off the expensive limestone.

I had no time to glove up, or even find more suitable cleaning equipment, so I quickly had shit on my hands. Shari was still shouting about the smell, how it would make her ill, even though she wasn't the one up to her elbows in it. "Do it quicker," she screamed, "I can't bear this smell."

"You need to get the dogs outside," I told her, "Just open the front door, let them out."

"I'll be too cold," she snapped back. "And don't tell me what to do. You're just staff, don't forget it." I fantasised about slapping her around the face with my shit-covered hand.

I was on my hands and knees, cleaning, when it all happened, so I couldn't see in what order events unfolded. I heard Shari scream as Roxy exploded with diarrhoea. I saw it spray up the leg of Shari's expensive trousers, as well as over the floor.

She became hysterical, screaming as though a bit of shit would kill her, shouting that she'd kill the effin' dog. Both dogs were pacing, clearly in pain and no doubt both very upset and ashamed.

"I have *got* to see to the dogs," I yelled. "They're in pain and they'll just go again. If you'd let me get them out in the first place when you stuffed them full of curry, it wouldn't have happened."

"Fuck the dogs, what about me?" She screamed. Bruno made the mistake of pacing near her. She drew her leg back to kick him.

That was when I became aware of Aaron and Marcus in the doorway. I had no idea how long they'd been there, or how much they'd seen. "Shari, don't you fucking dare," Aaron growled. "Get upstairs." She did as she was told, letting out a huge sob and running up the ornate staircase, leaving shitty footprints almost all the way to the top. Aaron strode after her, muttering "Sorry Sally" as he went past.

"Can you let them out please?" I asked Marcus. He sprang into action, leading the dogs out of the front door and onto the drive where they could let go and rid themselves of whatever had caused the problem. I surveyed the carnage in the hall. I needed more than a bit of kitchen roll to clean it all up.

In the utility room, I filled the mop bucket with hot soapy water and washed my hands. Back in the hall, I began by washing Shari's footprints off the stairs before tackling the main mess, all the while listening to the shouting and hollering going on upstairs. I'd just refilled the mop bucket with clean water when Marcus brought the dogs back in.

"What on Earth did they eat?" He asked.

"She said she gave them curry. I shouldn't have listened to her and just got them outside, but she was screaming at me to clear up first," I told him. I wasn't sure how long they'd been at the door, what they'd seen or heard. "I need to check them over."

Marcus took the mop from me, and began sweeping it over the few remaining smears. I felt around Roxy's tummy. It was gurgling like mad. "This must've been really painful," I commented. Both dogs pushed their muzzles into my shoulder as I checked them over, their expressions sad and ashamed. We could hear shouting upstairs, then a crash.

"I hope that wasn't the Orku vase going for a Burton," said Marcus. "It's a one-off. I just hope she's not such a philistine that she'd chuck it at him." We heard another crash and more shouting.

"I think I'll walk Roxy and Bruno back to the flat," I said. "It'll do them good, plus I'm sure they'll be up all night with tummy aches."

"What the Hell was in that curry? No wonder Aaron wanted to eat in the pub."

"Onions probably. It's poisonous to dogs, and gives them horrible tummy pains and rotten gas. Hopefully they've expelled it all quickly, but I'd rather keep an eye on them, just to be sure." I glanced down at my pyjamas. Not only were they vile to begin with, both knees had shit on them. I needed to get them off and get in the shower. The stench was firmly embedded in my nose and it was making me feel queasy.

"OK, and Sally? I'm sorry about her behaviour."

"Not your fault," I said, before leading the dogs out. We walked slowly back to the flat, even though it was bitter cold, just in case they needed to go again. They plodded along beside me, sorry for themselves. The walk helped though, as Bruno managed to clear out a bit more.

Back in my flat, I dug out my old duvet and set it down for them, as well as filling the washing-up bowl with fresh water in case they needed a drink.

I stripped off my pyjamas and jumped in the shower. As the hot water rinsed over me, the full impact of that night's events hit. The way Shari had spoken to me, the way I'd jumped to her orders, even though I'd known she was wrong. I cursed myself for having been such a weakling that I'd ignored the dog's plight in favour of appeasing her.

I was glad they were having a row. I hoped that Aaron was putting her in her place. She was the second rudest woman I'd ever come up against. Miss Gadd took first place, and I hoped I never met anyone worse.

With my body clean, I dried off and put on fresh pyjamas before making a cup of tea. The dogs had ignored the duvet and made themselves comfy across my bed. I smiled at them; pleased they'd felt well enough to get some sleep. I squeezed into the inch they'd left for me and sipped my tea. It was gone midnight.

They woke me up three times during the night to be taken out to expel a little more curry. The final time was at around four in the morning. I stood bleary-eyed on the lawn while Roxy had yet another poo. Bruno had joined us and was sniffing the ground, as though he was going do the same. We were interrupted by Aaron and Shari walking across the car park to the garage, both laden with bags. She looked as though she'd been crying.

"Hey guys," said Aaron, rubbing Roxy's head as she forgot about her poo and bounded over. "Still poorly?" He asked me.

"All night," I said. Shari blanked me as though I wasn't there. I watched as they loaded bags and a suitcase into her car. Aaron got into the passenger seat, I guessed to let her out of the estate, and sat grim-faced as she drove off. A few minutes later, he jogged back up the drive. I was just about to go back inside, but he called out to me.

"She's gone," he said. "I'm really sorry about last night, what she did to you." I just shrugged, not sure what I was meant to say. "Thanks for taking care of Roxy and Bruno for me."

"That's OK; it's what I'm here for," I said. "Listen, I'm frozen. I need to get back inside."

"Are you making tea?" He asked, following me in. "I've got to be at a meeting in the city in three hours, so there's no point going to bed. These two won't let you get any sleep either by the looks of it." He followed me up the stairs and sprawled on the sofa while I switched on the kettle. The dogs both jumped onto my bed and lay down, oblivious to the fact I'd had barely any sleep.

"I've ended it with her," he said. "I should've done it a while back really, Marcus told me she'd been acting like Queen Bee around the staff."

"So why didn't you?" I asked. I was curious.

He sighed. "I'm in the final stages of a big deal at work. I suppose I just couldn't be bothered with all the hassle. It's always a pain, saying goodbye."

"It's taken you all night," I pointed out.

"Only because Shari had squits as well," he said smiling. "She kept having to rush to the loo. Made packing her stuff up a bit slow. Fuck knows what she put in that curry."

I shuddered. "It smelt pretty rank when it was squirting out of the dogs." I paused. "So where did Shari go?"

"Her mother's. For all those 'friends' she purports to have, not one of them would put her up for a few days. Ironic that."

"Are you upset?" I asked, handing him a mug of tea.

"No, I'm pleased. I'd let it go on far too long. Marcus was talking about leaving earlier, over dinner. He just couldn't put up with her any longer, so it's done everyone a favour really."

"She was horrible to him. I heard her shouting at him. She was really rude to me too, before last night," I told him. He rolled his eyes.

"Now she told me everyone was really nice to her, and what a happy household I had. It was a bit of a shock being told by Marcus that he wanted to leave because of her and then walking in to hear her abusing both you and the dogs. She even tried to tell me you'd poisoned them yourself to get her into trouble."

I went cold, fear prickling the nape of my neck. "Did you believe her?" I asked.

"Course not. As soon as she said she'd given them food she'd prepared, I knew what it was. I'm just bloody glad I didn't have any." I could tell from his smile he meant it. I relaxed. "Why would you think I'd believe such an outlandish claim?"

"I'm one of life's unlucky people I guess. If there's a lie to be believed that'll cause me trouble, it's usually accepted as fact."

"You don't look unlucky. I mean you have an amazing figure, a pretty face. You've got a wealthy boyfriend. Personally, I'd say you were one of life's winners."

I gaped at him, processing his words. I could feel my cheeks turn a little pink with embarrassment at the compliment. "Thanks, but my body's pretty scarred up from an accident. I'm a bit shy about it."

"Mum told me you'd lost your parents in a car crash. It's how I lost Dad too. I bet the scars on my arm are worse than yours." He stood up and pulled his sweater over his head. Underneath, he was wearing a tight white T-shirt. He showed me his right arm, pulled the sleeve up to his shoulder. Two long, white scars snaked from his wrist to his elbow. Above that, the flesh was lumpy and misshapen, identical to my thigh. "Gross eh?" He said, seemingly unembarrassed by it.

"I see your arm, and raise you my leg," I quipped. If he could be blasé about his mangled arm, so could I. I rolled up my pyjama bottom to expose my thigh.

"Wow, that's a great scar," he said, "and an even better thigh. Is there any other parts of you I should see?"

I giggled nervously, shyness kicking in. "No," I said, quickly unrolling my trouser leg.

"Why are you so shy around me?" He asked softly.

"Because you're my boss," I said.

"If I wasn't your boss, would you still be as shy?"

I shrugged, "I don't know. What I do know is that I can't afford to lose this job."

"But you're Drew McCarthy's girlfriend?" He seemed genuinely puzzled as to why I needed my job so badly.

"So everyone keeps reminding me. It's a shame I don't get full girlfriend perks though," I blurted. Instantly I regretted saying it. I felt disloyal and greedy. Just because Aaron showered his girlfriends with money and gifts didn't mean that Andy had to.

"So what are you not getting from Drew that you'd like?" He asked, his voice gentle but insistent. I paused and thought about it.

"I wish he'd stop taking me out to eat and buy a bag of groceries instead," I said. Aaron laughed. "It's not funny," I snapped. "I'm on bare pasta until payday, while Andy thinks a meal out twice a week is taking care of me. I bet he won't be eating pasta for breakfast." Aaron laughed even louder, waking the dogs.

"Does he know?" He spluttered, trying to control himself. I shook my head. "Well then tell him. Doesn't he give you any spendsies?"

"Don't be daft. I wouldn't ask him either. I'm not a charity case." As soon as I said it, Aaron's eyes bored into me. He wasn't as pretty as Andy, but was handsome in a more masculine way. I shivered involuntarily.

"Are you cold?" He asked. "It's quite warm in here."

"I'm fine, just tired I guess. How are you going to cope with working after no sleep?"

He waved his hand dismissively, "I'll be fine. Used to regularly pull all-nighters when I was making a name for myself. I might come home early though. At least you can catch up during the day."

"I'm working," I reminded him.

"You've been up all night," he pointed out. "I'm sure those two'll be sleeping it off today. Use the time to get your own beauty sleep." He stood up. "I need to go get ready, I need to leave in an hour, and I'm bloody starving. Don't suppose you fancy sharing some bacon and eggs with me?"

"Better than pasta," I admitted. I pulled a dressing gown over my pyjamas and followed him back to the main house. He went off for a shower, while I cooked bacon, sausage, eggs, and toast. It was all very cosy and domestic.

Aaron polished off his breakfast at possibly the fastest pace I've ever seen anyone eat without being bad-mannered. I felt quite sorry for the dogs salivating by his side. They were on a strict twelve-hour starvation regime to calm their stomachs.

"That," he said, mopping the last bit of egg with his toast, "was delicious." I beamed at his praise, pleased to have managed such a nicely-turned-out meal despite a lack of practice. I also enjoyed the food, it being a considerable step up from what I was expecting to eat.

After he'd left for work, I cleared up, loaded the dishwasher, and nipped home to get dressed. Our walk was short, both dogs seeming a little tired from their upsets. I put them to bed in the boot room and prepared to head back to the flat for some sleep. Marcus, who

had fancied a latte and a good bitch about Shari,
interrupted me. He seemed as bright and perky as
normal. I wondered how he'd slept with all the noise
going on in the main house.

It was another hour before I finally fell into bed,
delirious with exhaustion. I never had been good at
staying up all night.

A loud hammering on my front door woke me up.
Disorientated and aware the light was starting to fail, I
glanced at the clock, it was nearly four o'clock.
Stumbling downstairs, I called out "Who is it?"

"Ocado delivery," said the voice behind the door.
Frowning, I opened it. A delivery driver was standing
surrounded by crates of carrier bags. "Delivery for Miss
Higgs. This is the right flat isn't it?" He enquired.

"Yes, I'm Miss Higgs," I confirmed, "but I didn't
place an order." He flicked through his paperwork.

"It was ordered by Mr Pryce, for delivery to this flat.
Shall I bring it all up the stairs for you before I tell you
about the colour-coding on the bags?"

I stood aside to let him in. Expertly, he carried in a
vast stack of crates, leaving only a few bags outside. I
grabbed them and followed him upstairs. "Are you sure
it's not for the main house?" I asked when I got to the
top.

"It says your name and address on the order, so I'm
certain it's for you."

It took a while for him to explain their systems, with
different types of groceries in different coloured bags,
then a further twenty minutes to put everything away.
Aaron hadn't stinted at all, buying expensive meats,
fish, and top-quality coffee. I wanted to cry at his
kindness. It was probably the most thoughtful, generous

thing anyone had ever done for me. He'd even included half a dozen bottles of wine and a huge bar of chocolate.

I headed over to the main house to feed and walk the dogs, having neglected them all afternoon. I found them in front of the fire in Marcus's office, flat out. They raised their heads when I walked in. "Hiya, just come to get them to give them their tea and a walk. Have they been OK?" I asked.

"They've been asleep almost all afternoon. I think everyone was shattered after last night."

"Did you organise that Ocado delivery for me?" I asked, "It was incredibly thoughtful."

He seemed genuinely puzzled. "Nothing to do with me. I can't lay claim to that one." He paused. "Why did you think it was me?"

"Because it was from Aaron's account," I replied.

"Must've been him then, probably felt bad 'cos you were up all night and got covered in shit."

"Yeah, probably."

I was just grating some swede into the dog meat when Aaron arrived home. His stubble seemed longer, making him look tired and weary. "Hiya. You OK?" I asked.

"I'm exhausted," he said, flopping down onto one of the kitchen chairs. Roxy and Bruno forgot their impending dinner for a moment and raced over to say hello. "Well, hello you two. Are you feeling better?" Bruno licked his hand.

"I think they're fine now. I'm going to give them their first feed since last night, then take them out to see if it goes straight through them."

"Good. I'll join you. Let me just get out of this suit." He disappeared upstairs.

The dogs ate with gusto, no signs of any residual soreness on show. As soon as Aaron reappeared wearing jeans, boots, and a padded ski jacket, we set off. The four of us walked in companionable silence for a while, enjoying the quiet of the woods in the dark. Eventually, I broke the silence. "Thank you for the Ocado order, it was incredibly thoughtful of you."

"You're very welcome. I hope I ordered the right things?" I could make out his Sphinx-like smile in the moonlight.

"It was perfect, thank you." I hesitated. "It was actually the nicest thing anyone's ever done for me."

"Really?"

"Yeah, really." I felt incredibly disloyal to Andy, but Aaron had shone a big spotlight onto his failings. Andy had only helped me when there'd been something in it for him. Aaron had just listened and done the right thing.

I was jolted out of my thoughts. "I know it's not my place to say, but what is Drew thinking? Letting you struggle, letting you eat pasta for breakfast and wear four layers of clothes to keep warm?" He paused, "I'm sorry, it's none of my business."

"I'm asking myself those same questions," I admitted. "I think he's ashamed of me, that's why he keeps me hidden."

"Why would he be ashamed of you?" He demanded, "You're beautiful, with a superb figure and a gentle nature. What's not to like?"

"It's because I'm poor," I said, "I was brought up in care after my parents died. I suppose I don't fit into his 'ideal girlfriend' profile."

"Then he's a bigger fool than I gave him credit for," Aaron snapped, the anger and venom in his voice shocking me. "He has it all: the wealth, the charisma, and a beautiful girlfriend, yet he can't even see what's in front of his face— unless it's a mirror."

"You really hate him don't you?"

He shook his head. "I'm generally indifferent to him. I mean, sure I enjoyed baiting him, but only the same as I would any stuck-up twat. What I'm struggling with is the way he treats you. It sounds like he just comes over, spends the night with you, then disappears again."

I thought about it. "I suppose when you put it like that... But he does take me out to dinner sometimes."

"But not to work functions, family functions?"

"No." My voice was small, and the seeds of doubt were sprouting at an alarming rate. I could see where Aaron was coming from. I was being treated like a fuck-buddy, and I'd let it happen, too enamoured by Andy's pretty face to question his actions. I felt a fool.

"I'm staggered you're putting up with it. I mean what exactly do you get out of this?"

"He's suing my ex-boss for me. I couldn't do that on my own."

"That doesn't cost much," he dismissed. "You could get a no-win, no-fee, lawyer for that. Next?"

"And he's chasing my uncle for stealing all my compensation money and spending it on a house." My voice sounded weak as I attempted to justify why I was allowing Andy to walk all over me.

"Again, no-win, no-fee. At worst you're talking about a couple of thousand pounds of legal work."

"Oh." My stomach sank. What with Marcus's revelation that Andy's firm owned my debt, and Aaron's revelation that Andy wasn't doing me any enormous favours by pursuing the people who owed me, I felt stupid, shamefully stupid. Yet again I'd been taken in and exploited.

"I'd just pay off your debt, and free you from it all. If you were my girlfriend, that is. Then I'd take you shopping for a ski jacket and other nice things."

"I see," was all I managed to squawk, stunned by his statement.

"Don't you think you deserve the best, Sally?" His voice was as smooth as silk. "Don't you think you should be cherished? Cared for? Shown affection?"

I stayed silent, unsure how to reply. If Aaron was coming on to me, I needed to be straight with Andy first. In my own mind, I wouldn't be dumping Andy for Aaron, I'd be leaving him because he made me feel inadequate. I mulled it all over in my mind.

"Well?" Aaron asked, interrupting my thoughts.

"I... I don't know. I know I've been questioning things in my own mind lately, but with Andy tackling my case, I thought I'd better not rock the boat." I cringed slightly. I'd made myself sound like a gold-digger, only with him for practical purposes. "That came out wrong," I corrected myself. "I just feel that I have very few choices right now and at least Andy shows a bit of kindness."

We neared the house, our walk at an end. "Leave him, and I'll pay off your debt. It's nothing to me, a drop in the ocean, but I know it'll free you. I'd like to do that for you."

I was shocked, stunned even. Gift horses don't come around very often and I wasn't about to look one in the mouth. "That's kind of you to offer, but I don't think you realise, it's fifteen thousand pounds I owe." I felt my cheeks begin their familiar burn.

He waved his hand dismissively. "Of course I knew that. It's nothing, a drop in the ocean. I wrapped a huge deal today, so I'm feeling generous. Tell you what, I'll even cover all your legal fees for those two cases as well." He turned to me and gazed down into my eyes. "I just want to see you happy and smiling. Is that so wrong?" The light from the kitchen window illuminated his face. He seemed sincere. I shook my head, mute.

"Good. Think about it. Just let me know."

"OK."

He opened the kitchen door and ushered me in. I set about cleaning the dog's paws while he shrugged off his jacket. "You out tonight?" He asked casually, his former intensity concealed under a breezy facade.

"No. Andy's coming over, so I expect we'll stay in," I said, noting his Sphinx-like smile creeping across his face. "You?"

"Marcus and I are going out to eat."

"Well, enjoy your meal," I said, before reaching for Bruno's toothbrush.

"You too," he said quietly before slipping out of the door.

CHAPTER 12

Andy beamed when I jumped into the passenger seat of his car after opening the gate. "Hi babe, you had a good day?" He asked.

"I've been asleep for most of it. The dogs were ill all night, so I was up every half hour taking care of them."

"They OK now?" He seemed genuinely concerned.

"Yeah. Aaron's girlfriend gave them curry. Once it was cleared out, they were fine." I didn't want to let on that Shari had been booted out. We pulled up outside the garage and headed into my flat. Andy was carrying a Chinese takeaway. He set it down on the coffee table and switched on the telly. For some reason, this irked me. He treated my flat as though he owned it.

I opened a bottle of the wine Aaron had sent, and poured two glasses. Andy was busy opening boxes and sorting out chopsticks, so didn't notice the other five bottles in the fridge. I took a slug to fortify myself before sitting down and making a start on the duck in pancakes.

"I spoke to Rupert earlier; some good news. He's given your boss the ultimatum of either paying you the money she owes or facing fines of double the amount. He's warned her that she'll be done for tax evasion as well as failure to pay minimum wage if she doesn't cough up within seven days."

"Do you think she will?" I asked. Andy nodded.

"I think so. As it stands, the minimum wage thing is a civil matter. She can be fined and stuff, but it's not that serious. Tax evasion is a criminal matter. It carries a jail sentence as well as fines and a criminal record."

"So I could get the money from her quite quickly?" I knew I wouldn't be seeing any of it, as it would go straight to Andy's company, so I didn't get excited.

"I'd expect so. Aren't you pleased?" He fixed me with a stare. I just shrugged.

"I won't see any of it will I? It'll go straight to you."

"To MVDI? Well, yes, but it's a good chunk paid back."

"Did your firm buy the debt from MVDI?"

He paused, his chopstick hovering in the air. "What a strange question."

I knew. I just knew at that moment that Marcus had been right. I owed the money to Andy, not the card company. I felt a profound sense of disappointment; primarily in myself for believing he was helping me for altruistic reasons. "Because I have to pay Alpha, not MVDI. It stands to reason doesn't it?" I didn't want him to know I'd been tipped off. "How much did you pay them for my debt Andy?" I put him on the spot.

"I don't know the exact figure," he admitted. "It's how it works, they pass it on and we collect it."

"I see. You never thought to enlighten me?"

"Listen, I could easily accept a reduced settlement, but it would be on your credit file for six years. If it's paid in full, it's noted as such, which is far better for you."

The Debt

"My credit file is shot, you know that. It's why I can't get another bedsit, or an overdraft to see me through to payday. I'm struggling with you not caring how much I suffer."

He looked incredulous. "How are you suffering? You have a great flat, a good job, even if I don't like your boss, plus I promised you a pair of boots tomorrow."

I lost it.

"Hang on, I've been living on plain pasta for the past few days because I couldn't afford food. I've been frozen stiff for the past fortnight walking the dogs because I don't have the money for warm clothes, and I'm feeling rotten and dowdy because you're treating me as if I'm something you're ashamed of."

"Have you been talking to Aaron?" He demanded.

"No," I lied. "I've been thinking about this a lot. I know you're wealthy and well connected. I've been wondering for a while why you just turn up, fuck me, and go home again, and the only conclusion I can come to is that you're ashamed of me. Whether it's because I'm scarred or because I'm poor, I can't decide."

"Don't be so ridiculous," he snapped. "I make time for you, drive over to see you, feed you, and help you with your cases. Isn't that enough?"

I shook my head. "You're only helping with those cases so I have enough money to pay you for my debt... aren't you?"

"Is that what you think?" I could see his anger flaring. Andy really didn't like being challenged.

"Yes, it is," I said defiantly. "I think you're ashamed to show me to your family, and you're only marking time with me until someone you deem more suitable comes along."

"You seem to have a very low opinion of me," he spat, clearly angry, but controlling himself.

"Really? Well tell me then, how do you feel about me?" I sat back, glaring at him, daring him to try and dodge the question.

He swallowed the chow mein on the end of his chopsticks. "I think it's quite obvious that I like you."

My heart sank. "You *like* me?" I said. "Andy, you fuck me. I'd sincerely hope you *like* me, or are you really only doing this for the money?"

"Now you're just being ridiculous, and would you stop using that word please? I don't 'fuck' you."

"What would you call it then?" I challenged. I waited with baited breath for him to answer.

"I'm not going there. I really don't do all this emotional stuff. I think you need a good night's sleep." He seemed to shut down, unwilling or unable to express any of his feelings. He spoke as if he was at a business meeting, talking to his secretary. This was a man who had seen me naked and exposed.

"Sleep has nothing to do with how I feel. I think you need to go."

I saw fear flash across his face; it was momentary and fleeting. He scowled at me. "You really are in a bad mood today."

"No, I just feel as though you are exploiting me and my situation. I know I'm not the girl for you, and I don't want to be the 'alright for now' shag. I'm worth more than that."

"Will you stop referring to yourself like that?"

I stayed silent, staring down at the remains of our meal. I wanted him to leave, but I knew I'd regret it the moment he was gone. I kept reminding myself of his duplicity in not informing me he'd bought my debt. I wanted to hate him for that, which was difficult given how much my heart lurched whenever I looked at his lovely face. I reached for my phone and placed it in front of him. "You'd better have this back."

"I don't want it," he said quietly. "I bought it for you. I don't attach strings to my gifts, whatever you think." He paused. I could feel his eyes burning into me, despite my lowered head. "Are you serious Sally? You want me to go just because I didn't tell you the nuts and bolts of collecting your debt? All the things I did for you don't count because of it?"

I nodded. "That debt ruined my life. It's on my mind every day. It meant I had to wear leaky shoes and thin, cheap clothes. It dictated my ability to feed myself properly. I thought you knew what it was doing, but you just didn't care." My voice was barely a whisper. "I fell in love with you, thinking you were my knight in shining armour, so realising you didn't care if I suffered the cold made me realise that you'll never care for me the way I do for you. By keeping me apart from your life, I'll never be allowed to actually love you, so I'd prefer it if you'd just go."

"You have no idea what you're talking about," he said, his voice cold and controlled. "I only ever did what was best for you. Just because I don't talk about my feelings in the way you'd like, well, it means nothing." He sat there stubbornly, making no move to leave.

"Just go... please."

"You don't mean that," he said confidently. I glanced up. He looked serious. I nodded silently and saw fear flash across his face. "You should have told me about not having food," he said.

"I did. You just didn't listen."

He stood up and strode over to the fridge, pulling it open and looking inside. "There's plenty in here?" He threw me a quizzical glance.

"Aaron got wind of how much I was struggling and sent an Ocado delivery this afternoon," I admitted.

Andy exploded. "That's what this is about isn't it? You've got the hots for him. All he had to do was pretend to be all kind and caring, and somehow you think everything I've done isn't worth a light. Well, let me tell you, the man's a snake. He uses people and shits on them from a great height."

"You're only saying that because he did something nice while you were too busy figuring out how to make money out of me," I yelled. "For the very first time since I was a child, somebody noticed I was struggling and did something about it. It's just a shame it wasn't you," I added.

He had the grace to look ashamed. "Stay away from him Sally, he's bad news. There's stuff I could tell you about him and Marcus…." He trailed off.

"As long as you get your money, what do you care?" I spat.

"I care," he murmured.

"Just leave... please. I can't do this anymore. You'll get your money, and I'll get my freedom." I felt weary, more tired than I had in years. I just wanted peace of mind, and knowing Andy effectively owned my future and hadn't thought to mention it felt shattering. I'd get over my feelings for him and move on to someone nice, who wouldn't be ashamed to introduce me to his family or friends.

I winced as Andy slammed the door, making the entire garage rattle. I ran down the stairs, knowing he'd need me to let him out of the estate. As I opened the door, I saw him standing by his car, talking to Aaron and Marcus, who were sitting in Aaron's car. Marcus caught my eye and nodded for me to go back in. They would let him out.

As soon as I got back upstairs, I let out a sob, the stress and emotion getting the better of me. I'd dumped the man I'd fallen in love with. I realised he'd never love me back. It had been a struggle to get him to say he liked me. I kept repeating it like a mantra in my head; *you're worth more than that*. I wished I had someone I could call for advice, to talk things over with, someone to reassure me that I'd done the right thing. Eventually, sleep took over, wrapping up the events of the past twenty-four hours and disposing of them in sweet oblivion.

I was awakened by a banging on my front door. I winced as the sunlight hit my eyes, making me squint. A quick glance at the clock revealed I'd slept until nine, late for me. "Hang on, won't be a minute," I yelled. I pulled on my dressing gown and trotted downstairs.

Aaron beamed at me, seeming to not notice my bed-head hair and bleary eyes. "Just thought I'd see if you were OK after last night," he said cheerfully.

"I'm fine, thanks," I said, standing aside to let him in. "I take it Andy told you I tackled him about some stuff?" I followed him up the stairs. The flat was a wreck, with the remains of our Chinese still on the coffee table and the bed unmade. I filled the kettle, switched it on, and then set about tidying up.

"Not in so many words, but reading between the lines, I figured it out."

"He didn't take it well," I said, my voice flat.

Aaron smiled. "I gathered that already. What did you say to him to make him flip out like that?"

"I'd rather not go into it." As angry as I was with Andy, I wasn't about to rat him out to a business rival.

"Loyal to the end, eh? I like that about you. Why don't we have our tea, you get ready, and we'll go get you that ski jacket I promised you?" He smiled hopefully.

"OK," I said warily. "Would you mind if I had a pair of warm boots instead? My feet are covered in chilblains because my trainers are leaking." I sat down opposite and placed his tea in front of him.

"You have *chilblains?*" He asked, incredulous. "Let me see." He picked up my foot and pulled off my slipper. His touch felt soft and warm. A shiver ran up my spine. He gently twisted my foot in his hand, looking at the purple patches covering them. "Do they hurt?" He asked.

I shook my head. "They itch like crazy when my feet warm up, but they're not too bad." I watched, hypnotised as he stroked my foot, cupping my ankle with his large hands. He glanced up at me, his piercing blue eyes capturing mine. I couldn't look away, mesmerised as I was by his gentle touch and intense stare.

"You have such lovely skin. I'd like to taste every inch of you," he murmured, shocking me. My belly squeezed, sending the signal down to that area between my legs that action was imminent. I shifted in the chair, pulling my foot out of his hands. He smiled his enigmatic smile and sat back to take a sip of tea. "I think we're gonna have a lot of fun today, don't you?"

I nodded, mute from the sensations he'd aroused. He drained his cup and stood up. "I'm just gonna walk the dogs, I'll see you in an hour."

"OK."

As soon as he'd gone, I leapt into the shower, determined to look my absolute best. As I lathered my hair, I contemplated what I was about to do. If Aaron paid off my debt, I could keep the money Ms Gadd paid as savings, which would act as a buffer if anything went wrong between Aaron and I. It wasn't strictly ethical, but when your back's against the wall and you face being homeless, being a good girl was a luxury I couldn't afford.

Aaron took me to Bluewater and spoilt me rotten. Not only did he buy me a pair of cosy, fleece-lined boots, he also treated me to a padded coat, several jumpers, and some super-thick woollen socks. "Not the most glamorous gift I've ever bought a girl," he laughed, as I chose the chunkiest, thickest ones.

"I'll think of you every time I walk your dogs," I told him. He smiled indulgently. I felt strangely comfortable with him, possibly because he wasn't as much of an enigma as Andy. After all, I'd met Aaron's mum and seen him at home.

Andy.

My heart lurched every time I thought of him. I wished it'd been him making me try on boots and laughing at my choice of socks. I wished it'd been Andy who'd admitted he loved Nandos as we searched for somewhere for lunch. I had to mentally slap myself and focus on the fact that I was with a gorgeous, fun man who seemed to really like me and was intent on making me smile. I didn't mention Andy, nor did he.

"We should get you a pretty dress this afternoon," said Aaron as he wiped his fingers with a napkin. "Then I can take you out to dinner tonight to show you off."

"I think you've spent enough," I said, not wanting to be greedy.

He laughed. "Sally, I did tell you I wrapped a deal this week. What I've spent... it's petty cash. You deserve lovely things. It's what all ladies should have, especially one as beautiful as you." His face was earnest, as though he was telling me a great truth that I should believe.

"I don't have any dresses," I admitted. "I generally try and keep my leg covered."

"Just put a pair of stockings on. I never let my scars stop me from wearing T-shirts. I don't really care who sees them."

"I wish I could be like that. I've always been embarrassed about mine."

He stroked his long, slender finger down my face and under my chin, tipping my gaze up to meet his. "Tell me, does my scar put you off?"

"No, of course not."

"Right. So why are you assuming yours will?" His bright blue eyes held my gaze. "Has anyone not fancied you, once they'd seen them?" I knew he was asking about Andy.

"No."

"Exactly. Sally, scars are never something to be ashamed of. They're just something we get. Yours and mine are on the surface. Other people get them buried deep inside. One thing you can be sure of though, is that everyone has them."

He bought me a dress. Not just any old dress either; a beautiful, fitted silk one that skimmed over my curves, showed off my waist, and covered the worst bit of my leg. He was waiting outside the changing room as I emerged wearing it. "You look gorgeous," he told me, beaming at me. I felt like a million dollars.

"It's really expensive," I whispered. "I'm sure I could find a cheaper one in New Look." I'd seen the price tag as I'd tried it on. It was two hundred and fifty quid.

"Doesn't matter," he said. "It looks amazing on you, which is all that counts."

Another hour later I had a pair of shoes, matching clutch, and some stockings, as well as a new lingerie set from Rigby and Peller which had been expertly fitted by a no-nonsense lady who'd taken just one look at me and told me my size. I'd been wearing the wrong size for years apparently.

Aaron treated himself to a couple of track suits from Massimo and a new pair of Timberlands as well, seemingly unconcerned about the cost of things as he chose them. I wondered how much he earned if he could spend seven hundred and fifty quid on three track suits without blinking an eye. He did keep getting phone calls though, which must've been annoying on his day off, having to duck away from me every half hour or so.

"Tomorrow, I need you to write down the payment details for Alpha for me. I'll call them first thing on Monday and pay them off," he said as we walked back to his car.

"Are you sure you want to do that?" I asked.

"Absolutely sure. I've enjoyed making you smile all afternoon. It's a small amount to me, but it means your first pay is yours to keep, with nobody getting their greedy mitts on it."

"I feel very spoilt," I admitted, beaming up at him.

"It's worth it just to see your beautiful smile," he said.

"Charmer," I quipped. "So tell me, what makes you smile?" He thought about it for a while as we strolled along.

"The dogs do, especially when they're naughty. I'm hopeless at telling them off."

"What else?" I asked as we hopped into the car.

"When I win a deal. I'm competitive in business; I always like to win." He flashed me a smile. "Plus, of course, there's always the pleasure of making beautiful women happy, both in and out of bed."

Cue another belly squeeze. Aaron struck me as an intensely sexual man in a way that Andy hadn't been. I expected him to be a dirty devil in bed; the type of man who'd studied how to make a woman scream. I pressed my thighs together to quell the growing insistence I felt. Even the way he handled the car was sexy, his long, slender fingers pressed the indicator with gentle precision, every movement sensual, almost languid.

"I'll pick you up around seven," he said. "We'll go to a great jazz club I know. They always have a band on a Saturday night. It's a fun place. The food's good too."

"Sounds great," I said as I got out the car. I carried my purchases into the flat and lay them on the bed. As I switched on the kettle, I checked my phone, which I'd left at home.

The Debt

Twenty-eight missed calls, all from Andy. There were also three voicemails and five texts. Gingerly, I listened to the first voicemail. It was just a rather clipped can-you-call-me-type message. As I listened to each in turn, it appeared that he'd twigged that I'd ended it and the messages sounded gentler each time. The last one was almost pleading. I could hear the anguish in his voice as he told me he'd sent an email.

I poured my tea and settled my laptop on the coffee table. I spotted his email straightaway and opened it.

From: Andy McCarthy
To: Sally Higgs
Time: 15.24 Saturday 7th February 2015
Subject: Sorry

Darling Sally

I'm sorry about last night, actually I'm sorry about so many things, it's almost hard to know where to begin. I should have told you about your debt, I know that now. In my defence, I've always separated business and personal. You owed Alpha, not me. I know a quick Google would reveal that I'm the CEO of Alpha, so I can't blame you for thinking it was me who you owed money to.

I did realise it weighed heavily on you, but in my stupidity, I figured you'd be happy paying it back from the compensation Rupert and I got for you, then you'd never be any the wiser.

I suppose I knew you were short of money, but it didn't really register. I've never experienced poverty, so I'm sorry I didn't try to understand. In hindsight, I thought I was helping you with the meals and things, but you were right: I wasn't listening, and now I really regret that. The idea that I let you go cold and hungry makes me feel ashamed. I'm sorry.

I should explain why I never took you home. I was never ashamed of you. I was ashamed of myself. I live an extravagant life, as do my parents. Set against your struggles, it felt flashy and greedy. I didn't want to rub your nose in our wealth. I also liked that you were oblivious to who I was. You landed Drew McCarthy, and you didn't even know. After years of gold-diggers and the cold, ambitious ex, it was something fresh and real, which I've never experienced before. I didn't want to enlighten you, as I was enjoying what we had. Rest assured it was never, ever because I was ashamed of you.

You told me you fell in love, and like a wanker, I told you I liked you. I'm so very sorry I said that, I'm just not good at talking about my emotions. Listen to the words in this: Rhianna-Stay and they'll explain it perfectly.

If I've really blown it, then I'd still like to run your cases, free of charge. It's the very least I can do for you in exchange for everything you did for me.

Miss you.

Andy xx

I read it several times, tears tugging the corners of my eyes. I clicked on the link to discover he'd sent a video of Rhianna singing "Stay."

"Funny you're the broken one, but I'm the only one who needed saving."

The Debt

That line did it for me. The tears began to fall freely, and for the millionth time that day, I questioned what I'd done. I read through the email another ten times, wondering if I should reply to it or not. The problem was compounded by the realisation that having encouraged Aaron, if I went back to Andy, I'd be both jobless and homeless. Andy had said nothing in his email about cancelling my debt or making any sort of firm promises. He appeared to like things the way they'd been, which had made me unhappy. Eventually, I hit reply and simply wrote: *Nothing's changed. You still can't give me what I need.*

With a heavy heart, I pressed "send," then set about getting myself ready for the evening, curling my hair carefully and applying my makeup to look seductive. The stakes were high, and I needed that debt paid off. Aaron was my best hope.

He looked amazing when he knocked on my door at seven, wearing what appeared to be a designer shirt, black trousers, and a black leather jacket. I felt a million dollars in my new dress and shoes. The heels were a little tricky as I was out of practice, but they made my hips sway as I walked carefully to the Porsche. "You look wow," he said, casting an appreciative eye over me. I smiled back.

"So do you." He even smelled seductive. A woody, citrusy cologne wafted over us as we closed the car doors. I'd used a sample of perfumed body wash I'd picked up in Boots, having used up all the perfume samples I'd managed to snaffle. I hoped the scent would last a few hours.

Aaron really knew how to show a girl a good time. He took me to a jazz club set in a basement in Mayfair.

The food was divine, the wine top quality, and best of all, once we finished eating, the tables were pushed back and a dance floor created. "Shall we?" He said, holding his hand out. The band was fantastic, doing a great cover of Amy Winehouse's *Back to Black*. Aaron was a good dancer, moving effortlessly in time to the music; his lean, rangy body swayed sensually to the beat.

I loved to dance, even though I wasn't particularly good at it. I loved to feel the beat deep inside and lose myself in the rhythm. The dance floor filled up quickly to become a seething mass of sweaty bodies grinding like puppets to the beat of the drums. Aaron was as in the moment as I, giving himself over to the music until we were both slicked with sweat. He motioned to me, asking if I wanted a drink.

We stepped off the dance floor and over to the bar. "Can I just have a lemonade please?" I asked, "I need a long drink." He ordered two lemonades and leaned back on the bar.

"Are you having a good time?"

"The best," I said, beaming. He grinned back.

"Me too. I've not been out dancing for a while."

"Me neither. It's fun though."

I drained my glass. The music changed tempo to a slow, sultry rendition of Marvin Gaye's *Let's Get it On*. Aaron grabbed my hand and dragged me back onto the dance floor. "I love this song," he said, as he pulled me into his arms. The sea of writhing bodies closed in on us, pushing me into Aaron's chest. He felt firm, his arms strong as they wrapped around my shoulders. I breathed in his scent, he smelt warm and masculine, testament to how much we'd been dancing. As I was crushed up against him, I felt his penis press against my hip. I glanced up to see him gazing down at me, a sly smirk grazing his face.

My body reacted independently of what my head wanted. I felt hot, horny, and wet. I could only pray that my aroused nipples weren't poking through my dress, announcing their interest to the world. Aaron was watching me intently and must have noticed my flushed cheeks, because as soon as the song ended, he whispered into my ear; "You ready to go?" I could only nod, not trusting my own voice not to come out as a high-pitched squeak. He made short work of paying our bill and collecting our coats. He held me tightly round my waist as we stepped outside into the frigid night air.

As we reached the car, he reached across me to open the door, our faces just inches apart. Before I had time to think, his lips were on mine, our tongues meeting for the first time. The problem of him being my boss faded away as we connected physically for the first time.

His stubble felt a little alien as I'd been used to Andy's perfectly clean-shaven skin, but the slight prickling felt unashamedly male. I forced myself to relax into his kiss. It didn't come as naturally as I'd felt with Andy, but Aaron represented a future free from debt, so I happily went along with it.

"I've wanted to do that from the moment I first met you in Marcus's office," he said when we came up for air. I smiled at him and ducked into the car. He slid into the driver's seat and switched on the ignition. "I can't wait to get you home," he murmured, before easing the Porsche out of its parking space. He drove home like a maniac. I'd already discovered he drove way too fast at the best of times, but on the empty London streets, he hammered the powerful sports engine almost to the point that my knuckles were white from gripping the edges of my seat. For a person who'd lost so much in a car crash, he seemed oblivious to the dangers he was putting us both in.

I was relieved when we stopped at the gates to Lakeswood to wait for them to swing open. Once through, Aaron floored the pedal to fly up the drive, before coming to a screeching halt in front of the garage. "There you go, home in one piece," he said brightly.

"Why don't you use a driver or a taxi?" I asked. It was odd that he always drove himself.

"We were in a cab when the accident happened. I'd rather die by my own hand rather than someone else's."

I understood.

I followed him into the house. "Drink?" He asked, rubbing the dogs' ears as they'd come to greet us.

"Please." The wine I'd drunk was beginning to wear off, and I needed something to relax me. I wasn't sure if I was shaking because of the journey home or due to fear of what was to come. In my heart of hearts, I didn't want to sleep with him. It was too soon after Andy, but I knew I had to seal the deal. A glass of brandy might help.

I'd been in the drawing room a few times, mainly chasing after the dogs. It was a large, luxurious room, furnished in shades of muted gold with black accents. Marcus had truly surpassed himself. Aaron strode over to the sideboard and poured out two glasses of amber liquid from one of the crystal decanters. He handed one to me. "Are you nervous?" He asked, after seeing my shaking hands. I nodded. "Why?"

"I'm not sure," I said.

He drew his finger down my face, gently stroking me. "You should never be scared of me. I'm a good lover, Sally. I'll make you scream, but only in a good way."

My traitorous body responded, sending an alert to all the requisite nervous systems. I felt my cheeks get hot and my nipples stiffen. I threw back my brandy, hoping for some Dutch courage. Aaron just smiled, amused, before plucking the empty glass out of my hand and setting it down. He kissed me again, a brandy-soaked kiss. His hands wound into my hair, anchoring me to him as our tongues stroked and danced. I felt him lift me up; his lips still on mine and carry me out to the hall and up the stairs.

It felt strange being in someone else's bedroom. For years, I'd only ever had sex in my bedsit. The types of men I'd attracted lived in grotty shared houses, which I hadn't felt comfortable in. As Aaron sat me down on the edge of the bed, I glanced around. It was an intensely masculine room, decorated in shades of rich chocolate and cream. In the centre of the room was a vast bed, the head- and base-boards covered with dark chocolate-covered leather.

I sat paralysed as Aaron unbuttoned his shirt and pulled out his cufflinks. His chest was covered in dark hair, which seemed groomed to show off his impressive muscles. He threw his shirt carelessly onto the floor. "Let me help you out of that dress," he said, reaching behind me to lower the zipper. With the back opened, the front of my dress sagged forward, exposing my lace bra, which he'd paid for.

With extraordinary dexterity, he reached one hand behind me and unclipped my bra. He slid it off and gazed at my naked breasts. "Spectacular," he breathed, before leaning down to capture a nipple on his mouth.

He suckled hard, causing me to arch into him and sending a spike of pleasure all the way to my groin. I gasped at the intensity of it, unsure as to whether or not I liked it. His hands roamed over me, feeling my skin, enveloping me in his innately masculine way. He lifted me slightly and pulled off my dress, flinging it on top of his shirt. The untidy pile jarred in that impeccably-polished space.

I watched as he undid his trousers, letting them fall to the floor. He was wearing grey jersey Calvins, which showcased his erection perfectly.

Then they too were removed, and his dick sprang free. My mouth went dry.

It was long. I mean really long. It wasn't particularly thick, but what it lacked in girth, it made up for in length. I must have been really staring, because he chuckled at my reaction. "Your turn," he said as he dragged my knickers down my legs and plunged a finger into me.

"So juicy," he remarked as he pumped his long finger in and out. "You feel ready to me."

I couldn't just lie there like a wet fish, so while he was opening a foil packet, I reached over and pulled the tip of his dick into my mouth. His breath hitched as I ran my tongue along the underside, licking along the whole length. He gave a little moan as I took the tip into my mouth and sucked. At that point, he pulled me off, practically throwing me onto my back. Within

The Debt

moments, he had the condom on and had plunged into me.

I gasped with pain as he hit my uterus. He was way too long to get it all in. I suspect it was a common issue for him as he pulled back and seemed content with being only two-thirds inside me. "Close your legs," he commanded. "I want you to try a new position." I complied. He lifted his legs over mine and used his thighs to clamp mine closed around his dick. It meant the shaft was rubbing repeatedly over my clit as well as increasing the tightness around him. I have to admit that it felt quite good, especially when he sped up. The man did everything hard and fast.

My body took over, and I came with a whimper. All my earlier misgivings were swept away by a surfeit of sensation. He carried on right through my orgasm, prolonging it to the point where I almost wanted to push him off to ease the intense throbbing. Thankfully, he came, grunting loudly, then slumped onto me, heavy and immovable.

Eventually, he rolled off and pulled off the condom. Even flaccid, his dick was strangely long, to the point of being peculiar. I pulled myself up onto my elbows and jumped when I saw two pairs of eyes watching from the side of the bed. "You know the dogs are in here?" I whispered. He glanced over at them.

"Hey guys, you can get in now. We're finished." Both dogs immediately jumped onto the bed and settled themselves down. I wondered if I should offer to go back to my own bed to sleep, but Aaron had already pulled back the covers and patted the bed next to him. I slid in, finding a gap between the dogs to put my feet. He switched off the light. "Sleep well, beautiful," he murmured as he spooned his front into my back, holding me tight. The unsatisfactory sex over for the night. He seemed quite happy with it and made no further overtures.

I lay awake a while, mulling things over. I knew I was shagging him for the money, which made me feel surprisingly sorry for him. He'd proven to be a kind, generous man, and I felt sad that I was using him. I also felt a bit ashamed of myself, partly for being with a man for his cash and partly for being such a mercenary. I was almost a prostitute. I prayed my parents weren't watching from Heaven.

I woke early the next morning, disorientated and unable to move. The room was too dark to see what was pinning me down, so I wriggled a hand free and felt along the top of the covers. A large dog, probably Bruno, stretched and yawned loudly as soon as I prodded him. He was sprawled out on top of me, his entire weight centred on my tummy. I gave him a little shove, and he shifted enough for me to wriggle out from underneath him. As my eyes became accustomed to the dark, I could make out Aaron fast asleep beside me.

I slipped out of bed and fumbled on the floor for my underwear and dress. I couldn't find either my bra or my stockings, so made do with my knickers and my dress. I padded downstairs to the kitchen. The clock in the hall said it was seven fifteen.

I strolled into the kitchen to let myself out the back door and was confronted by the sight of Marcus, sitting and drinking coffee with another young man. Marcus was wearing only a pair of tight Jersey boxers, while the other man was dressed in tight jeans and a skinny-fit shirt. I don't know who blushed first, Marcus or me.

"Sally."

"Marcus."

"Walk of shame?"

"Something like that." I looked pointedly at the young man sitting beside him who'd whipped his hand off Marcus's leg as soon as I'd walked in.

"Jonathan's just leaving," Marcus said.

"My cab'll be another ten minutes," Jonathan said in possibly the campiest voice I'd ever heard. Marcus blushed deeper.

"No need to leave on my account," I reassured him. "I'm just heading back to the flat to get changed."

"Good night was it?" Marcus asked, motioning me to wipe under my eyes. I licked my fingers and ran them under my lashes. A load of sticky gunk came off. I must've looked like a clown.

"Yes thanks. You?"

"We had *such* a good time," Jonathan interjected, smiling sexily at Marcus, "and your place here is *amazing*." He sniffed loudly.

"The house is beautiful," I agreed. "Marcus is very talented."

"In more ways than one," said Jonathan. I saw Marcus cringe. He turned to me. "So where do you live?"

"In one of the flats over the garages. I'm the dog-nanny," I clarified.

"So why are you creeping out of here?" Jonathan asked, rather tactlessly, I thought.

"I think she spent the night with my brother," Marcus told him. I twigged. He'd obviously told his date it was his house. I wasn't about to rat him out.

"You got me," I said brightly. "Now, if you'll excuse me, I need a shower and a change of clothes. If your brother wakes up, can you tell him I'll be back to feed and walk the dogs?"

Marcus grinned. "Will do."

I scuttled out before I said anything to drop Marcus in it. Back at the flat, I stripped off the dress and knickers and let the hot water wash over me. I felt incredibly dirty, the way you do when the dirt is on the inside and no amount of soap or scrubbing will make you feel clean.

I ached for Andy, for his forgiveness. I realised that not only had the sex been far better, our lovemaking had felt pure and born of nothing more than desire. It had made me aware of how tawdry my behaviour with Aaron had been.

I wrapped myself in a towel and made a tea before checking my phone. There'd been another three missed calls from Andy, but no voicemail. I checked my emails and found one he'd sent in the early hours.

From: Andy McCarthy
To: Sally Higgs
Time: 01:25 Sunday 8th February 2015
Subject: Never giving up

Darling Sally

I wish you would talk to me. Not speaking to you… It's driving me nuts.

I got your message, but I don't really understand it. There's nothing I wouldn't give you or do for you if it was in my power. I just wish you'd tell me what you need— help me out a bit when I'm a clueless dolt.

Today's song is Passenger- *Let her go*

Listen to the words. They speak for me. I'll send you a song every day until you at least talk to me.

Yours,
Andy

I clicked on the link and watched the video. "Only know you love her when you let her go." I wondered how Andy would feel if he knew what I'd been doing while he was composing that email. I wanted so badly to speak to him, ask for his forgiveness. What stopped me was the prospect of being homeless and jobless. The situation had gone too far, there was no way back for me.

I was just sipping my tea when there was a knock on my door. I tightened the towel around me, closed the laptop, and ran down to answer it, fully expecting to see Aaron. Instead, Marcus was standing there rather sheepishly. "I've just let Jon out," he said. "You won't tell Aaron I let him think it was my house will you?"

"Course not," I dismissed. I stood aside to let Marcus up to the flat. "Want a coffee?"

"Got any builder's tea? Two sugars please." He parked himself on the sofa while I made him a cup.

"He seemed nice, that Jonathan," I ventured.

"Yeah. Met him last night at Manscape. He's a bit skinny for me. I like them taller, more manly." "Like Aaron," I thought. The notion made me smile. "Quit the dopey smile, what were you doing creeping out of the house half-dressed?"

"Same as you probably."

Marcus scrunched up his nose in disgust. I just laughed. "Changing the subject, why are you seeing to the dogs? It's your day off"

"I may as well. I've got nothing better to do and no money till payday," I told him. He rolled his eyes.

"You should have said. I can give you an advance on your wages. It's only a few days away."

"I never thought to ask," I said, feeling foolish.

"Let me drink my tea and I'll transfer a hundred into your bank. Is that enough to tide you over?" I nodded, grateful for his kindness. I didn't even need that much, as I had plenty in the fridge, but I really needed to pick up some shampoo and toothpaste. Plus, I quite fancied a trip into Bromley. Being in the house all the time got a little stifling after a while.

Aaron was up when I went back with Marcus. The dogs were scoffing their breakfasts, and he was making coffee. "Hey you, I wondered where you went."

"Just went for a shower and a change of clothes," I said. I was wearing my new boots, a new jumper and my new coat. "I thought I'd join you on a walk."

"Excellent," he beamed.

We walked through the woods together, enjoying the sounds and smells. For the first time, I was warm enough to be able to relax and enjoy it. I spotted snowdrops along the edges, dangling their little white heads to announce that spring was imminent. Aaron saw me looking at the stiff green shoots of the daffodils poking their noses out of the soil. "Jed planted thousands over the years. It's quite a show when they all come out."

"Can't wait to see it," I said.

Neither of us mentioned the previous night. I didn't think it was because it was a taboo subject, or anything Aaron regretted, more that it wasn't something he felt the need to examine or discuss. The thought struck me that there was every possibility that the women who had come before me may have just accepted the lacklustre sex too, in exchange for his material generosity. Nobody had actually cared for him enough to guide him in what women actually like, which filled me with sadness.

"I'm going over to see my mum this afternoon, do you want to come?" He asked. I was torn, as I liked Maggie, but I also wanted some time alone.

"No, you go. I appreciate the invite, but I really need to pick up a few bits in Bromley."

"I've got a function next Saturday. I'd really like it if you'd accompany me," he said. "It's black tie, so you'll need a long dress. Marcus can order you one from Net-A-Porter if you like."

"OK, thanks. I'd like that." I felt quite excited at the prospect of getting all done up. I wondered if any salons would be open in Bromley for me to get a haircut.

It felt fantastic to hop on a bus back to the familiarity of Bromley Town Centre. Back at the house, Aaron had pulled out his wallet and peeled off a few fifties for me, telling me to treat myself. I wandered around for a while before walking into a salon for a luxurious cut and blow-dry, with an actual stylist as opposed to my usual dry trim with a trainee. She did a super job. My hair felt soft and bouncy as I wandered into Debenham's to look at makeup and get myself a bottle of perfume.

With Aaron paying off my debt the next day, I shoved all guilt aside and enjoyed myself, even stopping for a latte at Starbucks. I sat and ruminated how differently people treated me when I was wearing good clothes and had nice hair.

I felt normal.

I actually felt like the girl I'd wanted to be. With my bags of shopping beside me and with money in my purse, I felt like I belonged. I was no longer the dowdy, exploited little girl with the scars and the inferiority complex. I hadn't even cared when the hairdresser had combed my wet hair back off my face in public while she was parting it. Pulling my bags of purchases open, I found the new lipstick I'd bought and applied some, using the little mirror on the side of the cap. I smiled to myself and shoved all my doubts to the back of my mind.

CHAPTER 13

I spent that night with Aaron. He'd knocked on my door at nine, after getting back from his mum's, to ask for Alpha's details and my account number with them. The least I could do was spend the night with him, even though it left me feeling incredibly sad for the man. I even made him a nice breakfast the next morning to allay my guilt.

After he'd gone off to work, I fed the dogs and took them out, glad to have some time alone to think. I liked Aaron. I thought he was a kind, generous man with a wicked sense of humour and a down-to-earth manner. I just wasn't in love with him. I figured it was why the sex wasn't great. I mean, Aaron had a killer body: lean, muscular, and impeccably-groomed, but it didn't do it for me. I just couldn't get excited in the same way I did over Andy.

At half-ten my phone rang, making me jump somewhat. I saw on the screen it was Aaron. "Hi babe," I said.

"Put some champagne on ice, you're out of debt."

"Oh my God!" I squealed, "That's fantastic news. You've got no idea how happy that makes me."

He chuckled, "I think that squeal down my ear gives me an idea. Anyway, it's all done; you're free and I expect a big smile on your face when I get home tonight. I'll be quite late though, I've got a shareholder dinner to attend."

"Thank you," I said. "You have no idea what a weight you've taken off my shoulders."

"My pleasure. Now, go choose a dress for Saturday. Get Marcus to help you. He's good at that sort of thing."

I hugged myself as I walked around the perimeter. In some ways it felt anticlimactic in that I'd expected such a battle to pay it back; that the moment it was cleared would mark a major achievement, yet in other ways, it felt monumental, as though I was free again. I was temporarily tied to Aaron, but that in itself wasn't too bad.

Back at the house, after I'd done teeth- and coat-brushing, I made two lattes and went to find Marcus. He was sitting with his feet up talking on his mobile, which he put down the moment I walked in. "Hiya," I said, "Aaron said I should ask you to help me find a dress." I wondered if he'd be cross about being lumbered with another task.

"Yes, he said. You're going to accompany him to the Foxbury Ball apparently."

"I've never been to a ball before. I've got no idea what to wear or what to expect," I confided.

"It's just a big party, held at Foxbury Manor every year. It's a lot of fun." He had a strange look in his eyes, as though he wasn't telling me everything.

"Are you going?" I asked. He nodded.

"Wouldn't miss it for the world." He moved a package off his desk, then pressed a button that opened a flap. A large monitor slid up. He pulled a small keyboard out of a drawer and fired it up.

"This site's the best one. I'll order a few and send the ones you don't want back. Just don't look at the prices or you'll lay an egg. Now, what size are you?"

With Marcus's help, we ordered five ridiculously-overpriced dresses, four pairs of designer heels, and three handbags. He pulled out a credit card and paid for them as if they were nothing. I was astonished.

"Aaron won't be cross, will he?" I asked nervously as he tapped his number in.

"Nah. He'll want you to wear something spectacular. He's pretty well known, so people will be checking you out."

His words struck fear into me. I'd never liked being centre of attention, and being Aaron's date would mean every hungry girl in the place would be examining me in minute detail. It was a scary thought.

"Should I book to get my hair done?" I asked nervously. Marcus shook his head.

"I'll organise someone to come to the house. You don't want to be travelling home from a salon with fresh hair. She'll do your makeup too. Can you get your nails done in the morning though? There are a couple of places in Locksbottom that'll do it. Feet as well. I'll book you in and organise a taxi."

"You're being very bossy," I told him. He just smiled.

"Just doing my job. Aaron will expect you to be the belle of the ball. I'll be getting a fresh haircut and a hot towel shave. Can't let the side down."

Aaron didn't get home till nearly eleven that night, still as bright-eyed and bushy-tailed as he'd been when he'd set off that morning. He walked in wearing a tux, his bow tie undone and dangling around his neck. I had to admit, it was a look that suited him. He insisted on toasting the end of my debt with champagne, making a celebration of it. I'd rarely tasted real bubbly, but knocked it back, not wanting to be ungrateful.

He practically had to carry me up to bed. The blasted stuff went straight to my head. I wasn't too pissed to give him a nice shag though to say thank you.

The next day, another email from Andy awaited me. I cringed when I saw it, thinking he'd know about Aaron paying his firm off, but it seemed he didn't, or he didn't mention it. That day's song was *The First Time* by Roberta Flack, which made me cry.

Each day that week, he sent a different love song. Some were full of angst, such as Say Something by Christina Aguilera, while some were more romantic and sweet. What bound them all together was that each one provoked more tears. I wished I could reply or even talk to him, but I just couldn't risk upsetting Aaron; at least until I'd got some sort of money behind me. Ms Gadd was still refusing point blank to pay, saying she couldn't afford my wages owed. Rupert had begun proceedings for tax evasion, which meant it would become longer and more drawn out. At least I got my first month's pay, which was a relief. I decided I'd try and resist the temptation to splurge it and try and squirrel as much as possible away as savings for when the inevitable happened, and I had to move on.

When Saturday came, Marcus got me up early, telling me I needed a bath and exfoliate, as he'd booked a spray tan for each of us before my taxi arrived for my nail appointment. Ten minutes later, a girl in a black tunic arrived with a pop up tent and what looked like a fence sprayer. She proceeded to spray foul-smelling tan solution all over me and made me stand in a starfish shape to dry off. She then did the same to Marcus, who was quite insistent that she give him two thorough coats of the darkest one possible. By the time she'd finished, he looked like he'd been mud wrestling. "Give it eight hours to develop, then wash off the guide colour," she instructed, before folding up her tent and disappearing.

"So you shower and wash your hair at four. Got that?" He said. I nodded. "Make sure they just do your toenails. You want a dry pedi. No water." I nodded again, not daring to argue.

I was prodded, poked, and primped all day. I'd never spent so long getting ready for a night out. By the time I slipped on the long, red silk dress Marcus had chosen and the red Jimmy Choos, I was unrecognisable. I stared at the sophisticated girl in the mirror; with perfectly blow-dried hair and immaculate makeup and stood a little straighter. I really had nothing to be ashamed of.

Carefully and with some trepidation, I made my way over to the main house. Aaron and Marcus were in the hall, waiting for me. They both looked me up and down as I walked in. Aaron whistled.

"You look... wow. Good job Marcus." I beamed a smile at them both.

"You two look very handsome too," I said. They were both in tuxedos, which made them both look very sophisticated, although I did wonder why Marcus had been so picky about his tan when I could only see his face and hands.

As there were three of us, Aaron had decided to drive his Bentley, which was a beast of a car. He explained how difficult it was to handle compared to his Porsche as we drove at alarming speed through the suburbs. I had no idea where I was. Eventually we turned up a track that was signposted "Foxbury Manor," with a makeshift sign for the Foxbury Ball tied to the hedge beside it. "So this ball is held every year?" I asked.

"Oh yes, it's a fundraiser for a local charity," Aaron explained as he dodged all the people walking up the track in high heels and party outfits. It wasn't quite the grand entrance I'd expected.

"What charity?" I asked as we passed a sign announcing the entrance of "The Old Elthamians Rugby Club."

"Just a local sports club," he said.

He parked the car directly outside a vast marquee and switched off the engine. I got out carefully, checking first for puddles. I noticed a few people watching, no doubt because of the car. Aaron offered me his arm "Shall we?" He said, smiling. I hooked my arm through his to make the short but perilous walk across the car park and into the venue.

Aaron pulled our tickets out of his inside pocket and handed them to the doorman. He nodded us through to an area where I could leave my coat. Aaron took the chit for me and put it in his pocket. We walked on through another short corridor, teeming with people, then into the main marquee itself. It was enormous and packed with people. Round tables dotted the hall, with people clustered in groups around them, drinking bottles of champagne, which were set in ice buckets beside them. Several people accosted us, primarily to say hello to Aaron. A few girls blatantly looked me up and down, their lips curling in envy. "You go find our table, I'll go to the bar," Aaron yelled over the music to Marcus. He nodded and weaved his way through the crowds to where a large table plan was pinned up. Aaron led me to the bar. "Quite an entrance you made," he said into my ear. "I bet they're all gossiping about my lady in red. Now, shall we have some champagne?" I nodded and smiled at him gratefully. The staring, whispering girls were making me a little paranoid. Some champers would blot them out. Marcus returned just as we were served.

"Table one," he said, "We're with the Quinells and a couple of celebs from that show, The Only Way Is Essex." Aaron just nodded.

"Better make that three bottles of Krug," he said to the barman, peeling a load of fifties from the wad in his wallet. I trotted along as Marcus led us to our table, in front of the stage. The others were already there and were delighted to see Aaron.

"Aaron, darling, so glad you could come," said an older lady as she kissed both his cheeks. "I'd like to introduce you to Amy, Gemma, and Lauren."

They seemed a bit star struck as Aaron shook their hands and pecked their cheeks. Each of them wore gorgeous dresses and was really glamorous. I was beyond excited. "This is Marcus, my friend," he said, allowing Marcus to peck them all as well, "and this is my girlfriend Sally." I had my turn air-kissing everyone.

"Your dress is to die for," Amy said, "and I love your hair." I almost burst with pride. The older lady, whom

Aaron introduced as Sherry, joined in by asking who designed it.

"It's a McQueen," Marcus chimed in. "The shoes are Jimmy Choo."

"Is he your gay best friend?" Amy whispered in my ear, making me laugh. "Well, that dress is totes gorge," she said loudly so that Marcus could hear.

Myriad people came over to shake Aaron's hand. He kept his arm casually but firmly around my shoulder, introducing me to so many people it made my head spin. I admired how easily he chatted, and how confident he was, almost a born politician. I pretty much kept quiet and just smiled sweetly at everyone. Marcus was equally popular, disappearing off with various people every few minutes.

The table next to us intrigued me. I couldn't see who was sitting there, but throngs of people, mainly preening women, seemed to be flocking to them. "I wonder who's on that table," I said to Sherry. She peered over.

"The McCarthy boys by the looks of it. It wouldn't be Foxbury without them." My blood ran cold.

At that moment, the crowds parted, leaving a clear view directly at Rupert. He saw me, his eyes widening when he saw whom I was with. I watched him elbow someone next to him, who peered around a group of girls.

Andy.

I felt sick.

He looked me up and down, taking in every detail. Despite his poker face, I could see he was struggling to contain some sort of emotion. As the crowds closed back in, I became hidden again. I hadn't been able to read him, whether he was angry I'd intruded into his world, or livid because I was with Aaron. I even toyed with the idea that he was cross with himself for not being the one to put me in a posh dress.

I tried to remind myself that he preferred me in ragged clothes and leaky shoes, not beautiful outfits. If Marcus was to be believed, he could have easily done what Aaron did. I needed to pull myself together.

We were interrupted by the compère asking us to take our seats, as the food was ready to be served. From my chair, I had an almost perfect view of Andy's table. When I saw that he was the only one without a date, I was relieved. Selfishly, I would've been upset to see him with another woman, despite the double standard of me being his rival's date for the night, although judging by the number of women flirting around him, he could take his pick.

Rupert was sitting next to a pretty, blonde girl, who had an effervescent air about her. She had to be the new girlfriend who hadn't been taken home. On the other side of Andy was an obvious brother, the older one by the look of it. He didn't have Andy's extraordinary good looks, but he had an air of authority about him. His wife had her back to me, so I couldn't examine her.

On the far side of the table sat a younger man, the only one close to Andy in the looks department. Beside him was a stunningly attractive Asian girl in a vivid teal-coloured dress. Her brunette hair shone in a glossy, dark curtain down her back. I remembered Andy telling me that she was the one his mum adored.

I glanced at Aaron. He was busy chatting to Sherry's husband, John, about some business they were doing. Marcus, on my other side, was watching proceedings with great interest. "Did you two know he'd be here?" I asked.

"Not specifically, no. He usually is though," Marcus said, a little too gleefully for my liking. I wondered if I'd been set up, the pair of them getting me all done up so that they could rub Andy's nose in the fact I was there as Aaron's girlfriend.

"You'd be amazed what I can steal from under your nose McLoser."

Aaron's words popped into my mind. I wondered if he'd bother to spend almost twenty-five thousand pounds, my debt and the outfits he'd treated me to, just to get one over on Andy. I had no idea what he earned, or for that matter what he actually did for a living.

"You OK babe? You're a million miles away," Aaron whispered into my ear.

"I'm good, thanks. It's a great party. Some fabulous outfits on show."

"It's where the great and good of Chislehurst come to show off. My old school sports club gets enough cash to see it through another year and buy some equipment, and the wives all get to outdo each other."

"I see. Everyone seems to know you," I pointed out.

He smiled, "I suppose they do. I went to school nearby and played sports here. I even used to drink in the local pubs once I was old enough."

"And you're a famous businessman," I added.

"Well, yes."

"What exactly do you do?" It had been bugging me. I should've read his bio a bit more closely when I Googled him.

"It depends which side of a deal you're on really. I buy companies which are struggling, and either turn them around or break them up. If you were a businessman wanting to retire, and I came along and bought your lacklustre company, you'd think I was an angel from Heaven. Those people call me a venture capitalist or private equity buyer."

"So what's the downside?" I was puzzled.

"Well, if I went to investors and got them to pump a load of cash in, and it didn't work, when I broke up the company, they'd be calling me a corporate bandit or a raider."

"But wouldn't you lose money as well though?"

He shook his head. "I never lose on a deal. It's a bit complex, but I take control of all the assets, so the investors just get paper bonds, which they can trade. They never actually own very much. Sometimes they make shit-loads, sometimes they don't. Like anything in finance, it's a gamble."

I didn't really understand. Rather than reveal my inability to get my head around his explanation, I decided to change the subject. "Did you know Andy's here?" I asked.

He shook his head. "I've not seen him. He often attends, as it's his Alma Mater too. Where is he?" He asked, a little too innocently.

"He's on the next table." Aaron looked over.

"He can't take his sad little eyes off you. Shame he was only happy when you were suffering."

I fought the urge to look over. Thankfully our food arrived.

The auction was held during the meal. Any pretence that the two men weren't aware of each other's presence was dropped as they battled it out, bidding ridiculous amounts for pathetically stupid lots. Even Marcus groaned when Aaron paid twenty grand for a signed rugby shirt.

"You're gonna have to find a wall to hang that on," I sniggered.

"No chance, that hideous thing has no place on a wall. I'll donate it to next year's auction. He'll have forgotten about it by then," Marcus whispered. I snorted trying to suppress my laughter.

The final lot was a pair of tickets to some football final. A few people started off bidding, but as the bids climbed to ten thousand, the early bidders began to drop out. Only Aaron and Andy were left. I watched, horrified, as the bids climbed to forty thousand, then fifty. Aaron bid sixty. Andy seemed to hesitate before saying loudly, eighty.

It was Aaron's turn to hesitate, I guess he came to his senses and shook his head. Andy smiled for the first time that night as the over-excited auctioneer brought his gavel down. I didn't even know Andy liked football; he'd never wanted to watch it on telly.

He'd just spent eighty grand.

The irony wasn't lost on me. For a fraction of that, he could've had me sitting beside him. Instead he was all-alone with his cash, sending me soppy songs every night. He caught my eye and dropped the poker face just long enough to show me he was in pain, a man with regrets.

I looked away, unable to stand it.

Why had he let it all go so wrong? That was the question I couldn't get my head around. Just trying to figure it out made my head hurt. I took another swig of champagne instead. Ever the gentleman, Aaron refilled my glass.

The Debt

"I need to find the ladies'," I said to him. He pointed over to the far corner.

"I'll come with you," said Sherry, "the queue will be massive." We made our way over and discovered Sherry was indeed correct. The line snaked out of the door. We joined the end of it.

"Aaron seems happy," Sherry said, "apart from losing out on those tickets."

"Ridiculous to spend so much money on one pair of tickets though," I scoffed.

"It's more a way of donating," she pointed out, "plus it's tax deductible, so more efficient than making a private donation."

"I didn't realise." I felt a little stupid.

"Neither did I at first. John did it once when he had a big tax bill, I had no idea how it worked and kicked his arse all the way home that night." She smiled at the memory. I liked her a lot.

"Have you known Aaron long?" I asked

"Oh yes. He went to school with my boys, my David was good friends with him and Marcus, so when they all left Eltham, they stayed in touch. Aaron bought our company several years ago, which was fantastic as it allowed John to semi-retire and start some of the projects that really interested him. I think Aaron's interested in investing in one of them."

She chattered on about the business her husband had started, which seemed to have something to do with extracting metals out of old phones. I nodded in the right places but wasn't really listening as I was tuning into the conversation behind me.

"What's up with Drew? I've never seen him so miserable. Thought he was well over that Charlotte by now."

"Rupert said he met someone a little while ago."

"Really? So why didn't he bring her tonight?"

"Not sure, but I think she left him. All Rupes said was that it was his own fault for being an arse to her. Tried to keep who he was a secret, but it backfired. I think it's that girl with Aaron Pryce. Drew can't take his eyes off her."

"I wondered why he's been staring over my shoulder all night. I'll get a good look at her when we go back."

"If it is her, then pulling both Drew *and* Aaron? I'll have a bit of whatever she's got." They both laughed.

I was glad when a cubicle became free, ducking in without turning around. Once inside, I turned it all over in my mind. If it was true, that Andy had been hiding *his* identity as opposed to hiding me, then I could understand him a little. With my relationship with Aaron out in the open, I would see if Andy still carried on chasing me. If he did, as soon as I had the money from Ms Gadd, I'd do a runner from Aaron. He deserved better than I could give him.

With a plan in my mind, I finished up and washed my hands, checking first that the two women from earlier weren't around. I re-applied my lipstick and fluffed up my hair. As I stepped out of the ladies, I came face to face with Andy himself.

"I just wanted to speak to you," he said. "I wanted to tell you how beautiful you look tonight."

"I'm with Aaron," I hissed, "and he won't be too impressed if I'm seen talking to you."

"I know," he said, chastened. "Have you been reading my emails?" I nodded, glancing around to see if anyone was watching. "I mean them, every word."

"Well maybe you should've been a bit more honest at the start," I snapped. "You knew how distraught I was over that debt, how it nearly killed me, yet you let me suffer real hardship to keep your deception going. Aaron has his faults, but at least I have warm feet these days."

He blushed. "I'm truly sorry. I wanted you to know that. It's just, well, being without you... It's hard."

"Being cold and hungry was hard too. You'll get over it, just like I had to, plus of course I was stupid enough to fall in love with a man who I didn't even know. I was an open book to you; it was you who deceived me remember?" I could feel my temper rising.

"Do you hate me?" He asked softly. I shook my head. "So come back to me," he said.

"I can't. I'd be homeless, penniless, and jobless. I'm just not willing to go there."

"I wouldn't let that happen," he said, his voice taking on a pleading tone. I raised my eyebrows at him.

"You let it happen once," I reminded him. What I really wanted was to throw myself into his arms and begin again, only with our lives out in the open. I desperately wanted to trust him, but the little spark of self-preservation that every orphan develops held me back. Aaron was kind and generous. I just wasn't in love with him.

"I beat myself up every day over it. I know I put my own agenda above your needs, but what we had, it was... special, pure. I know I was selfish and stupid. I don't really blame you for dumping me. I bet you think I'm pathetic," he said.

"No. I just wish it had been different. Story of my life really." I spotted Aaron scanning the room for me. Without another word, I walked away from Andy and towards our table. As I got close, Aaron spotted me and smiled warmly. "The queue was massive," I told him, feeling a little shaky and off-centre.

"Sherry only just got back too. John and I thought the two of you had wandered off. Shall we go check out the fairground rides? The celebrity girls are having a go on the dodgems." He took a swig of champagne.

I had no idea they had dodgems and Wurlitzers at posh do's. I was even more shocked to see a bucking bronco. Girls were hitching up their long dresses and having a go, flying off after a few minutes, legs akimbo, much to the onlookers' amusement. It was quite surreal.

"Are you gonna have a go?" Aaron asked.

"No way. Both my dress and my dignity are too precious." He laughed and pressed a kiss on my temple. We wandered over to the dodgems, where the celebrity girls had quite an audience as they raced around the track, followed by Marcus. We watched them laugh as they hurtled around. I was envious of their confidence, their sense of fun, and their seemingly carefree existence. As my envy grew, I was transported back to Chapter One, being in awe of all the women there, imagining their perfect lives, then the realisation that everyone had problems. To those girls, I had a rich, generous, handsome boyfriend who treated me like a princess. The actual reality was a world away. I was with him because I'd been effectively bought and paid for. I'd never felt such a strong urge to run away in my life.

Everywhere Aaron and I went, I was aware of Andy watching us. I think Aaron saw it too and delighted in making a big show of either affection or ownership. Eventually we bumped into Rupert and his girlfriend.

"Hey Sally, Aaron, you having a good time?" Rupert said in his jovial way. "Have you met my girlfriend Michelle?" I smiled and shook her hand.

"Nice to meet you," she said, before turning to Aaron. "Hey babe, not seen you for ages. Things OK?" She leaned forward to let him peck her cheek. They obviously knew each other. As they chatted, Rupert took me aside.

"I think that nasty bitch you used to work for is gonna settle this week. Andy's really turned the screws."

"Good, but I'll believe it when I see it."

"Oh ye of little faith," he said. "We promised you we'd get it." He paused. "Have you spoken to Andy tonight?"

I nodded. I checked Aaron wasn't listening. "I did. He's apologised for a lot."

"I slapped him upside his head. The twat thought you wouldn't like him if he revealed what a flash little git he really is. Telling you to go on the dole was a step too far, and he's only got himself to blame. Poor bugger's suffering though; he's never been dumped before."

"What about Charlotte?" I asked, puzzled. I thought she'd instigated their split.

Rupert gave me a puzzled look. "He caught her with another bloke. Didn't he tell you? Dumped her arse quicker than you could blink. You are genuinely the first girl to leave him, which after years of women chucking themselves at him, is a bit of a shock to his system."

I liked Rupert a lot. He had a slightly more common touch than Andy, a deeper understanding of how people behaved. "He'll get over it," I assured him.

"Losing you to Prycey of all people. That was insult to injury I think. We used to tease him something rotten at school."

"Why?" I was intrigued.

He leaned in closer, "Andy told me that in the first year, Aaron was seen in the showers after rugby practice and from then on was known as 'pencil dick.' He never got changed in public again."

I tried to keep a straight face.

"He's probably filled out a bit now..."

I blinked, trying not to react. Rupert grinned, using that silence trick to get me to speak. It was obviously a McCarthy family trait.

"You know what upsets me?" I said, "I know full well that if I was still with Andy, I'd be sitting indoors tonight, in my bedsit above the garage, with my socks drying on the radiator, eking out some plain pasta or the previous night's Chinese and watching telly. Instead I'm in a lovely dress at a great party, feeling as though I'm a member of the human race. Which would you prefer?" Rupert sucked in a breath.

"I did warn him. I could tell he was falling for you and concealing who he was. Well, let's just say that deceit never ends well."

"I had no idea how he felt. I got him to admit that he liked me, but that was all," I confided. Rupert just shook his head.

We'd been so busy talking I didn't notice Aaron walk over to Andy. The music was too loud to hear what was being said, but I could get a pretty good idea from the triumphant sneer on Aaron's face. Andy said something back, then turned and walked off. "Wonder what that was about," said Rupert.

"I can take a pretty good guess," I remarked.

Aaron wandered back over, a big smile on his chops. "Rupert, how's it going?" He said. "I've just been catching up with Michelle. You still working at the tax office?"

"Sure am," said Rupert in his usual jovial way. "I was just complimenting Sally on how lovely she looks tonight."

Aaron wrapped his arm around my shoulders and planted a kiss on my cheek in a show of ownership. "She does indeed."

He steered me over to another group of people he wanted to introduce. I couldn't help but admire how good he was at making small talk and how many people appeared to regard him as a good friend. It seemed everywhere we went, people were stopping us to chat, pressing champagne on us at every opportunity. I was getting a little light-headed. I caught a glimpse of Marcus chatting up a beautiful young man, who was equally as tanned as him. I wondered if looking like a Wotsit was some sort of gay code, so they could identify each other. The thought made me giggle.

"What's funny?" Aaron asked.

"Marcus is chatting up some orange fella. I wondered if, oh never mind," I said. His mouth twitched.

"I think you need some water young lady," he whispered as he steered me to the bar, where I downed a pint of water gratefully. Aaron disappeared to the loo, so I used the opportunity to just take in the sights around me: the myriad beautiful dresses and the people dancing and having a good time. I felt part of it, not an outsider. A DJ had taken over from the band and was playing *Valerie*, the celebrity girls were all up dancing with a group of fellas. Even Sherry and John were boogying. In my slightly drunken state, I could see Andy seated at his table watching me.

I became aware of a kerfuffle at the other end of the bar. A short, bald man was gesticulating, ramming his pointed finger into someone's chest, whom I couldn't see. The bald man was clearly livid, his features twisted, his skin purple with rage. People crowded round to watch. I moved closer, wondering what was going on. As I reached the crowd, I realised it was Aaron he was berating.

I guessed it was business they were arguing over, rather than a woman, due to the age of the man. As I got closer, I heard him shout "fifty grand, you fucker!"

Aaron simply shouted back, "You gambled, you lost. Not my problem," as he swatted the jabbing finger away from his chest. The man made a move to try and punch him, which was a bad one considering Aaron was about a foot taller and at least twenty years younger. He caught the feeble punch in his hand quite easily, and forced the man down onto the floor. Aaron then turned and walked away, nonchalantly, as though nothing had happened. He smiled at me, unruffled by the encounter. People crowded around the man, helping him up. He glared at me and stormed off.

"What was that all about?" I asked.

"Investor who held onto his bonds just a bit too long. He got greedy, ended up losing a chunk of his gains. Don't feel too sorry for him. He made nearly a quarter of a million in profit."

"And he's angry it wasn't more?" I asked, incredulous. It really was a different world.

"Shall we make a move?" Aaron said.

"Sure. Do you have a number for a cab?" I asked. I didn't have my phone.

"Don't be daft, I'm fine. I haven't had that much. Let's go find Marcus and see if he's ready to leave."

We wandered around, eventually finding Marcus snugged up with the beautiful young man I'd seen him with earlier. He waved us away, telling Aaron he'd be fine and blowing us both drunken kisses.

As we walked to the car, I asked; "Did it never bother you that Marcus was gay?" Aaron had never seemed remotely fazed by it, nor at the way some people could have assumed they were boyfriends, living together.

"Nope. I always knew really. Personally, I don't *understand* it, but it's never bothered me. I just think that who Marcus shags is his own business."

"Is he in love with you?" I asked. Aaron laughed.

"I doubt it. I mean, we're close like brothers, but I've never even been curious about the gay thing, and he knows that. He likes his men small, sleek, and pretty, all of which I'm not."

I thought about his hairy chest and had to agree. Aaron was a physically imposing man with an intense masculinity. I was surprised he'd dismissed the notion of being fancied by Marcus so easily, especially given what an arrogant and cocky sod he was.

I was also concerned he'd had too much to drink and shouldn't be driving. "Are you sure you want to drive?" I asked nervously.

"Sally, would you stop behaving like my mother? If I say I'm OK, then I'm OK." Meekly, I got into the passenger seat and made sure my seatbelt was fastened securely. Aaron fired up the engine and pulled out of the space, before accelerating much too fast down the track, narrowly missing a gaggle of girls who were walking towards the main road.

Whether he drove too fast because I'd questioned his fitness to drive, or whether it was recklessness borne of too much alcohol, I wasn't sure, but he pushed the powerful car hard as we crossed Chislehurst common, causing me to grip the edge of my seat in fear. I noticed the car kept drifting as he struggled to control it.

"Aaron, I really think you should either slow down or stop and get a cab," I squeaked. To my horror, he seemed to forget he was driving and turned to face me.

"Will you stop nagging? You sound just like my mother. Where's your sense of adventure?"

Then it happened.

He mounted the kerb, jolting us both and careened towards a group of people walking along.

In films, accidents are always portrayed in slow motion. In reality, they happen faster than a blink. We came up behind the group, leaving them no time or opportunity to jump out of the way. Aaron noticed at the last moment and pulled the wheel in a vain attempt to avoid them, only partially succeeding. I heard a sickening crunch as we made contact with someone, sending him flying.

"Shit!" Shouted Aaron, as he realised what had happened. "Fuck fuck. It's your fucking fault for distracting me."

He carried on driving, speeding up slightly. "You need to stop," I shouted, trying to look behind me to see what had happened. It was too dark to be able to check if the fella was OK. We'd hit him at such speed that I was dubious anyone could possibly survive. Aaron kept going, gripping the wheel so tightly that I could see his knuckles turning white. "Aaron, what's wrong with you? You can't just drive away from an accident, and if you don't slow down, we'll have another one." I was panicking, verging on hysterical by that point. Aaron simply ignored me. He seemed to be in some sort of trance, just staring at the road ahead.

"Please let me out," I begged as he pulled across junctions without even checking to see what was coming. I prayed the lights on the A21 would be red and I'd be able to jump out of the car. I unclipped my seat belt in readiness.

He screeched straight through the red light at about eighty miles an hour, narrowly missing a lorry coming in the opposite direction. I screamed in fear.

"Will you keep. Fucking. Quiet!" Aaron berated me.

"You're scaring me," I shouted. "You nearly fucking killed us."

"Mind your language," he snarled.

Instead of heading towards Lakeswood, he turned off towards Keston Common. "Why're you going this way?" I demanded. He didn't answer. He just pointed the car towards a large tree a hundred yards away and put his foot down. Two seconds later, everything went black.

CHAPTER 14

I became aware of light shining brightly onto my face. I tried to turn my head away, but it felt leaden and immovable. The light was irritating, preventing me from going back to sleep. I guessed it must be morning. I tried to shift myself off my back, to roll over away from the sunshine, but my body seemed stuck, as though the covers were hemming me in. I tried to grip them to move them out of the way, my hand grasping at the sheets covering me.

"Sally, can you hear me?" A foreign accent permeated my dream. I felt a warm hand wrap around mine. "Sally, can you open your eyes?"

They felt as though lead weights were holding them closed. It took almost superhuman strength to lift the lids and peer at whoever it was waking me. A small Asian girl in blue scrubs was standing by my bedside. "Sally, you're in the hospital, you had an accident." She smiled at me, her eyes like two molten chocolate buttons set against pale coffee-coloured skin. In my confusion, I wondered if all angels were Asian. "Can you see me?" She asked.

I tried to reply that I could, but my voice was barely a croak. "I'm going to get the doctor to come and have a look at you, then I can give you some water to help your throat," she said. She bustled off, and I was left to look around at my surroundings. The hospital smell was horribly familiar, that nasty mixture of antiseptic and stale food which gets right up your nostrils and embeds itself in your brain, never to be forgotten. I was in a bay, with a window and a portable table. What was odd was that my bay had a door, so it made it into a private room. I wondered if Aaron had insisted on it. I wanted to check that my arms and legs were still there, but I couldn't move, which made me panic.

My nurse returned, accompanied by a doctor. "Hello Sally, Iris tells me you've woken up. Shall we take a look at you?"

"Cut... anything... off?" I managed to rasp out.

"Goodness, no. You had a nasty bang on the head though. At least you're alive, not like the other poor devil."

"Aaron?" I rasped. I tried desperately to remember what had happened but my brain was just a fog.

"No, the man you hit. He died at the scene, massive head injuries." The doctor shone a light into my eyes and noted down the results. He seemed cold and impersonal, as though he was going through the motions. He turned to the nurse "She can have water now. I'd give it another twenty four hours before she's well enough to be interviewed." With that, he went.

"Your name's Iris?" I rasped, as she brought a jug of water and a paper cup over to my bedside. She nodded and smiled as she poured a small amount and helped me drink it. The water felt like cool nectar, soothing my parched throat.

"Is there someone I should call?" She asked. I looked at her quizzically. "To tell them you woke up."

"What day is it?" I asked.

"It's Monday morning," she told me. "We didn't know who to call to say you were here. The man who was your passenger, he came yesterday, but didn't give us his number."

"What happened?" I asked, "How did I get here?"

"You crashed your car," she said softly. "There was a lot of alcohol in your blood. The police think you hit a pedestrian first."

As soon as she said it, the memory came flooding back. I remembered Aaron driving like a maniac after drinking champagne. Begging him to stop after he hit the man, sending him flying into the air.

"I wasn't driving," I said. "Aaron was."

"The policeman, he said you were pulled out of the driver's seat," she said.

"I wasn't driving," I repeated. I sank back into the pillow as despair hit. I knew I hadn't gotten behind the wheel of that car. I wondered if Aaron had crashed deliberately to put me, unconscious, into the driver's seat to pin the blame on me. As I lay there, alone and in deep trouble, I tried to think through what I should do, but my head was pounding so much it was hard to keep focus.

I was dozing when Aaron strode in. He had a serious scowl on his face, nothing like the smiling, kind person I'd known just a few days before. "You're awake," he barked, "good." He said it like he didn't mean it. The thought flashed through my mind that maybe he'd tried to kill me too, so I'd be a dead person taking the rap, meaning he'd never get any comeback.

"I brought you some coffee," he said. I eyed it warily.

"Thanks. I'm not sure if I can drink it or not. I only woke up an hour or so ago."

"So have you spoken to the police yet?"

"No. The doctor said 24 hours till I'm well enough." I paused. "What happened?"

"How much do you remember?" He asked.

"I remember you hitting that pedestrian and me begging you to slow down," I said. I noticed he had a small plaster on his jaw. He obviously hadn't been badly hurt.

"You're not gonna tell them that though," he said, his voice taking on a more sinister tone. "You see, if I went to prison, all those people who depend on me for their livelihoods, well, they'd all be destitute. You know what that's like, don't you Sally? If you took the rap for this, you'd get two years tops. I'd give you enough to buy a nice house. It makes sense."

"I wasn't driving," I said firmly. "I didn't kill that man."

"Just don't forget how much you owe me Sally. You were fast enough taking my money, now it's time to pay it back. You were pulled out of the driver's seat of that car. I've testified that you were driving because I'd had too much to drink. Nobody on Earth will believe you over me, and we both know it, so you can make this easy, and make yourself rich by taking the blame, or you can do it the hard way and end up a penniless ex-con. You decide." With that, he strode out of the room.

As soon as he'd disappeared, Iris, the nurse came in. "I was listening," she confessed. "I heard what he said. It's no fair what he done. Is there nobody can help you?"

"What happened to my bag?" I asked. I needed Andy. I could only hope and pray that he'd still be willing to help me. Iris shook her head.

"Police must have it. It not with you when they brought you in."

"Iris, can you call someone for me? He works at a law company called Alpha. His name is Andy. Can you tell him Sally Higgs is in trouble and I need him? Tell him where I am... please."

"Is he your lawyer?"

"No, he's my ex. I'm only hoping it's not too late."

"I get him for you. Now try to rest and not worry too much. I tell the desk that the tall one with the scruffy beard is not allowed in again." She smiled her radiant smile and went off to try and find Andy.

Andy. I wondered if he'd help me, or leave me to languish in my own stupidity. Tears leaked down my bruised face as I contemplated going to prison. I knew full well that drunk driving, on a ban and running someone over would be far longer than two years. My life really was well and truly over. Twenty minutes later, Iris returned. "I left a message. They wouldn't let me speak to him. I'm sorry."

"Let's hope he gets it," I said.

"I can tell the police what I heard the devil-man say. I hate liars."

"Where are you from Iris?" I was intrigued by her accent.

"Myanmar, but I've been here a long time." She saw my puzzled look. "Used to be called Burma," she clarified.

"I've never met a Burmese person," I said.

"It's a beautiful place, so not many people leave. I'm only here because my father took up a post in London. I go back very year for a holiday, to see my grandparents and family. Do you have a family?"

"Nope, nobody. I'm an orphan." I didn't often use that term, but at that moment, it was an apt description. Nobody would even notice if I went to prison, let alone worry. I'd just become another ex-care home statistic in the prison system.

"That's such a shame." Her molten chocolate eyes were filled with compassion. "One day you can make your own family," she said.

"Maybe." Inside I was calculating how much fertile time I had left. If I got twenty years in prison, that would be that dream scuppered.

Iris gave my hand a little squeeze and set about taking my vitals.

Two hours later, I was lying still, trying not to move my head, when the door opened. Andy stood in the doorway, sweating profusely as if he'd been running. "I'm sorry, I didn't get the message straightaway. What the Hell happened?"

"You were right," I told him. "He shit on me from a great height."

He sat on the edge of the bed and grasped my hand. I winced as I became aware of some new bruises. "What do you mean? Did he do this to you?"

"When we left on Saturday night, he drove like a maniac; he'd had too much to drink. He ran someone over and just drove off. I begged him to stop, or at least slow down, but he wouldn't listen."

"I see, where does you being in trouble fit into all this?"

"He drove the car into a tree. I was knocked out. Apparently the police pulled me out of the driver's seat. He told them it was me that killed that man." Andy's eyebrows flew up. "He came in here today to pressure me into saying it was me. He said I owed him, plus that it will be my word against his, nobody will believe me."

Andy sucked in a breath. "I believe you." He paused. "I was watching as he drove away. I saw you get into the passenger seat."

"The nurse heard him threaten me. It's why she rung you. I'm in so much trouble, and I'm so sorry." Tears coursed down my cheeks. "I only went with him because he paid off my debt, then it was too difficult to call a halt because I'd have been homeless as well as jobless." I could barely get the words out through my sobs.

"Oh Sally, you should have come to me sooner," he said. "I wouldn't have let you live on the streets. I know I'm an ass, but I'd have never allowed that." He paused. "And he didn't pay off your debt."

We were interrupted by Iris bustling in carrying some pills in a paper cup. "I have your painkillers." She stopped when she saw Andy. "Andrew, I didn't realise it was you I was calling. I'd have just got Phillip to call you direct."

"You two know each other?" I asked.

"Iris is Phil's girlfriend," he explained.

"Here I'm Nurse Winn," she said sternly, before flashing her lovely smile and kissing Andy lightly on the cheek.

"Were you wearing the teal-green dress on Saturday night?" I asked. Without her makeup on and with her hair in a neat bun, she looked completely different.

"Yes, that was me," she said. "So Andrew, you help Sally with the liar-man, yes?"

"Of course. I'm not a criminal lawyer, but I happen to know the best in the business."

I wasn't listening, his statement saying Aaron hadn't paid off my debt was racing around my mind. Everything I'd done, the bad sex, selling my soul, it had all been in vain. Apart from my dress, Aaron hadn't had to pay anything. I felt well and truly "had." "Hang on," I interrupted, "He told me he'd paid it off, and now you're telling me he didn't?" I'd wondered why they hadn't written to me to confirm it was settled and the CCJ lifted.

"He didn't pay it, because I'd already done it," Andy mumbled, embarrassed for some reason. "I cleared it when I got into work on Monday. By the time Aaron called, you had a nil balance. He obviously lied to you. Bastard."

"Why did you pay it?" I asked, puzzled as to why he'd do that for someone who'd just dumped him.

"Two reasons really. First off, he's not a good person to owe. I know he's all charming and pretends to be nice, but you don't get that rich by being a nice guy."

"Are you that rich?" I asked. It was a loaded question. He nodded warily.

"It's how I know he's not a nice guy," he admitted. He avoided my eyes. "Second was my mum. Rupert ratted me out during Sunday lunch when she wanted to know what was bothering me so much. I was a wreck. Rupert told her exactly what I'd done."

"What did she say?" I asked.

"Oh where do I start? That I was a fool, I'd let the family down, I was selfish and mean, that she didn't bring us up to be thoughtless to women. It went on for over an hour."

"So why did you lie to me?"

"I didn't outright lie, I just avoided telling you the truth. What we had..." He tailed off.

"You never had before?"

He nodded. "Everyone knew us, the McCarthys, loaded, high achieving and cocky. I either had hungry, ambitious women throwing themselves at my feet, or the cold sociopath who treated me like a retard. I'd never had the chance to meet someone like you."

"Poor, hopeless, and facing a prison sentence?"

"It won't come to that. Listen, I need to make some calls, get the ball rolling. Whatever you do, don't speak to Aaron. If he gets in here, press your buzzer for help. I don't want you alone with him under any circumstances. He possibly tried to kill you once..."

I went cold at the thought.

"Sally will need something to wear to go home in," Iris said. "We cut her dress off, so she only has a pair of high-heeled shoes with her."

"Of course," muttered Andy. "I'll get Mum on it. What size are you?"

"Eight, medium length, shoe size five," I said, reeling from the horror of the red dress being cut up.

"OK, leave it all with me. I'll make a start, then I'll be back later on." He kissed me softly on the lips, waved to Iris and hurried off. I sank back into the pillows, exhausted.

He came back a few hours later, lugging a load of bags and accompanied by an older man, who was casually dressed in an anorak and slacks. He certainly didn't strike me as a hotshot criminal lawyer. "This is my dad, William," he began.

"But everyone calls me Bill," interrupted his dad. "Andrew tells me you're in a spot of bother?"

I nodded, "Seems that way." Inside, I died a little. I knew my fringe was sticking up, my hair was greasy, and I was covered in bruises.

Andy dumped the bags in the corner and pulled up two chairs, one on each side of my bed. "Dad was one of the top criminal lawyers in the UK," he explained. "He's semi-retired now, but there's nobody sharper to have on your side."

"Now, what I'm going to do is ask you to talk me through the events of that night. Don't leave out any details and certainly don't keep quiet about anything for fear of upsetting Andrew. I know his side of the story too." He threw Andy an exasperated glance, then switched on his voice recorder. I tried to keep events in sequence, racking my brains to remember details and approximate times. He then began asking me questions. Odd things such as which hand I opened the car door with, that sort of stuff.

"What shoes were you wearing? How long was your dress? Were you wearing gloves?" His attention to the minuscule details was astonishing. He turned to Andy, "Have the police still got the car? Have forensics been over it?"

"Yes and yes," he said. "Aaron requested it back in order to send it to Bentley to be fixed, but I've scuppered that. I've also requested forensics double-check the prints on the wheel and any flecks from shoe leather in the foot wells. I spoke to the doorman who was working that night. He also remembers seeing

Sally and Aaron get into the car. I've sent Mike Ritrovato over to get a statement from him and an affidavit."

"At the moment, the police are simply looking for evidence of a hit and run, so we need to direct them that we believe there was an attempted murder involved in order to frame Sally. I need the shoes you were wearing."

"Bedside cabinet," I said. Andy bent down and pulled them out. He handed them to his dad, who examined them carefully.

"If she'd have been wearing these while driving, the back of the heel would be slightly scraped. It's why ladies often have driving shoes. We can see that these are still pristine. Sally obviously had her feet flat on the floor." He placed them carefully on the end of my bed and turned to me. "The police will interview you tomorrow. I will be present throughout. You don't speak unless I'm there. Understood?" I nodded. "Good. Now, they may well arrest you tomorrow, but don't worry, I'll immediately apply for bail. Before that, I'm meeting with the chief inspector for a swift nine holes, first thing tomorrow. I'll have a chat with him in confidence; steer the investigation a little."

"Will that work?" I asked, panicking about being arrested.

"Of course it will. This was the clumsiest fit up I've seen in years. He didn't have a lot of time to get his ducks in a row. Plus of course, he was drunk. He made a lot of mistakes. The police are only looking at you right now because they haven't had any other evidence put in front of them, nor has Mr Pryce's version of events been challenged."

"Wouldn't I be better not asking for bail? I mean, I've got nowhere to go, I can't go back to Lakeswood." I didn't particularly want to go to prison, but it was better than living on the streets.

"You're staying with me," Andy said rather gruffly. His dad shot him a daggers look.

"What did your mother say about being a bit more emotionally intelligent? No wonder the poor girl got herself into a scrape with you being so kind and welcoming."

Andy rolled his eyes. It was funny seeing him told off by his Dad, although it was pretty tongue in cheek. "Is there anything at Lakeswood of value? Anything sentimental?"

"My phone and laptop, that's all, plus of course my clothes."

"Can all be replaced," Andy stated, "It's safer to have no contact. We don't know what lengths he'll go to for your silence. You'll be safe at mine."

"Okay... if you're sure. I know I've been enough hassle."

There was an awkward pause.

Bill stood up. "Right, well, I've got enough to be going on with. I'll see you tomorrow afternoon. Andrew, think about what your mother told you to do." He blew me a kiss and left.

"I'm sorry," I said. "I just lurch from disaster to disaster. You must be so fed up with me by now."

"I like saving you," he said, still rather gruff. "It's what I do best." I went to speak, but he put his hand up to stop me. "When you left me, it was physically painful. I've never experienced anything like it before. I missed you terribly."

"I missed you too," I murmured, "and I loved all those songs you sent."

He shifter closer and held my hand gently. "I meant every word of them. Can you believe I actually missed your disasters? Wondering if you needed me... it drove me insane."

I let his words sink in. "Andy, if you want me, then you need to be honest with me." I paused and took a deep breath. "Are you only with me because it makes you feel superior?" I half-expected him to either laugh, or be cross. Instead, his lovely face was etched with concern.

"Is that what you think? Of course not. I want you because you're the right woman. You're smart, funny, caring, and incredibly kind. I'll accept that you're a Calamity Jane, but to be honest, if I'd had your upbringing, I doubt I'd have coped half as well as you have." He brought my fingers up to his lips and kissed them. "Just so you know, I never, ever thought you were with me for money. I thought you were with Aaron for his, but not me." His eyes bored into me, searching out the truth. Fat tears rolled down my face, partly because I was ashamed of what I'd done, and partly because I knew I'd hurt both of us. He gently ran his thumb under my eyes.

"You were right," I said, "and I feel shitty for having to admit it. I planned to wait until I had my back pay in the bank, and then do a runner. I just didn't think I had any other choice." I brought my face up to look at him. His eyes were a little glossy. Silently, he opened his arms and I fell into his embrace, breathing in his wonderful scent and enjoying being in my safe place. Tentatively and oh-so-gently, his lips found mine. He poured all his emotion into that kiss, trying to communicate what he just couldn't do with words.

We sprang apart the moment the door opened. Iris bustled in. "I'm so sorry for disturbing you, but I've brought you a cup of tea and I need to take your blood pressure." I could see she'd blushed a little and was wearing a sly smirk. She took my vitals quickly and efficiently, noting them on the sheet at the end of the bed. "So you have clothes?" She asked, pointing at the heap of carrier bags. "Did you shop or did your mum do it?" She asked Andy.

"Mum. I wouldn't have a clue," he admitted.

"Then you're safe," she said to me with a wink. "If Andrew had done it, I don't know, lots of lingerie and not much else."

"Cheek!" Andy exclaimed. "We're not all like Phil you know."

"I know all about McCarthy boys," Iris said, smiling at me. "Too many good looks, too much charm, and they all have cheeky smiles. They all run rings round us girls."

She bade us goodbye, as her shift was finished. Andy went off to find the nurse who'd be covering the night duty to warn her not to let Aaron in, and then he found the hospital Starbucks and bought us both large lattes.

As I sipped mine, grateful for his comforting presence, he showed me what his mum had bought. She'd truly thought of everything. Comfortable yoga pants, a soft, warm sweater, socks, warm boots and a quilted coat, as well as hospital stuff like a nightie, dressing gown, and toiletries.

"She said to say sorry it's only Marks, but she didn't have much time to get it all."

"It's perfect," I told him.

It felt wonderful to put on a clean nightdress after wearing the open-backed hospital gown. I'd had quite a severe concussion, so was getting a sort of sea-sick effect when I stood up. The doctor had assured me it would disappear in a day or two, and I'd have no lasting damage. In the meantime, getting to the loo meant gripping hold of anything solid within reach, with my arse on full show, so the nighty instantly made me feel better.

Andy stayed until the night nurse threw him out. Leaving me with a soft kiss and a promise to be back the next day. His dad would be there for my police interview.

I woke early the next morning, the noises of the hospital jolting me awake. With some trepidation, I got out of bed and made my way to the loo. The dizziness I'd experienced the day before had definitely eased. I decided to attempt a shower.

I had to wash my hair ultra-gently, the bruises on the side of my head where I'd hit the passenger window were still tender, but I managed to lather up my hair and let the hot water run through it to rinse. Just being clean again made me feel better.

I was drying off with the cardboard-hard hospital towel when Iris came in to find me. "I would have helped you," she told me. "Now, do you want to put normal clothes on rather than your nightdress?

"Please. I wasn't sure if I'd be allowed."

I sat in my bedside chair, fully dressed, and ate the rubbery scrambled eggs and cold toast served for breakfast and ruminated on the prospect of having lost every possession I owned. In a peculiar way it felt cathartic. I was rid of the leaky shoes and useless coat forever, along with the girl who'd had to buy them because it was all she could afford. I made a vow to myself to only shop carefully in the future. In fact, all my fears about losing everything felt small now that it had actually happened. The only fear I had to face was the possibility of losing my liberty, which struck terror inside me.

The doctor came round late that morning and after checking me over, announced I could leave. He seemed warmer than he had previously, which I put down to Iris telling him what had really happened. "I hear the police will be here soon. Let's hope that the truth comes out, eh?" He said as he examined the egg-sized bump on my left temple. "Thinking about it, you couldn't have got this bump unless you'd been in the passenger seat, given that the driver was unharmed." He frowned as he gave me a last check-over. "Well, good luck."

I thanked him and watched him sign my discharge form. I briefly contemplated doing a runner, but quickly dismissed the idea. I needed to face the problem head-on, otherwise I'd be limiting my options even more.

Bill showed up at mid-day, just ahead of the police. I sat in silence as one formally arrested me, stating that anything I said would be used as evidence. Even though I knew it was coming, I was shocked and scared. I was glad Bill was there. The list of charges was a long one and included driving without a licence as well as driving under the influence and most importantly, manslaughter.

We were driven directly to Bromley police station, a new building which the architect had attempted to make modern. The high walls and security spikes gave it a forbidding appearance, and the lack of windows rammed it home that this was a place for prisoners. Bill guided me in, gently holding my shoulder in a very fatherly gesture. He could probably see me shaking.

We were taken to an interview room, where we were left alone for a while. "Are you alright?" Bill asked. "You're very pale."

"I'm scared," I admitted. "What if they don't believe me?"

"They'll believe you alright," he said very quietly. "The chief inspector, this morning, let me in on a little secret. Aaron Pryce is being investigated for a string of insider dealing and dodgy bond-trading scams. If they can get him for this, it'll blow open the rest of his empire for the fraud squad to investigate, so they're keen to accept the truth about the accident. Just let them get their ducks in a row Sally. They'll need to do this a certain way. Be aware of that. Just remember, they're not after you."

I let out the breath I was holding and tried to calm down. When two men walked in, grim faced, my stress levels ratcheted back up. One switched on a tape recorder, reeling off the date, time, and who was present. "So Sally, would you tell us about the events of Saturday fourteenth of February, more specifically from the time you left the Foxbury Ball."

I began haltingly, trying hard not to leave out any details. Bill didn't interrupt or try and steer me on what to say. The detectives asked a few questions, mainly about timings, until the nicer one asked; "did Mr Pryce argue with anyone on Saturday night?"

"Yes, a middle-aged bald man. I didn't know his name. He confronted Aaron. I was standing some way away and it was loud, but I heard him shout something about fifty grand. Afterwards, Aaron, Mr Pryce told me that the man was cross because he held onto some bonds too long and his greediness cost him fifty grand of profit, but he still made a quarter of a million."

"Did you know about any of his business deals?" I shook my head.

"I was his dog-nanny; it's how we met. He never discussed business with me."

"What do you know about Marcus Brookes?"

"He's the housekeeper for Aaron. Well, he organises the household and designs all the interiors."

"Was he present with you Saturday night?"

"Yes, he came with us, but didn't leave when we did."

"Why was that?"

"He was chatting up some fella, said he wanted to stay." I wondered why the nice cop was interested in Marcus. He'd had nothing to do with the accident. Bill seemed puzzled too.

"Can I ask why you're asking my client these questions? Mr Brookes wasn't in the car when it crashed," he asked. The copper ignored him.

"Were you ever offered cocaine by Mr Brookes?" He asked. I gasped.

"No, never," I squawked. "I don't take drugs, you can do a blood test if you like." The copper just blinked at me.

"We already have. You tested clear for narcotics, positive for alcohol." He pulled out a file. Inside was my red clutch, held in a clear plastic bag. "Is this your bag?" He asked.

"Yes."

"What was in it?"

"A Rimmel lipstick and my door key."

"Where in the car did you place your clutch?"

"On the seat, wedged under my thigh. Why?"

"Do you recognise this? He reached into his file for another plastic bag, and showed me a small rectangle of foil. I shook my head.

"Can you say 'yes' or 'no' for the recording, please?" He said.

"No, that wasn't in my bag."

He placed it all back in the file and closed it carefully. "Did you check the wheel for prints?" Bill asked.

"We did indeed. I'll need to take your client's to see if they match. The duty Sergeant will arrange it. Now, Sally, while you were at the house, were there any suspicious comings or goings?"

Bill butted in straightaway. "This line of questioning is not relevant to the case in hand. Given that there has already been an attempt on my client's life, I'd like to know why you're asking about this?"

The policeman gave Bill a hard stare. "Cocaine was found in your client's bag, which was on the back seat of the car. I'm trying to ascertain where it may have come from."

"My client is not a drug user, you have the evidence, plus the bag was, in her words, wedged under her thigh on the front seat. Has the bag been tested for prints?"

"Yes, we found three different prints on it."

"Marcus unwrapped it when it was delivered," I said. "I don't think Aaron ever touched it."

The policemen left the room. "You OK?" Bill asked. I nodded.

"So Aaron was a drug user?" I said, more to myself than Bill. "Explains why he did everything at a hundred miles an hour."

Bill just did the McCarthy family smirk. He really was just an older version of Andy, with the same mannerisms, which I found fascinating. The tape was still recording, so we stayed quiet. I took in the bare, featureless room, with its nailed-down, utilitarian furniture and oppressive decor, designed to be as bland and featureless as possible, offering no pleasant distractions to people accused of being the criminals of society.

When the policemen returned, they'd been joined by another, uniformed copper who proceeded to take my fingerprints and a swab of my DNA. He handed Bill a sheaf of forms to fill in to apply for my bail. It was all a bit of a blur. I struggled to take in the things they were telling me, focusing only on the part where I'd be appearing in front of a magistrate in a week or so time.

"That's it," said the duty Sergeant, after swabbing my mouth. "You're OK to go."

CHAPTER 15

We got a taxi over to Andy's house, which Bill had named as my bail address. Despite my horrible predicament, excitement rose in my belly at the prospect of seeing where he lived and getting a true insight into the man I'd fallen in love with.

We pulled into a turning marked Yester Park, which had large gates barring the entrance. The gates opened automatically, making me wonder why anyone would bother having them. We drove slowly down a road lined with large detached houses, each different, but all nicely kept. We were in affluent Chislehurst, the money plainly on show.

"Keep going till you get to the end," Bill said to the cab driver. At the end of the road was a dead end, with another large pair of gates. Bill jumped out and entered some numbers into the keypad beside them. They began to open and he jumped back into the car.

"Andy lives here on his own?" I asked, trying to take it all in.

"Yes. I told him it was too big for one person, but he insisted on it. I think he rattles around in it." We carried on up the drive. As we turned past some trees, the house revealed itself. It wasn't as huge as Lakesview, but it was possibly more beautiful. It was also more modern, with pretty cream-coloured render and a tile-hung second floor. The total effect was breathtaking.

Bill paid the cabbie and told him how to get back out of the gates. I was busy gazing up at the building, wondering why Andy had chosen to hide it from me. Bill proceeded to knock on the front door. "Monica's in there waiting for us," he said. I wondered who Monica was, but as soon as I heard yapping, figured it was Andy's mum and her dog.

A small, but elegant blonde lady opened the door, clutching a yapping Maltese terrier. "Come in, how'd it go? You must be Sally? I'm Monica, but everybody calls me Mon. Lola just did a widdle in the kitchen, bloody typical. Can't take her anywhere. Come on in out of the cold."

She was nothing like I expected at all, but I thought she was great. For some reason I'd expected her to be tall, but she couldn't have been more than five foot two. I wondered how on Earth she'd produced four big strapping men. She stepped aside to let us in.

"It went fine. Sally's on bail while they check out more forensics. I think they're going for Brookes as well as Pryce. They found a wrap of coke planted in her bag, but none in her bloodstream. It's quite damning." He led the way into the kitchen, which was a vast room separated into zones. He sat himself down on a stool at the island, while Monica filled the kettle, one handed, as she still had the dog tucked under the other arm.

"And Sally," she addressed me, "how are you holding up? This must've been a Hell of a shock."

"It's pretty scary," I admitted, "on all levels. I just hope they believe me."

The Debt

"The truth always comes out eventually," she said sagely. "Andrew told me to tell you he'll be home soon. He wanted to be here when you got back, but had something come up at the office. Bill and I are under strict instructions to make sure you have someone with you all the time due to you being a witness. Goodness only knows what that man's capable of." She set out three cups and dropped a teabag in each one.

I was sipping my tea and listening to Monica's description of Lola the dog's routines, when Andy got home. His eyes crinkled into a smile when he saw me sitting in his kitchen. "How'd it go?" He asked.

"I'm out on bail," I said, "they're looking into the case a bit more closely, plus there seems to be a bit of another issue going on."

"Oh?"

"My bag was found on the back seat with a foil wrap inside it, which was probably cocaine."

"Yes, I know. I spoke to the police this afternoon. They invited Aaron in to give his witness statement. As soon as he got there they arrested him. They're raiding Lakeswood as we speak."

"They asked me if Marcus offered me cocaine."

"Doesn't surprise me. He was dealing it in sixth form, low-level though back then. The rumour is that's why he liked living in such a high-security house. He'd stopped dealing as such and moved up to supplying."

"I had no idea," I said. "I'm so bloody naive." I watched as he plopped his briefcase on the island and pulled off his tie. He really suited formal business wear. His mum made him a coffee in a very swanky built-in machine that seemed fiendishly complicated.

He sat on the stool beside me and squeezed my hand. "You're very pale. How's your head?"

"A bit tender. I've got a headache, but not a bad one," I admitted.

"Good. Now, Mum's gonna take you shopping tomorrow, to start replacing everything you lost at Lakeswood. It's probably best you don't go anywhere alone right now, given there's been one attempt on your life. Aaron's got a lot at stake, and he's a ruthless man. I don't want anything else happening to you."

I didn't want to argue, especially in front of his parents, but with only twelve hundred pounds to my name and the very real possibility of going to prison on the horizon, I didn't feel that splurging on new clothes was top of my agenda, although I had to concede I needed a few things. Monica clapped her hands together, excited at the prospect of shopping, which made the dog jump.

"Put it on your card Mum, and I'll drop the money into your account," said Andy.

"Do I have a budget or limit?" She asked, a steely glint in her eye. Andy blushed before shaking his head. Monica grinned at me. "We'll go to Bluewater; nicer shops and better places for lunch."

With a promise to pick me up at nine the following morning, they left. As soon as they were gone, Andy pulled me into his arms and pressed a featherlight kiss to my lips, almost seeking permission to kiss me properly. I wrapped my arms around his shoulders and deepened the kiss, letting him know I still wanted him. Our tongues met in an erotic dance, tasting and teasing each other as we reconnected.

Eventually, he pulled away. "I'm sorry all this happened to you, it's not going to be fun having to be chaperoned everywhere, but I just can't risk anything happening to you. You're the lynchpin in three separate investigations now, the hit and run, the insider dealing fraud, and Marcus's coke dealing. They're bound to want to silence you."

"Well your mum is hardly gonna be much of a bodyguard is she?" I pointed out. He just laughed.

"Dad was a lawyer dealing with some of the worst, most powerful criminals in the UK. They got used to living with protecting themselves. Don't let the little fluffy blonde appearance fool you, she's as sharp as a tack."

I pondered his statement. "Have you had the guided tour yet?" He asked, interrupting my thoughts. I shook my head. "Come on then, I'll show you around." He held his hand out. I placed mine in it and let him lead me out of the kitchen.

The house was big, too big for a single person, or even a couple. It was more comfortable than Lakeswood in the way it was furnished: the sofas were squashier, the colours warmer. Andy told me that his Mum's friend had done it, and her work had been featured in Homes and Gardens magazine. "Why did you want such a big house?" I asked as he showed me around the bedrooms. He shrugged.

"It was a bit of a pissing contest really. A group of us, all typically cocky high achievers, we were all competing I suppose. I wanted Lakeswood originally, but I needed a mortgage to afford it, hence why I was outbid. By the time the mortgage company agreed to up my borrowing facility, the house had been sold to someone else. I didn't know it was Aaron until you worked there. He wasn't part of our group."

"Your house is far nicer," I told him, "but why keep it a secret? It's the bit I don't understand."

He pulled me into his arms, wrapping them around me. "I was selfish, just enjoying the purity of what we had. Sitting in your little bedsit, just hanging out together, it meant I got a break from being Drew McCarthy, flash git and all-around bastard. What I didn't take into account was that your need for a break from the poverty you were in was far greater than my need for a bit of escapism. I'm sorry I did that to you."

"You expect me to feel sorry for you?" I asked, exasperated.

"Nope," he said, popping the 'P.' "You should never feel sorry for me. My only concern is that you think I'm a certain type of person. I just wonder how you're gonna feel about the real me."

"The same I expect. Maybe you showed me your true self, not the mask you wear for the world."

He just shrugged. "Are you hungry? I could eat a horse."

The moment was broken. I followed him back down to the kitchen to see what there was to eat. He had an enormous American fridge, which, upon inspection was pitifully empty, containing only milk and a couple of out-of-date ready meals. "I should've asked Mum to fill it up for me," he said.

"Isn't there a supermarket up the road?" I asked. "We could go now; it wouldn't take long."

Andy pushed the trolley, while I chose some shopping. It meant we wouldn't be living on takeaways and I'd get to have a play with the beast of a range

cooker in his kitchen, which was so pristine. I guessed
it hadn't seen very much action. As we wandered
around, Andy seemed to relax and enjoy himself,
choosing some expensive steaks for that evening.

Back at the house, I unpacked the shopping and
worked out how to use the fancy griddle plate, while
Andy opened a bottle of wine. He sat at the island while
I prepared our meal. "This is very cosy and domestic,"
he remarked, as I checked on the oven chips.

"You say it like it's a bad thing."

"Not at all."

As I cooked, I felt his gaze the whole time. I
wondered if he regretted having me stay, disrupting his
solitary existence and using his showroom-fresh cooker.
I felt awkward, a bit tongue-tied around him, knowing
I'd invaded his space by virtue of circumstance,
knowing he'd done his best to keep me away. I dished
up our food carefully and placed his plate in front of
him.

"Talented little thing aren't you?" He said, before
digging in. I stood on the opposite side of the island,
picking at mine, unsure if I should make myself at
home too much. He didn't seem to notice.

"Is my being here going to annoy you?" I asked
nervously, "I can go and look for a room tomorrow."

He put his fork down for a moment. "Course not. I
like having you here. I told you already I wish I'd been
honest from the start. If you cook like this every night,
you can stay. I've not had proper oven chips in years."
He smiled tentatively. I relaxed, silently chastising
myself for being so needy.

After we'd eaten, I cleared away and tidied up the kitchen. "What would you like to do this evening?" Andy asked.

I shrugged. "Whatever you like." I fully expected him to suggest some telly or a film. Instead he surprised me by suggesting a bath.

"I never really use it," he said as he sat on the edge filling it. He even tipped in some bubble bath, which scented the air in his large ensuite beautifully. I twisted my hair up into a knot, having to secure it with one of his tie clips, as I had no grips. As I slid into the hot bubbles, the enormity of the task ahead crashed over me. I didn't have so much as a hairbrush, let alone all the various clips, grips, and accoutrements girls acquire from years of dealing with wayward hair. I barely noticed Andy sliding in behind me, until his arms gently wrapped around me. For some reason, this tender gesture caused the dam to break. I let out a sob. "Hey, you're safe now," he said softly, pulling me in tighter.

"It's not that," I managed to say. "I realised I don't have a hairbrush, or any makeup, let alone a change of clothes." I sounded dumb, given how worried he was about my life being in danger, but to me it was important. I may have only possessed cheap stuff, but it was my cheap stuff, bought from my own labours. I'd never seen it as vital before, but now that it was all gone, I longed for the safety of my little bedsit. It was the first night in the children's home all over again.

"My mum will help you, I'll even take you again at the weekend if you like."

I picked up the flannel and wiped my face. Leaning back onto his chest, I felt warm and comfortable. "The first day I arrived in the kid's home, I had nothing at all.

The Debt

My nurse had got me a dress and shoes from a charity shop, but I had no underwear apart from a pair of hospital paper knickers. It was like my life had been erased. I became invisible, worthless even. It was three days before anyone realised I had no clean clothes and my feet were blistered from the plastic shoes worn without socks."

"What happened then?" He asked.

"I was given some hand-me-downs from the other girls," I said. "The horror of having to wear second-hand knickers has never left me. I bought my very first new clothes with the money from my Saturday job."

He kissed my shoulder. "You, my darling, will have the best of everything. You'll never have wet feet or blisters ever again. I'll make it my mission." He began soaping my back, working the lather into my tense muscles, trying to relax me. "Now that you have the McCarthy clan seal of approval, you get the considerable resources available to you, namely, my mum. She's the most efficient, organised person on the planet. She'll have you kitted out in no time."

"I'll get a few bits to tide me over, but I can wait until Ms Gadd pays out to really have a splurge." I felt his hands slow to a stop.

"I've already said I'd pay for new things. You don't need to wait."

"I don't want to be in debt any more. You of all people should understand that."

I heard him suck in a breath. "You won't be in debt."

"I still think I should wait until I know whether or not I'm going to prison first. No point having a wardrobe of nice clothes if I'm in the clink."

I let my words sink in. He needed to understand that however well-meaning he was, my situation was dire and no amount of platitudes would cover up the fact that I was in deep shit, plus jobless and homeless for good measure.

"It won't come to that," he tried to soothe. It was exasperating.

"How do you know? You don't seem to get it. I'm homeless, jobless, and pretty much skint with a huge court case hanging over my head. I actually don't think it could get much worse." The tears were falling again. Big, fat ones dripped into the bubbles. "And I'm placing all my trust in a man who doesn't even love me. You *like* me, remember?" Sarcasm dripped from my tongue. I was so far down the black hole I no longer cared what he did. For all his knight-in-shining-armour routine, he hadn't actually managed to achieve anything of substance for me.

"Do you really believe that?" He breathed. I turned to face him and let him see my tears. I nodded. "Is that why you left me for Aaron?" He asked, realisation dawning.

"I thought I was your fuck-buddy, just a girl you could casually see on your terms, without having to involve me in your life. Aaron could see it too, pointing it out at every opportunity..." I trailed off, mindful he could kick me out, and I'd be sleeping in a shop doorway.

"I hate that I made you feel like a casual shag. I never meant to. I'm just not good at expressing myself. Didn't you listen to the words of the songs I sent you?"

"I did, but as nice as they were, they weren't coming from you. As things stand, I feel awkward here, knowing you didn't want me in your house, with your family. I've been imposed on you through circumstance, and it's not what you would've chosen, I realise that."

He shook his head. "You're completely wrong. I like you being here. I should've been open from the start, and I know that. You can trust me though. I'd never risk losing you again. That week you left me; I've never known pain like it. I was a wreck, sitting in here, plotting which songs to send you because I'm too emotionally stunted to actually say the words myself. I just wish I knew how to make you realise..." He trailed off. I could see how worried he was, the little line between his brows had appeared.

I used the McCarthy trick. I stayed silent, mentally willing him to open up. "Do I need to spell it out to you?" He snapped, annoyed at my silence. "OK, I'm in love with you. I'm stupidly, totally obsessed by you. For the very first time in my life, the controlled, cold Drew McCarthy is completely helpless. Happy now?" He held my gaze, apparently unsure how I'd react.

I stroked his face, watching as he leaned into my touch. Then I brought my mouth to his and kissed him. As I rested my hands on his chest, I could feel his heart hammering. It'd taken a lot for him to open up. Eventually I pulled away. "I'm in love with you too, but you already knew that," I reminded him.

"Let me take care of you," he whispered, his voice hoarse with emotion. "Let me be the one to give you all the things you've never had."

It was everything I needed to hear. The bath water sloshed as I lay on him to kiss him again, pouring all my feelings into the connection between our lips. His hands roamed the length of my body, touching as much skin as possible, setting nerve endings alight as they stroked and kneaded. Without another word, he pulled me out of the bath, picked me up and carried me to his bed, still soaking wet.

He wasted no time plunging into me. I gasped at the sensation of him filling me, stretching me inside. As he began to move, I understood that he needed to take back what was his. It was a show of dominance as he grabbed my hands, pinning them above my head with his as he thrust into me hard and fast. My hips moved with his, meeting him thrust for thrust. It was raw, animalistic fucking, and we both wanted it.

I let go first, the sheer sexiness of being so needed by this beautiful, complex man, coupled with the pace and power of his lovemaking, pushed me over the edge. I came with a shout, arching off the bed as he continued to buck into me. "You. Are. Mine," he said as he rode my orgasm mercilessly, before letting go himself. He buried his face in the crook of my neck as he pressed in deep. I could feel it pulsing inside me.

A horrible realisation dawned.

I hadn't taken my pill for four days.

He must've felt me freeze. "What's the matter?" He mumbled.

"I've not taken my pill."

He raised his face from my neck and kissed me on my lips. "Morning after pill. Get it from Boots tomorrow."

"I'll have your Mum with me," I hissed.

"Oh, she won't mind. She had four boys remember? She's marched more girls to the chemist than she could count." He resumed his position in the crook of my neck. I liked his weight on me.

The next morning, I woke early and rolled over to see an angelic, sleeping Andy laying on his back, his arm carelessly resting on the pillow. He appeared younger, more relaxed than he'd been when sleeping at the bedsit. I slipped out of bed and went hunting for his bathrobe or a shirt to put on.

I padded down to the kitchen to make a cup of tea. Sitting at the island, I allowed myself to daydream about living there, sharing his beautiful house, his big, friendly family, and his successful life. I thought about his declaration the night before with a big, dopey grin on my face. If he loved me as much as I loved him, everything else could pale into insignificance. The only thing that could part us would be if I was sent to prison, the thought of which made my stomach churn.

At around seven, I made Andy a bacon sandwich and loaded a tray with coffee, juice, and his breakfast and took it up to him. As I placed it on his bedside table, he stirred, and then opened his eyes. As soon as he saw it was me, he smiled. "Good morning beautiful," he muttered, before spotting the tray. "I am being spoilt this morning." He picked up the juice and drained the glass.

"Thought I'd better make myself useful. What time do you need to leave for work?" I handed him his coffee.

"I'll wait till Mum gets here. Aaron may have been bailed by now. I'll know more once I've spoken to Dad.

I frowned, "Surely if the truth's out there, backed up by forensics, there'd be little point him bumping me off? I mean, I'm sure he doesn't want another murder charge added to the list."

"Quite possibly. It depends on whether they've charged him or not. In the meantime, I'd like to take as few risks as possible."

Monica arrived at precisely nine o'clock, dressed immaculately in a smart trouser set and lightweight jacket. Inside, I died a little, given I was wearing my one and only outfit and my hair was held in a tiepin due to Andy only possessing a comb.

"I've made a list ready. I just went round my dressing room noting everything in there. It's amazing how much women amass isn't it?" She smiled brightly at me. "Now, Andrew, I need an idea of our budget. Your dad warned me about getting carried away, told me to clarify it with you first."

I could see Andy blush at being put on the spot. "I don't know how much it all costs," he whined. "Just... knock yourselves out."

"I really think you need to specify," I pointed out, "can we spend a thousand? Two thousand?"

"Twenty thousand? Thirty thousand?" His mum chimed in, shocking me. I didn't expect anything near that amount.

Andy was visibly uncomfortable as he muttered to his mum, "Don't go over fifty eh?" My mouth dropped open, and the familiar sensation of being out of my depth washed over me.

"I don't need anything near that amount, I can go to Primark and get a whole wardrobe for a thousand quid, really. They do jumpers for three pounds each." I was babbling. His mum frowned at me.

"Don't be silly, let's go spend his money. Andrew won't mind treating you, will you?" She turned to him.

"Course not," he said, trying his best to sound happy about it. "No bargain basement stuff either Sal, best of everything, remember?"

We all left the house together, Monica and I in her sporty, red Range Rover, and Andy in his BMW, which he said he'd leave at the station. As the gates closed behind us, I glanced around nervously, but nobody was there. "Bill's playing golf with the chief inspector this morning," Monica told me, "He objected to bail yesterday, on the basis that Aaron and Marcus both had the means to leave the country, and of course, put your life in danger. We should be safe, but keep your wits about you, just in case."

We got to the shopping centre before the shops opened, so nipped into Costa to form a plan of action. I confessed the pill situation to Monica, who seemed unfazed and just added it to her list, promising to get me an appointment with their doctor first thing next morning for replacement pills or a shot. I relaxed and concentrated on her shopping list. She really had thought of everything.

We were in John Lewis buying a pair of straighteners when Monica's phone rang. She fished it out of her pocket and checked the screen before answering, whispering that it was Bill. I stood awkwardly, not wanting to eavesdrop, but desperate to hear the news. Eventually, she clicked her phone off. "We have to get you back by five, the police want to speak to you again."

My face fell. I wondered what Aaron had said.

"Bill thinks they're gonna drop all charges. The police didn't find a single fingerprint of yours on the steering wheel, and none of the flakes in the footwell of the driver's side came from your shoes. They've charged Aaron with your attempted murder, perverting the course of justice, as well as driving under the influence, and manslaughter. Looks like you're in the clear."

"What about the drugs they found in my purse?"

"Given that you had none in your bloodstream, I think they'll accept that Aaron planted them. They know Bill would demolish them in court over it. Marcus has been charged and remanded in custody. Apparently they found a significant amount of cocaine in the safe at Lakeswood."

I let out the breath I'd been holding. "To think, all that was going on around me and I didn't have a clue," I muttered. "I'm so sick of being the naive, gullible one. I wish I was a bit more streetwise." She patted my arm. "I know Andy's well off... He did make his legitimately, didn't he?"

She laughed. "Of course he did. Our law firm has been in the family for three generations, so we were comfortable before Andrew joined. He had the brains to become the collection agency for card debt, positioning the firm to be number one in that field. How he made all that money may be morally questionable, but it's certainly legal. He's done extremely well."

"I'm sorry, I didn't mean to question you," I said, cringing at how I'd sounded.

"I don't blame you after what you've been through. You wouldn't want to be jumping out of the frying pan into the fire, now would you?" I shook my head, glad that she'd understood.

Monica was a whirlwind, whisking me from shop to shop, ticking purchases off her carefully-prepared list. We stopped for a quick lunch in Carluccio's to refuel.

"We'll have this, then do another drop off to the car," she said, before pulling out her little glasses to read the menu.

I surveyed the array of bags. We'd already dropped one lot off. I'd never spent so much in my life. "Do you know what we're up to, budget wise?" I asked. I'd lost track. She shook her head, seemingly unconcerned.

"I'm not sure whether to have the linguini or the gnocchi. You really shouldn't worry about it Sally. Andrew confessed what he'd done to you, so you should let him make it up to you."

"I feel like a charity case," I muttered. "I'll have the tagliatelle if that's OK."

"I don't think he sees it that way. He sees it as being given an opportunity to take care of you, something he should have done at the start. I'm appalled at his behaviour. Rupert told me Andrew instructed you to sign on, letting you panic over a £350 rent bill. Ridiculous behaviour."

The waiter came to take our order. I was relieved Monica didn't order a bottle of wine, although she asked if I wanted a glass. She stuck to mineral water as she was driving. As we waited for our food, I asked her what Andy had been like as a child. I felt as though I didn't really know him properly, so prompted her to fill in the blanks.

"I love all my boys," she began, "but Andrew was always the beautiful one. He was always self-contained though, in his own little world. He didn't need praise like Matthew, or mothering like Rupert. Phillip needed constant stimulation or else he'd get bored easily. No, Andrew was just content to amuse himself, play with the others when it suited him, and walk away when it didn't. He was bright though, found schoolwork too easy, found everything too easy really. Girls flocked round him from the age of about fourteen, hanging around outside our house. The other three used to get a bit disgruntled about it, probably because Andrew never really took much notice of the girls, picking them up and dropping them without a care."

"He was with Charlotte a long time though?" I asked.

Monica laughed. "Mainly because she was as cold as he was, plus she wasn't there most of the time. Travelled a lot for her work, which suited them both I think. I knew she wasn't the one for him, mothers know these things. We were all relieved when they split."

"Andy said you didn't like her," I remarked.

"She didn't even try and make him happy. I'm a bit old-fashioned I suppose, but I do believe a relationship should be a partnership. I never saw her make the slightest effort to be nice to him, or the family. My boys are all close, so I figure when Bill and I have gone, they'll always have each other to lean on if needs be."

"Maybe some people just don't appreciate a family. Not having one is far worse."

"Andrew told me what happened to yours. It's such a shame. Girls need their mums as they grow up. Charlotte just didn't understand how close Andrew is to his brothers, she was scathing about him meeting up with them."

"Meeting his brothers? What could possibly be wrong with that?" I asked.

"Goodness knows. I think she knew he didn't love her, so she wanted him on a short leash the whole time.

Drove us all mad, ringing constantly, checking up on
him."

"Where is she now?" I asked. Monica just shrugged.

"Last I heard, she'd married some investment banker.
Met and married him within three months. I'm not sure
if she thought Andrew would be jealous, but he was
delighted. No, I've never seen him fall in love until
now. Poor boy was a wreck when you left him. Came
round for lunch all mopey and unshaven. I was terribly
worried until Rupert ratted on him."

"I understand why he did it," I told her.

"I understand it, but I still slapped him upside his
head, as the boys say, and gave him a stiff telling off.
He might be all grown up, but he still listens to his
mama."

We both giggled. I. Just. Loved. Her.

The afternoon was another whirlwind, with
footwear, casual clothes and underwear on the agenda,
before we raced back to the car at four in order to be
back at the house for when the police arrived.

The traffic on the M25 was appalling, and we only
just made it back on time. Andy and his dad were
already sitting in the lounge chatting to two coppers.
"Sorry, are we late?" Monica asked, looking pointedly
at the large clock that said five to five. The copper
shook his head and stood up to greet us.

"PC Bentlock and DC Thomas. We were early. You
must be Miss Higgs?" We shook hands. I sat down next
to Andy, who seemed quite relaxed. I began to shake.
"The forensics have come back now and there is no
evidence that you ever drove that car, plus one of the
group walking with the deceased has come forward and
said quite categorically that she saw you in the

passenger seat as Mr Pryce drove off. He has been charged with numerous offences, and I'm pleased to confirm that all the charges against you have been dropped."

"What about the drugs planted in her bag?" Asked Monica.

"Again, none of Miss Higgs's prints are on it, but both Mr Pryce's and Mr Brooke's are. No charges will be brought against Ms Higgs. You will however be called as a witness."

Andy was gently rubbing my back as I relaxed, relieved beyond belief. For some inexplicable reason I wanted to cry. The stress and tension of the past few weeks got the better of me. I managed to bottle it up until the policemen left, but the moment I heard the front door close, the tears became unstoppable, which was embarrassing with Andy's parents present. Andy pulled me into a hug while Monica fished around in her bag for a tissue, handing it to me before announcing she needed to bring the shopping in. I think Bill was grateful for an excuse to escape.

"Hey, why're you crying?" Andy asked.

"I don't know," I admitted, which sounded stupid. The poor man was probably sick to the back teeth of my copious waterworks. "I think it's just relief and stress. I've been so scared."

"I know baby, I have too," he said, which surprised me. He'd seemed so confident I'd be exonerated that I hadn't expected him to have his moments of doubt. "I was so scared he'd be let out on bail, that they'd be slow to build the case against him. I just couldn't bear the thought of anything happening to you. I'm just glad my dad was on the case; he can pull strings like nobody else." He took the tissue from my hand and began tenderly wiping my tears. "Now, I've got two more surprises for you, so I want to see your beautiful smile."

"I think we spent too much," I blurted out. "We lost track."

"The best of everything, remember? I really don't care how much it costs. I just want you to feel loved and cared for, although I do hope you bought good lingerie."

I smiled at him. "Of course, top of my list." I heard the front door slam and Bill muttering about being a pack pony.

"I'm putting the kettle on," Monica yelled. "Do you both want a cuppa?"

"Please," Andy yelled back. "Come on, I want to see all these new things you've got."

"My surprises?" I reminded him.

"Oh yes, if you check your account, you'll find Ms Gadd has paid out. I did some serious arm-twisting. She settled on thirty-five grand. Rupert cancelled her investigation after supervising the transfers to both you and your colleague."

I flung my arms around him. "That's amazing news!" Then of course it hit me. "My bank card's at Lakeswood."

"Ah, now, about that. Dad mentioned a couple of things to his friend at golf, so the search officers liberated your phone, laptop, and bank card, as well as your birth certificate and photo album. They couldn't get any more out I'm afraid as it wasn't strictly... the done thing."

I kissed him hard. It felt like Christmas, only better. "I can't believe you did that for me. I can pay you back for the clothes and stuff."

His expression hardened. "No way. I don't want it."

We were interrupted by Monica, "Tea's ready. Great news about your old boss isn't it? Bill's just told me. It's another chapter closed, so you can move onwards."

Seeing all the bags laid out on the kitchen floor was a bit of a shock. We'd been offloading into the car all day, so I hadn't really got a grip on how much I'd actually bought. Andy, of course, made a bee-line for the Rigby and Peller bags, nosing at the lovely underwear I'd purchased. Monica rolled her eyes.

"I've ticked off about half of the list, we ran out of time, so I suggest we go back tomorrow after the doctors," she said.

Andy frowned. "Doctors?"

"Replacement pills," I muttered, hoping Bill wasn't listening. "Tomorrow would be great. After that, I need to start looking for another job."

"No, you don't." Andy was scowling. "Have a break at least, you could do with a rest."

I ignored him. "Bill, do you know what happened to Aaron's dogs?" I asked.

"I think his mother's looking after them. Apparently she was in the house when they raided it."

It was a relief knowing Roxy and Bruno were being cared for. I wondered if Gerry and Jed had been sacked. So much had happened that it was starting to feel like another life.

Monica and Bill left soon after, leaving Andy and I with the piles of bags. As soon as we were alone, he snaked his hands around my waist and kissed me. I melted into him, tired from both the shopping and all the crying I'd done. "Why don't we eat out tonight? It's still early."

"I should sort through all these bags first."

"I'll help you later. I'm starving and I think we have a lot to celebrate."

CHAPTER 16

We held hands as we walked through the golf course to a little pub in Old Hill that had a small restaurant attached. The first signs of spring were all around us as we skirted the fairways, giving us both a very real sense of optimism. I'd changed into a pair of new jeans and a cashmere jumper that felt luxuriously soft and warm under my new coat. Even my hair was glossy and sleek, thanks to new top-of-the-range straighteners.

Andy seemed to know a lot of people as we waited in the bar for our table, introducing me to various acquaintances and friends. I watched as he chatted happily about the rugby on telly that weekend. A few of the women looked me up and down a few times, no doubt curious as to whom I was, and how I'd nabbed the gorgeous Andrew McCarthy.

After being seated and ordering, he dropped a bit of a bomb. "You really don't need to work, I'd prefer it if you didn't," he said.

"Why?" I asked.

He thought for a moment. "The last two jobs you had, they didn't work out so well. I just thought you might like to take some time out from getting yourself in trouble."

The Debt

"I knew you'd get sick of my fuck-ups," I said dejectedly. He leaned over to grasp my hand.

"How can you possibly say that? You're beautiful, kind and compassionate, you have a great wardrobe of outfits, a handsome boyfriend who loves you beyond all reason, and more importantly my mother adores you. I really think you need to change the record now. You've got no debt, money in the bank and nothing hanging over your head. I'd call you one of life's winners myself."

I blinked, trying to take it all in. He was right, all my life I'd been the poor little orphan girl with the scars. It was time to re-write my inner monologue. I'd already come a long way, thanks to his love, no longer caring who saw my forehead or knew about my leg. It dawned on me that I was un-self-conscious sitting in the restaurant, a million miles away from the awkward girl he'd taken to Chapter One. I'd transformed into the sort of girl the old me would've been watching, marvelling at her sense of belonging, envious of her hair, clothes and poise.

"Thank you," I said. I couldn't have loved him any more than I did at that moment.

"You're welcome," he said glibly, a glimpse of the cocky devil coming through. "Now, practicalities. There's a spare dressing room off the bedroom down the hall. It might be better for you to use that rather than squashing your things in with mine. Second, we need to get you a passport. I'll download the forms, if you can get a photo done at Bluewater tomorrow."

"Why do I need a passport?" I asked, half-knowing the answer.

"We need a holiday. Also my parents have a place in Puerto Banus. We all go for a week in June. Mum likes it when we're altogether."

"I've never been abroad," I said, "well, actually I've never really been on holiday as such."

"Not even the seaside? Or camping?" He was incredulous.

I shook my head. "We used to get a sunshine coach to Margate, but it was only ever for a day trip. There are a lot of things I've never done."

"Then I'll enjoy showing you," he said, raising his glass to me. We clinked. "To seeing the world," he murmured.

I decided not to mention moving out. Given that he didn't want me to look for a job, I figured he'd feel the same way about me searching for a new bedsit. The evening was so happy and celebratory that I didn't want to spoil it.

We were both a little tipsy walking home. The golf course was too dark, so we walked down to the caves, then back up the hill, laughing like kids at stupid, drunken jokes. It was nearly midnight by the time we got back, and we were both exhausted. "I wanna see your knickers," he blurted out as we climbed the stairs. I stood still for a moment and popped the top button of my jeans. "You're teasing," he said, grabbing my hand and dragging me up. I giggled as he pulled down the zip and yanked my trousers down. "Oh, that was money well spent," he remarked as he exposed my lacy, black thong.

"I'll let you see my bra too, dirty boy," I taunted. I began a striptease standing on the landing, flashing glimpses of my new bra. Eventually, he grabbed me and threw me over his shoulder before carrying me to the bedroom. "Put me down," I squealed, laughing at his impatience.

"With pleasure," he growled, as he plopped me down onto the bed. I watched as he began to unbutton his shirt, my mouth going dry as he revealed his toned, muscular torso. "I," he said, as he unbuttoned his jeans, "am going to make you beg for mercy."

As soon as he was naked, he began to take my boots off, flinging them on the floor carelessly. He peeled my jeans down my legs, stroking the skin reverentially as he went. "You have such lovely legs," he murmured, "so slender and long." He kissed his way up to the apex, then buried his nose and inhaled. I began to giggle, the combination of the drink and his naughtiness tipping me over.

"That's so rude," I spluttered.

"It makes me really horny," he confessed, a touch sheepishly, before pulling my thong to one side, and stroking me with his tongue. I gasped, throwing my head back, revelling in the sensation.

"That's what you like, isn't it?" He said, before dragging my knickers off and pinning my legs wide open. I couldn't move. In fact, I couldn't do anything other than try and absorb the pleasure he was inflicting. I was horny too, turned on by his obvious desire as he lapped up my juices and stroked my clit repeatedly.

I felt the mother of all orgasms building, that fizzing sensation you get when all you want is a big cock inside you to salve the ache. "Please fuck me," I begged. He ignored me, continuing to torment me with his mouth. He thrust his tongue into me, while his nose continued the pressure on my clit. With my legs pinned apart, I had no choice but to come, my body exploding into a mass of convulsions as I writhed, devoid of all control. I felt him slam into me, filling me totally. He fucked me so hard and fast that I came again.

He cursed as he let go, pressing in deep. Afterwards, he kissed me softly and tenderly, before switching off the light and wrapping his arms around me.

Monica calling up the stairs the next morning rather abruptly awakened us. "Hello, anyone up yet?"

"Down in a minute," Andy yelled. I sat up to see the time; it was half-seven, and we'd overslept. I cursed, knowing I needed a shower. My plan had been to get up early and make myself presentable for once.

I showered in three minutes flat, dried off, and put on the same jeans and jumper I'd been wearing the previous evening. I cringed knowing she'd see that we hadn't even moved the bags out of the kitchen. For some strange reason, it felt as though I was being ungrateful. I braced myself to go downstairs.

Andy was sitting at the island and sipping a coffee, wearing just his bathrobe when I walked in. Monica handed me mine and smiled as I rummaged through the carrier bags searching for the ponytail bands I'd bought the previous day. "Did you forget your doctor's appointment?" She asked.

"No, I think the wine last night went to my head and sent me into too deep a sleep," I confessed. "Shouldn't you be getting ready for work?" I asked Andy.

"My first meeting is at ten, funny enough it's with your uncle," he said.

"Why didn't you tell me?"

"I'm telling you now. I meant to tell you yesterday, but it went out of my head, with all the other stuff going on. He's asked to see me face-to-face, so I'm driving over to his house. Any message you want me to pass on?" I shook my head, mildly annoyed that he'd sprung it on me like that.

"Come on, we need to go, the traffic in Chislehurst might be bad," his mum urged. I checked my bag to make sure I had my phone and purse, and pulled on my coat.

"Ring me when you have news," I muttered before kissing him goodbye.

I decided on an implant at the doctors, much to Monica's approval. I figured it would be one less thing to worry about, given my track record with fuck-uppery. With that job completed, we decided to head straight over to Bluewater to continue where we'd left off the day before, as there was still a huge amount to get. While we were having coffee and waiting for the shops to open, I decided to ask her advice. "Andy asked me not to look for a job for a while. I can understand why, but it makes me feel a bit... useless. I've never not worked. Do you think he was just saying that?"

She thought about it for a few moments then shook her head. "Andrew never says anything he doesn't mean. If he says you don't need to work, then embrace it. Bill never wanted me to work either. It's a pride thing. It shows the world they're good providers."

"I wasn't sure if I should start flat hunting or not. I don't want to outstay my welcome." I knew I wouldn't exactly be thrown out onto the street if he got sick of me, but it meant having the whole "how committed are we" conversation, which kind of scared me. It was safer to ask Monica.

"I thought it was all settled that you'd moved in. At least I believe that's what Andrew thinks. He's like a different person when you're around. It's lovely to see. Even Bill remarked about how happy he is with you there, and public displays of affection from Andrew have always been unheard of. Unless you particularly want your own place, I wouldn't worry about moving out." She sipped her coffee while I marvelled at what a difference having a mother around could make.

"I don't want to move out, I like being with Andy. I just don't want anyone to think I'm sponging off him," I said anxiously. She patted my hand and smiled.

"Nobody at all thinks that. We were just relieved you took him back. He was the most miserable little devil without you. Now, finish your drink, we've got shopping to do."

Andy called me later that morning. "I've got good news," he said, sounding excited. "Your uncle caved straightaway. Well, I put the proof in front of him, so he couldn't do much else. He knew going to court would cost him even more, so he's agreed the full amount."

"The whole hundred and twenty thousand?" I was incredulous.

"No, the whole three hundred and sixty. I went for top whack, so I could come down if needs be, but he agreed on it, especially when I pointed out that what he'd done amounted to fraud. I think he's keen to make that particular accusation go away quietly."

"He'll have to sell his house though, so it'll take ages," I pointed out.

"No, here's the thing: he was selling it anyway to move in with his girlfriend. He's already exchanged contracts, completion next week. We both spoke to the solicitor dealing with it and he's agreed to pay it across to you in full, given I haven't had time to get a charging order on it, which I threatened to do this afternoon. I think he was planning to buy some flats as buy-to-lets, but given the alternative was a prison sentence, he's prepared to rethink things."

"What if he just runs off with the money again?" I asked, feeling a little faint.

"He won't. He signed a settlement contract. He knows, because I spelt it out, that if he reneges, not only does he face a fraud charge, but also the high court bailiffs. They don't mess about. He was shitting himself Sal, so don't worry."

"I'll try not to... Thank you. For everything." I knew I'd have never been able to confront my uncle on my own.

"All part of the service. Now, go buy more nice lingerie, that's an order."

"Yes sir," I giggled.

With nothing to rush back for, we cleared Monica's list, then went "off piste" as she called it, checking out the designer concessions in House of Fraser. By the time we finally left to go home, I was exhausted. Monica was as perky as she'd been at the start. I wondered how she did it. "Poor Lola will be missing me," she said. "I mean she loves her Daddy and all that, but he doesn't brush her coat twice a day, or slip her bits of cheese for good behaviour. He even shouted at her last night for having an accident in the lounge. She was so upset she did a wee in the kitchen, poor little thing."

Sneaky little thing, I thought, I kept my opinion to myself.

It took ages to unload the car; if anything we had more bags than the previous day. I surveyed the piles in the kitchen, vowing to spend the evening hanging it all up and putting things away. Andy arrived home about five minutes after we'd unloaded everything, so Monica waved goodbye and hurried home to see to her spoilt dog.

I concentrated on fixing dinner, determined to fit myself into Andy's life in any way I could. He sat at the island, telling me all about his meeting with my uncle, while I made a stir-fry. I admired his ability to face down people, to confront a wrongdoing, rather than hide away as I'd always done, suffering the consequences of the liars and con-artists of the world. I wondered if he'd been born that way, or if his confidence was the product of his superior education.

"I talked to your mum today. She's very easy to talk to," I began. He did the McCarthy silence, so I carried on. "I asked her advice as to whether or not I should look for a flat. I don't want to be a nuisance or anything and outstay my welcome..." I trailed off.

I expected him to ask what Monica had said, but he didn't. "I don't want you to go, I like having you here. It makes me feel more relaxed. I can look after you properly if you're with me." His eyes burned into mine, "Do you want to leave?" I shook my head. "Good, in which case, stay."

"As easy as that? What if I annoy you?" I'd never lived with just one person before, having gone from the home, where I'd just been a quiet shadow, to living alone in the bedsit. I had no idea if I was one of those people who got on other's nerves or not.

The Debt

"I don't think you will," he replied, "but if you do, we'll talk it out like adults. Whatever happens, I'll never throw you out onto the streets, I know it's a fear of yours, and I know I'm asking you to trust me after I've been a selfish dick, but I hope we can get past all that."

I thought about it for a few moments. I desperately wanted to be with him, which meant trusting him not to throw me out on a whim. Having that money in the bank made the decision easier. It gave me choices. If he slung me out on my ear, I could afford a hotel until I'd found myself a flat. He dangled a set of keys in front of me. "I need to give you this. Mum won't be around tomorrow, so you need to be able to get in and out."

I took them hesitantly, afraid of the reality of having to let go of the girl I used to be. With those keys in my hand, I was the lawful inhabitant of a beautiful home. I couldn't hide behind my insecurities or my past. I had to face the world as the girl I'd become. As I turned them over in my hand, I marvelled at how quickly fortunes changed, for both good and bad. In only six weeks, I'd gone from the tragic, depressed debtor in the county court to the excited girl holding a set of keys to a lovely life.

Andy might have been a complex, thoughtless, and rather clueless bloke, but he loved me, I was certain of that. Plus, he seemed to like having me around, which was a bit of a mystery to me, but I refused to question it. Instead, I just dished up his meal, smiled, and said thank you.

"For what?" He asked, pulling a quizzical face.

"For the keys," I said glibly.

After dinner, I set about my unpacking while Andy worked in his study. I pressed everything carefully before hanging it all up. By the time I'd finished, my new wardrobe room was quite respectably full. He came up to find me just as I was peeling the labels off a pair of shoes. "I've got those forms for you to sign, did you remember to get photos done?"

I nodded towards the dressing table. "On there. They're pretty horrific though. It might have been better to have got up early enough to put some make up on." I watched as he cut one out, and then scribbled something on the back of it.

"Just verifying your identity," he said. "It's handy being your lawyer." He handed me a pen and showed me where to put my signature, having filled it all out on my behalf. I scanned through it quickly before signing. He already had a stamped, addressed envelope prepared, which tickled me for some reason. For all his bravado and slickness, he was really a Boy Scout at heart. "Rupert called earlier, said the girl you used to work with was trying to contact you. Apparently I'm to tell you that Bessie made it, whatever that means."

I smiled at the news. "I'll email Maria tomorrow with my number."

"The cleaner, Janet, and her husband Fred, who does the garden will be in at eleven tomorrow. They've got keys, so you don't need to worry about letting them in. You can have a whole day to yourself."

I awoke the next morning strangely excited to have a day off in my new home. I was used to a lot of solitude, so being around other people non-stop for a week or so, as nice as it was, had left me craving a bit of time alone. I made Andy some breakfast and waved him off as he drove to the station. The moment I was alone, I allowed myself the luxury of a bouncy happy dance, revelling in

The Debt

the space of the magnificent hallway. With that out of the way, I made myself a latte in the complicated machine, and sat down at the island to fire up my laptop and check my emails.

Andy had still been sending me a song every day.

On the Saturday of the ball, he'd sent me a beautiful video of a Russian dancer, performing to Hozier's *Take Me to Church.*

"Take me to church, I'll worship like a dog at the shrine of your life, I'll tell you my sins so you can sharpen your knife."

"I was born sick, but I love you."

I played the video four times. It was beyond beautiful in an angsty, painful sort of way.

The following day, after the ball, while I was lying in the hospital, out cold and unaware, he'd sent me Bruno Mars', *When I Was Your Man*, which I thought was rather fitting. I hummed along as I played it, feeling a sense of the regret he must have felt seeing me on Aaron's arm. I was guilty of dismissing his feelings, which had clearly run deeper than I'd been aware. If I had seen a girl on his arm, I'd have probably spent the evening in the loo being a blubbering mess.

Since our reconciliation, the songs had changed. He'd focussed on love songs, sending me John Legend's *All of Me*, which was a favourite of mine.

"Love your curves and all your edges, all your perfect imperfections..."

I clicked on the latest one, which turned out to be Adele's *Make You Feel My Love*. I swallowed back the lump in my throat while I listened to the lyrics.

"When the rain is blowing in your face, and the whole world is on your case, I could offer you a warm embrace, to make you feel my love."
I wondered why Andy couldn't say the words himself, preferring to let the music communicate how he felt, until it dawned on me that I hadn't exactly been demonstrative either, only telling him I was in love with him twice.

I quickly emailed Maria my number while I racked my brain as to what to do. In the end, I figured I could take a leaf out of his book and send him a love song, mainly to make him smile at work. I found a few on YouTube, and spent half an hour checking out the lyrics, until I found the perfect one.

Eva Cassidy could say it for me. Her angelic voice, filled with love and emotion could deliver the lines perfectly.

"For you, there'll be no crying. For you, the sun will be shining, cos I feel that when I'm with you, it's alright. I know it's right."
Satisfied, I hit "send."

It was great to talk to Maria again. She called whilst on a tea break at her new job. Miss Gadd hadn't exactly sacked her, preferring to make her life so miserable and difficult over the wage issue that Maria had searched for something better. Ironically, she'd gotten the job at the Bromley South surgery that I'd originally gone for. "It's so well-equipped, and they're really nice people," she gushed, "I'm even getting nine pounds an hour, it's fantastic."

I was really pleased for her, delighted that my own good fortune had created an opening for her to get her dream job. We'd agreed to meet for coffee sometime for a proper catch up, which I'd look forward to, as I kind of missed the camaraderie of surgery life. I'd kept quiet about my own news, assuring her that I'd fill her in when I saw her.

Janet and Fred arrived later that morning and to my surprise, they seemed a little nervous of me, promising they wouldn't get in my way as they did their work. I was transported back to how Shari had treated us staff at Lakeswood, with her imperious tones and unreasonable demands. Being on the other side of the equation was totally new to me, so I mentally swore I'd never behave like her as I smiled sweetly at Janet and offered to put the kettle on for her, which seemed to break the ice nicely.

With Janet beavering her way through the upstairs and Fred busy sweeping the drive, I felt a bit of a spare part. I wondered how I'd be expected to fill the days while Andy was at work. Cooking a meal each night wouldn't take more than an hour or so. I wasn't into keeping fit, being naturally skinny, and I'd always been rubbish at sports. I toyed with the idea of volunteering to help in a charity shop and resolved to discuss it with Monica the next time I saw her. My thoughts were interrupted by Andy calling. "I love that song," he began, "cheered me up no end and got me through a difficult decision."

"What decisions that?" I asked.

"I was toying with the idea of giving up the collection work, our contract's up for renewal shortly, and I wasn't sure if I wanted to carry on, mainly after seeing what it did to you."

"Are you mad?" I barked. "I was in that debt whether you collected or someone else."

"That's very true, only it made me feel like the lowest human being who ever walked the Earth, preying on the poor and desperate, but knowing you don't see me that way, well, it made me think again."

I stayed silent.

"Knowing you don't bear a grudge over it," he said eventually. "You think I'm still worth loving, even after seeing the worst of it."

"Of course you're worth loving, I'm sorry I don't tell you often enough. This is all very new to me too. I've never fallen in love before and, well, you know my track record with fuck-uppery..." I trailed off. He laughed down the phone.

"You don't say? I'll bear it in mind. Listen, would you mind if we went out tonight? Phil and Iris have invited us to dinner. I think they all want to get to know you better, find out about the woman who's made me go daft."

I smiled at the thought. "Sure, I don't mind at all. I was only going to cook that chicken you bought, but I can do it another time. I have got one question though."

"Go on."

"What am I supposed to do all day? I feel a bit useless here. Janet's doing the housework, and I don't need to cook..." I trailed off.

"Well, my mum gets her hair done, beauty treatments, she goes shopping, sees friends, goes up to town to galleries and stuff. You can do any of those things, or just watch telly, read a book. I know you like reading."

It was a revelation. I'd be able to browse the library to my heart's content and curl up in front of the fire with a good book, without the ever-pervading money

The Debt

worries clouding my mind. I glanced at the clock. It was still early. I could nip into Bromley and get half a dozen. "I'm gonna do that this afternoon. Do you know where the bus stop into town is?" I asked.

"No idea. For safety's sake, get a taxi. The number's on the hall table. There's some cash in the drawer in my study, just take what you need." I didn't need telling twice.

EPILOGUE

It didn't take long to get into the swing of things. I seemed to fit into Andy's life without too much more drama, joining him on Sundays at his mum's big lunches and getting to grips with the whole not-working thing, although I was volunteering at a local animal rescue centre a couple of days a week, which I adored. The simple act of caring for the most neglected and disadvantaged animals was an antidote to any guilt I felt over my good fortune.

My uncle had paid up meekly, the whole three hundred and sixty thousand he owed me. I can only speculate on what Andy had said to make him do it. To me, Andy was a gentle, thoughtful man, with a strong sense of right and wrong. I'll take everyone else's word for it that he's hyper-competitive, aggressive, and a master arm-twister, I don't see any of that. I only see the kind, generous man who tenderly kisses my scars and still sends me a soppy song every day. I can't imagine my life without him now. As it is, he's accompanying me to court to support me as I give evidence against Aaron. The authorities decided to prosecute for the hit-and-run incident separately from the financial crimes. At least in prison, he wouldn't be able to thwart their attempts to unravel his labyrinthine financial affairs.

The Debt

I shook as I was called to the stand and sworn in. I tried not to look at Aaron, seated in the dock, but my eyes were inexplicably drawn to the man who allegedly tried to kill me. I still had nightmares about that night, usually involving me being eight years old again and begging the doctors not to cut me up. Several times I'd been gently woken by Andy, worried by my calling out and thrashing around. The doctor said it was post-traumatic stress, possibly laying latent from my childhood accident, unleashed by Aaron's actions. I prayed that seeing him sent to prison would lay those particular demons to rest.

Aaron had lost his cocky swagger, appearing sullen and stroppy as I answered the myriad questions posed by the barristers for both the prosecution and the defence. It took the entire morning. After lunch, the judge would begin his summing up, and then it would be a wait for the verdict.

We decided to eschew the cafeteria in the court and headed outside to Hays Galleria, a pretty shopping courtyard on the river, where we could enjoy a glass of wine and some great food while I got myself together again. "I think the barrister for the defence went easy on you," Andy said after we'd ordered. "He could've tried to twist you in knots to attempt to discredit your testimony. I think he knew he was on a hiding to nothing."

"What if he gets away with it?" I asked. It was my biggest fear, that Aaron would somehow be acquitted and chase me down, angry I'd testified against him.

"He won't. Besides, he'd be the number one suspect if anything happened to you. He might be an angry cokehead, but he's not stupid. Just hold your nerve."

His words soothed me. I knew it wasn't anywhere near over, as Andy planned to launch a private prosecution for his attempt to put me in the frame, with a view to getting me some compensation. It meant I'd be giving evidence again at some point in the future. The first step was Aaron being convicted in Crown Court.

As we sat through the judge's summing up, I couldn't help but imagine how I'd have been feeling if the truth hadn't been told, or I hadn't been believed. I knew I'd have been shaking from head to toe, terrified and despairing. Aaron, on the other hand, just appeared bored by the whole thing. I saw him smile at his mum, who I spotted in the front row of the public gallery. He completely ignored me. Eventually, the judge finished, and the jury were discharged to consider their verdict.

"I could kill for a coffee," said Andy, taking my hand as we all stood to leave. "It'll probably be hours. Verdicts are rarely quick." We wandered down to the public area, where I found us seats and Andy went to the coffee concession to get drinks. I smiled as he arrived back bearing a tray of cookies and cakes as well as bucket-sized lattes.

"Are you trying to get me fat before our holiday?" I asked, perusing the various baked goods, before settling on some millionaire's shortbread.

He beamed his film-star smile. "I gather Iris is panicking about standing next to you in a bikini, Phil said she's been on lettuce leaves all week."

I laughed. We were off to the McCarthy family villa in Puerto Banus after Andy finished work on Friday, which would be my first time flying and my first-ever holiday. I was beyond excited. The preparations had succeeded in taking my mind off the trial, especially after Monica provided lists of what I'd need to take, and what I'd need to have done at the beauty salon in preparation. She'd even insisted I should wear bikinis and shorts for the first time in my life, dismissing my concerns about showing my scar as "It's only family." I'd bitten the bullet and purchased several bikinis and pairs of shorts in addition to several full-length maxi dresses for evenings out. All of us were going, including Rupert's girlfriend and Iris, so it would be a blast.

We'd barely finished our coffees when the announcement came through that the jury was about to deliver their verdict. My stomach turned as we walked hand-in-hand back to the gallery.

The lead juror was a middle-aged lady with a kindly face. She reminded me a little of Maggie as she stood to address the judge. I could feel my heart pounding as he read out the first of the charges to her.

Guilty.

I stole a glance at Aaron. They may as well have been discussing the weather for all the reaction he gave. As the judge read out the list of charges, the juror replied "Guilty" to all of them. People in the front row of the gallery cheered. I figured they must have been the family of the poor man who'd been killed, delighted to have garnered some justice for him. I hoped that they too had the sense to sue him for compensation.

He got five years. Andy whispered into my ear, "he'll serve two and a half. Let's hope they put him in a cell with Brooksy." Marcus had already been sentenced to seven years for supplying class A drugs.

It didn't seem much for taking a life and attempting to take mine too. I could only hope that the fraud squad could build a compelling case while he was in prison and prosecute him for that too. As we stood to leave, I caught sight of Maggie crying, her only son taken from her. Andy saw me looking. "She can visit him. Just keep your eyes on that poor lady down there who only has a grave to visit." He nodded towards the woman who'd cheered the sentence, supported by a sad, grey-haired man and a young woman. He was right, of course; only a death is final.

Two days later, I took my seat next to him on my first-ever trip in an aeroplane, fizzing with excitement at the prospect of leaving the UK for the very first time. I'd been antsy all day, worried he wouldn't be home from work on time, or that we'd somehow miss our flight. As it was, he'd only made it back with ten minutes to change out of his suit before our taxi to the airport arrived.

Gatwick was much bigger than I'd expected, rammed full of people making their weekend getaways. I'd been fascinated by the departures boards, announcing flights to exotic places such as Casablanca and Vienna. I'd dutifully followed Andy through check-in and the myriad security sections until we reached an enormous shopping mall. With half an hour to spare until our flight was called, we perused duty-free, purchasing aftershave and perfume, as well as a new pair of sunglasses each. It was enormous fun.

Nerves began to kick in when the engines on the plane fired up and the doors were closed. I grasped his hand tightly, much to his amusement, as the plane taxied to the runway. I felt the sweat drip down my back as that stupid song went around in my head on a loop. Bloody Alanis Morrisette.

"He waited his whole damn life just to take that flight, and as the plane crashed down, thought 'well isn't this nice?' Well isn't it ironic, don't you think?"

"Are you alright?" He whispered, probably alarmed at the beads of sweat gathering on my nose. His voice interrupted the earworm of a song playing on repeat in my brain.

"Talk to me," I pleaded as the plane began to speed up.

"OK. You know that Rupert wears speedos? Did Mum not warn you? We laugh at him every year, telling him he looks like a fat German, but he insists they're more comfortable for swimming."

I turned to face him, forgetting about hurtling along the runway for a moment. "Monica never mentioned it. What's the etiquette? I mean, where do I look? It'd be creepy if I kept staring at his crotch by mistake."

Andy began to laugh. "I'm having you on. It's hilarious that you believed me though. I'm gonna tell Rupes when we get there. Knowing him, he'll go and buy a pair, just to see where you put your eyes."

"Don't you dare!" I began… until I realised we were airborne.

By the time we'd landed, got our bags, and found a taxi, it was getting late. I trailed along, marvelling at Andy's competence at travelling. He seemed to know exactly where to go. "Have you been here many times before?" I asked.

He looked at me a little strangely. "Of course I have. Mum and Dad have had the villa over twenty-five years. We spent whole summers here when I was a kid.

Mum still insists we all come out for at least one week together every year, but everyone uses it other times too. I think Matt and Mel are planning to come out for at least four weeks of the school holidays."

Eventually our taxi pulled up outside the gates to a rather magnificent villa, situated right on the beach. As much as I liked to think I'd got used to the extreme wealth of the McCarthys, it still caused a sharp intake of breath. The villa was enormous, painted a soft cream, with white embellishments. Andy hopped out of the taxi and tapped a number into the keypad to open the gates.

We drove past a central fountain in a circular drive, surrounded by lush gardens. Waiting at the front door were Monica and Bill, dressed in shorts and t-shirts, looking tanned and remarkably relaxed, considering they'd only arrived the day before. "Hi Mum, Dad," Andy said as we got out of the cab. He kissed his mum on the cheek as the driver pulled our bags out of the boot.

"Sally, I'm so delighted you're here. Isn't it great news about the trial? I did tell you the truth always comes out." Monica kissed both of my cheeks. "Come, let's show you round the villa. Everyone's already here."

She led me down a frankly magnificent hallway, through an elegant lounge and out onto a large terrace, where the entire McCarthy clan, plus girlfriends, were lounging on massive outdoor sofas drinking bottles of beer. The large, rectangular pool glittered under the outdoor lights. It looked extraordinarily inviting given how sweaty I was after the flight and subsequent taxi trip.

After saying hello to everyone, and having an icy cold beer pressed into my hand by a slightly tipsy Phil,

Andy took me upstairs to show me our room and unpack our stuff. Our room was delightful, with a large picture window and a gorgeous, marble ensuite. "I chose this room when I was six," Andy told me. "Just wait until daylight, the view is astonishing."

"How many bedrooms does the villa have?" I asked, taking it all in.

"Eight altogether, so we all fit in quite easily. When we've all got families of our own, it might be more of a squeeze, but it meant we could always fit in lots of friends and visitors when we stayed out here for long stretches in the summer."

Back downstairs, Monica had prepared some supper for everyone, passing round plates of ribs and barbecued chicken, as well as providing a large bowl of salad, coleslaw, and some bread. I wondered how on Earth she did it, catering for such an enormous family, while making it look so easy, as well as always being immaculately-groomed and neatly turned out.

We sat up until two in the morning, chatting, laughing and drinking beer. I lounged on the sofa, nestled between Andy's legs, his arm slung casually around my neck. "I think it's an imposter," slurred Rupert, who clearly couldn't handle his beer as well as the others.

"Who's an imposter?" Asked Michelle, his girlfriend.

"That bloke there," he pointed at Andy. "You know I've never actually seen him cuddle a lady before." He turned to Andy, "Who are you, and what have you done with my brother?" Everyone laughed.

I woke up with a banging head the next morning. Rolling over, I saw Andy scrubbing at his face, trying to wake up. "Morning," I said.

"I feel rough," he replied. "My mouth's full of cotton wool. Is there any water on your side of the bed?" I gently rolled back and grabbed the bottle from my bedside table.

"It's a bit warm," I warned him.

"Don't care." He took it and glugged it down, before wiping his mouth with the back of his hand. "Hopefully Mum's got the coffee on." He swung his legs out of bed and stood up gingerly. Satisfied he could stay upright, he pulled on a pair of shorts and slid his feet into his flip-flops. "Come on, I'm ready," he said. Huffing slightly at having to actually lift my head from the pillow, I got up and started ferreting through my wardrobe. "Just bung on a bikini and a pair of shorts," he said, impatient at my having to fix my fringe, which had scrunched up in the night.

I did as I was told, cringing slightly at my scars being on show. I reminded myself I was with family and followed him down to the kitchen. Monica was cooking up a storm, flipping eggs while grilling bacon and making toast, clearly extremely well-practiced at catering for a large group of hungry men. Mel was making a pot of tea and pouring coffees from a cafetiere, while Iris was setting the table out on the veranda. "Anything I can help with?" I asked, praying that she'd say no.

"Can you slice those peaches and strawberries please?" She asked, pointing at some punnets on the surface. I set to it, arranging them neatly on a plate. It wasn't too onerous. "The children often prefer fruit to a big fry-up, she explained. I took the plates outside and placed them on the table. Andy had poured me a strong coffee, which I sipped gratefully as I watched Matt and

The Debt

Mel's two kids play in the pool with various inflatables.
They were having a whale of a time.
Breakfast was heavenly, sitting in the sunshine,
listening to everyone chatting, laughing and joking
around. The banter between the four brothers fascinated
me as they ribbed each other mercilessly, Rupert getting
the brunt of it. It was the family life I'd dreamed of,
actually, it was better than my meagre imagination
could have ever dreamed up during my darker, lonelier
days.

After a large breakfast and copious amounts of
coffee, we all made our way to the sun loungers for
some serious lazing about. Following the other girl's
leads, I slipped off my shorts and lay back, soaking up
the Mediterranean sunshine. I felt incredibly happy.

"What's wrong with your leg?" Little Josh couldn't
have shouted it much louder. I opened my eyes to find
both him and his sister staring at my thigh. I glanced at
Andy who was shifting on his lounger, looking
extremely uncomfortable.

"It's a scar," I told him. He leaned forward to
examine it more closely.

"How did you get it?" Asked Amelie, his little sister,
who was staring at it. A sudden tension in the air was
almost palpable. Even Monica froze.

These people were family, I told myself.

"I got it fighting a dragon," I told them. "It was a
really fierce one, nearly chewed my leg off."

"Wow," said Josh, his eyes big and round. "That's so
cool."

"Yeah, better than Uncle Rupe's one," Amelie
chimed in. "Did you kill it?"

I nodded solemnly.

Satisfied, they ran off to play with an orange inflatable dragon in the pool. I caught Andy's eye. Smiling, he blew me a kiss.

The end

Also by D A Latham

A Very Corporate Affair Book 1
A Very Corporate Affair Book 2
A Very Corporate Affair Book 3
The Taming of the Oligarch (Corporate Affair Book 4)
Salon Affair
The Beauty and the Blonde
The Whore of Babylon Cay

All available from all good e-retailers

Find out more at:
Facebook: The Novels of D A Latham
Twitter: @dalatham1
dalatham.wordpress.com

Please consider leaving a review for this book on the site you purchased it, or on Goodreads. Reviews help others discover new books.

Do stick around for a bonus chapter from A Very Corporate Affair Book 1

D A Latham

A VERY CORPORATE AFFAIR BOOK 1

CHAPTER 1

I stood on Welling station shivering in the cold, and trying to calm the butterflies fluttering around in my stomach. Today was the day of judgement at work. The day I would find out if my training contract would turn into a fully fledged job at Pearson and Hardwick, one of the big four law firms in London. If today went well, I would become a qualified, and gainfully employed, corporate lawyer. If today went badly, then six years of studying would be down the drain.

It had been a real slog to get this far. I came from a working class family, who didn't believe in social mobility, and thought I was wasting my time. I had worked hard at Bexley Grammar to get top grades and secure a place at Cambridge to study law and business. I had kept my head down through university and had put in enough effort to gain a first. A year long legal practitioner course led to my traineeship, and another two years of intense concentration at Pearson and Hardwick had followed, as I threw myself into the opportunity they had given me.

I looked around the grey, featureless platform. At six thirty in the morning, only the early bird commuters were present. Pale, pasty looking men in badly fitting

The Debt

suits looked resigned to another miserable day in mundane jobs. There was not one exciting or interesting looking person there. Suburbia doesn't really breed the people who make you sit up and take notice, I thought to myself. All the more reason to escape as quickly as possible.

I'd enjoyed Cambridge as it had been a huge relief to be around intelligent, informed people who had been passionate about academia. My mum had never understood a thirst for knowledge, and had tried to get me to lower my aspirations and take a 'nice shop job' at sixteen. The thought of returning home tonight unemployed and a failure, confirming all her warnings about 'getting ideas above my station', made the butterflies ten times worse.

I arrived at the offices at quarter past seven, pausing in the stunning wood panelled lobby of the ancient law firm, and wondered if it would be the last time I would walk through on my way to work. I ducked into the cloakroom to change into my heels and shed my coat.

"Good morning Elle," said Roger, the security man who was based in the lobby, as I waited for the lift up to my floor.

"Morning Roger, today's the day."

"I wish you the best of luck. I'm sure you'll be fine, the time you get here everyday must have shown them how conscientious you are."

"Thanks. Hope so." I smoothed the front of my neat pencil skirt, and gripped my handbag a little tighter.

Once I had reached my floor, I made my way straight to my desk to switch on my computer, check my emails, and just wait. All the cases I had been assigned to work on had been completed, and as my traineeship had been near its end, they hadn't given me any new ones. For the last week or so, I had just been assisting the other trainees with their cases, doing their drudge work, and helping out in the filing room. I had felt that the lack of new cases being put my way was a bad omen, and if they were keeping me, they wouldn't have worried about giving me fresh work.

Checking my emails, I saw one from Mr Lambert, my line manager. I opened it.

From: Adam Lambert
To: Elle Reynolds
Subject: Interview
28th March 2013

Dear Ms Reynolds,

Your interview today will be held at 11am in room 7 on the 4th floor. In attendance will be Ms Pearson, Mr Jones, and myself.

Kind Regards

The Debt

Adam Lambert

I stared at the email for a minute or two. It wasn't giving anything away. I decided I need a cup of tea. In the small kitchenette area, I realised that my hands were shaking as I filled the kettle. I needed to get a grip. The last thing I wanted to do was show nerves or weakness when the rest of my workmates arrived. Cool, calm and collected was the image I wanted to project at work, not needy, insecure or scared, no matter how I felt inside.

As the other trainees filed in, I could see how rattled they were. It was interview time for all of us who began in 2011, and usually only a quarter of the intake would be offered permanent jobs. Scanning the faces, I tried to figure out who had screwed up, who had excelled, and who would be a tough call.

"Why are you looking so pensive?" Lucy demanded, standing in front of my desk, "we all know you'll be ok, miss perfect," she teased.

"I don't know about that, they could easily decide I'm not posh enough to fit in," I said, fully aware of my lack of private schooling and accompanying posh accent.

"Don't be daft, the fact that you have a perfect record and are a bloody genius will easily outweigh the problem of a glottal stop." She smiled to let me know she was teasing.

"Wha times yuh mee-ing?" I said, in full south London accent, taking the piss.

"11.30. You?"

"11. Good luck."

"You too. If its good news, I'll treat us both to lunch in Bennies." Lucy came from a wealthy background and didn't have to watch the pennies as I did. She sauntered off, seemingly unconcerned about her fate being decided upstairs.

At ten to eleven, I rinsed my hands in cold water to avoid a sweaty handshake, and made my way up to the floor above. The secretary directed me to take a seat just outside the meeting room to await my turn. The door swung open, and a fellow trainee, John Peterson, came out looking as white as a sheet. I caught his eye, and he gave an almost imperceptible shake of his head. He had been one of the 'sure things' I had judged earlier that morning. My stomach sank into my boots.

"Miss Reynolds, you may go in now," said the secretary. I plastered on my best fake smile and entered the room. The three interviewers sat behind a long table, with a single chair placed in front of them. Mr Lambert smiled at me, and asked me to take a seat. I shook their hands, and sat down.

"Good morning Miss Reynolds, I'm sure you must be nervous, so I won't waste time on pleasantries," began Ms Pearson. My heart sank. "You have the highest work output rate of your year group, the best attendance and punctuality rate, and the best report from your superiors." My heart hammered, and I tried to stop myself blushing at her compliment. Ms Pearson was a managing partner, so remaining in control in front of her was extremely important.

"So I'm delighted to be able to offer you a permanent position at Pearson and Hardwick. Now your report states that you would like to specialise in corporate law, is that correct?"

The Debt

I pulled myself together quickly enough to answer her, "yes, that's correct."

"Good. We have an opening in our corporate department at Canary Wharf. You can begin there on Monday. For the rest of this week you will be on paid leave, as Mr Lambert has indicated that you have taken no holiday at all this year. The salary will be eighty thousand per year, plus the grade 3 benefit package. Do you have any questions?" Ms Pearson looked at me intently.

"No questions, and thank you Ms Pearson, I won't let you down," I said, barely able to take it all in.

"I'm sure you won't. Now, please head over to HR, where they have your new contract ready for you to sign, and sort out your package, then I suggest you have some rest until Monday."

I smiled widely at the panel, "thank you for this opportunity," I said before heading out.

Over at HR I signed my new contract, collected the details of my new workplace, and perused the list of benefits I could choose as part of my package. As I didn't have a car to be subsidised, I chose gym membership, private health care and an enhanced pension. The HR lady assured me that the gym at the Canary Wharf building was superb, and useful for showering and changing facilities if I needed them. On my way back to my floor, I bumped into Lucy, who was sporting a wide grin

"Great news Elle, I got family law, just as I wanted. What about you?"

"Good news for me too, I got corporate, so Canary Wharf here I come," I replied with an equally big smile.

"Wow! They are the most prestigious offices in the firm, you must have done really well. I'll come and visit you there. Now, shall we meet by your old cubicle as I have to see HR before we go to lunch?"

"Great, see you in a bit."

I went back to my cubicle with my shoulders back, and a lightness I had never felt before. Success felt fantastic, and for the first time ever I could escape my background.

Bennies was a bistro type bar tucked away down one of the tiny passages that characterised the city. Lucy ordered a bottle of Moët while we waited for our overpriced sandwiches. We clinked glasses and gossiped about who got kicked out and who was kept on. It turned out that out of a hundred who began the training contract with us, only fifteen had been offered full contracts.

"So, what's your next plan? Are you moving nearer work?" Lucy asked.

"Sure am, I have the rest of the week off, so it's a good opportunity to look for a flat share or a studio. Mum's boyfriend wants to move in, and it's too small a flat to have all three of us there, so it's time to move out." I hugged myself with glee. Escape from the moaning about my getting up early, use of hot water and aversion to junk food.

Lucy broke my reverie, "my brothers friend is looking for a flatmate, he lives near Canada square. Would you like me to call him?"

"Oh yes please, that would be great." She pulled her phone out of her bag and prodded the screen.

"Hi James, it's Lucy Elliott. Have you still got that room available? Only one of my friends is looking for a

The Debt

flat near Canary Wharf." She listened to the other
person, injecting a 'mmm' every now and then. "Yes it's
a she, and she is a nice, hardworking, quiet, corporate
lawyer. Yes I work with her.....yes.....no......ok I'll send
her along this afternoon. Text me the address yeah."
Lucy ended the call.

"Rooms still available then?" I asked.

"Yep. He's a bit fussy about who he shares with.
James is a nice guy, and likes a quiet life. He works
from home, so needs a flat mate who goes out to work,
and isn't too noisy." Lucy's phone chirped as a text
arrived with the address, which she forwarded to me.

A couple of other trainees from our year arrived to
celebrate with us, nicking our champagne, much to my
relief. I didn't want to view a flat half cut.

After lunch, I headed over to the docklands, taking
the DLR. I had to double check the address, as the
building looked way too swanky to be a flat share type
of place. Pressing the buzzer, a voice came through,
"who is it?"

"Elle Reynolds, Lucy sent me."

"I'll buzz you in. Take the lift to the fourteenth
floor. My door is right in front of you." The buzzer
sounded, and I pushed my way into a marble and glass
lobby. I took in the silence, the deep carpet, and sense
of restrained opulence. The lift was large, mirrored and
silently sped straight up to floor fourteen, which I
noticed, was the highest floor.

The door in front of the lift was open, and what
could only be described as a bear was standing in the
doorway. It was hard to gauge his age with all the facial
hair, but I took a guess at early thirties. He was tall and
broad, dressed in jeans and an old T-shirt which showed

off muscular, hairy arms. Through all the long, curly hair and copious beard, a pair of twinkly blue eyes reflected a smile. "You must be James? I'm Elle," I said, extending my hand out to him. He shook it warmly and invited me in.

"Did you find it alright?" he enquired, "and would you like a coffee?"

"Yes it was easy to get here, and yes I'd love a coffee if you're having one." He showed me through to what could only be described as a state of the art kitchen. James pulled two cups out of a cupboard and pulled two pods out of a drawer.

"What sort of coffee? I can do Americano, espresso, latte or cappuccino."

"A latte would be lovely," I said, awed that there was a choice. If my mum remembered to buy fresh milk it was an event, and yet this hairy, bearded, bear-person had fresh coffee and fresh milk. I was impressed.

I found out that James was an app developer, and had built a few hit apps, which had enabled him to buy the apartment. He was working on a new app, and worked from home, so needed some peace during the day. I told him all about my promotion, and we toasted my success with fresh coffee, which made me giggle. He explained that Canada Square was quite literally round the corner, and my walk to work would be around five minutes.

"So why do you want a flat mate?" I asked.

He squirmed slightly, "I work from home, and sometimes barely speak to a living soul from one day to the next. I guess I get a bit lonely here on my own." He looked a bit sad.

"No girlfriend?" I wanted to make sure there was nobody to get jealous that a woman was moving in. The last thing I wanted was to put anyone's nose out of joint.

"Nope. My last girlfriend went to live in Australia, so don't worry, nobody to get arsey about a girl living here. I have to ask, any boyfriend?"

"No. I've been working like a demon for the last few years. No time for a man." Much to my mothers disgust, I thought.

"Well, I have no issue with you bringing friends back, but I'd rather not have a man move in here, so if you get serious with anyone, please bear that in mind."

"Will do. Can I see the room?"

"Sure, this way." James led me down a short corridor and opened a door. The room was enormous, with floor to ceiling windows covering one wall. There was just a large bed and a cabinet with a TV in the room. It looked a bit sparse. I walked over to the windows and stared at the view of the Thames.

"There's a dressing room through here, and an ensuite through that door," said James, pointing at two doors. Looking in the first one, I found a beautifully fitted out walk in wardrobe, with acres of hanging space, shoe racks and a dressing table. My paltry clothing collection would take up about a tenth of the space.

The ensuite was lovely. It had a large, deep bath, a separate shower, and a heated towel rail. It all looked brand new and pristine.

"How much is the rent?" I asked, suddenly nervous that I wouldn't be able to afford to live in this luxury.

"A thousand a month, but that includes all bills. Does that suit?" I breathed a sigh of relief.

"Fantastic, it's a deal." We shook hands. I arranged to pay the deposit and first months rent into James bank account via my laptop, and he gave me a key.

We bonded over another cup of coffee. I really warmed to James. He was just the right mixture of intelligence, geekiness and humour. We had thrashed out some basic house rules which, thankfully, didn't include hot water usage or rationing the gas. He also mentioned that he was an early riser, and hoped that it wouldn't be an issue for me to be quiet late at night. We both laughed when I pointed out that ten pm was staying up late for me.

I headed back to Welling with a spring in my step, eager to begin my new, London life. As predicted, my mum could barely contain her excitement at my moving out. She dug out the News Shopper and found an ad for a 'man with a van' who would be able to move all my belongings at short notice. He was able to do Thursday, so that left Wednesday to pack up, and get everything ready. I would still have a few days to unpack, settle in, and explore before starting work.

Mum was eager to help pack my belongings, and I actually didn't have much. The whole lot took us a morning to box and bag up. I had invested carefully in good work clothes, but apart from that, I didn't really buy a lot. Plus I had used the money I earned during my training contract to pay off my student loans, and build some savings, rather than blow it on clothes and makeup.

The Debt

That afternoon, I decided to hop on a bus to Bluewater and treat myself to a haircut and some new work outfits ready for Monday.

I went into the swankiest salon there, and booked in for a trim. I kept my hair long, but the stylist added layers, and the whole effect was classy and grown up. Delighted with my new hair, I wandered round the boutiques trying on clothes until I found a fabulous navy dress and jacket combo which fitted like a dream, and projected just the image I was aiming for. I stocked up on tights and toiletries and bought a pair of navy heels to match my new dress. In a mad moment of optimism, I even bought a box of condoms before heading home.

The next morning a slightly grubby van pulled up outside the flat, and an even grubbier, skinny man got out. He wasted no time flinging my stuff in the back while I wrote out my new address for mum.

"You have fun, and don't work too hard," were her parting words of wisdom. No doubt Ray, her boyfriend was waiting round the corner for my van to pull away before rolling up with his bags.

As we pulled away from Welling, the excitement rose in my belly. This was the moment I had worked towards for six long years. My life could finally begin.

James helped van man with my bags and boxes, so with the three of us, it didn't take long. It took a further two hours to unpack and neatly hang my clothes in the closet.

"You don't have much stuff for a girl," said James, wandering in with two glasses of wine.

"I'm not a great shopper, and I've not had much spare cash to spend on clothes and stuff," I replied, a bit embarrassed by my meagre use of the dressing room. I aimed to spend 10% of my new salary on clothes every month to make sure I looked the part.

"Not criticising, just saying. I've got even less clothes than you," he said in a good natured way. He sat on the dressing table seat sipping his wine as I checked all my shoes for dirt before stowing them on the rack. He told me all about the new app he was working on, which sounded great, and described the other occupants of the building.

"The only unfriendly one is the fella on the floor below. Never says hello, and seems to bring lots of different women back. I saw one crying in the lobby once, said he threw her out. He's definitely one to stay away from."

"Thanks for warning me. He sounds delightful, not. Now is there a grocery store around here? I need to pick up a few bits."

"There's a small mart round the corner. What do you need?"

"Milk, bread, that kind of stuff."

"I had it all delivered today. There's loads in the fridge. I get everything ocado'd in. I have everything sorted for dinner tonight, thought you might be too busy with the move to worry about it."

"James, that's really kind of you, thank you. I'll pay you back."

"Nonsense, it's only a few groceries, and besides, I love to cook, but I never have anyone to cook for, so indulge me and let me prepare something." He smiled warmly, and wandered back to the kitchen area.

I hugged myself with glee. Sipping wine in a gorgeous apartment overlooking the river, with a new friend, and a new job. It was everything I'd imagined it would be.

"Elle," James yelled, "foods ready." I hurried into the kitchen as he dished up a pasta and tiger prawn concoction. He poured another two glasses of wine, and pushed one over to me.

"Bon appetite little Elle, and welcome to Canary Wharf. I hope you'll be very happy here." We clinked glasses.

"Thank you big James, and I'm sure I'm gonna love it." I took a bite of my pasta, it was all lemony and buttery, and delicious. "Wow, you are a great cook, this is gorgeous."

"You look like you need a bit of feeding up."

"I'm not a great eater. My mum only ever heated stuff up out of the freezer, so it was often better to go without than suffer the nightly unidentified breadcrumbed fare."

James laughed, a rich, deep, hearty laugh, "no wonder you're skinny. You need good, healthy, hearty food, especially with a pressurised job. Will they have you working all hours of the day and night?"

"Probably. I'm going in there as the lowest in the pecking order, so I'm in no doubt that I'll get the donkey work. Law is like that, hierarchy is everything. I'm pretty certain that I'll be given a cubby hole next to the bogs for my office, and the secretaries will be sly bitches. I don't mind though, I'm prepared to earn my stripes."

"I hated corporate life," James confided, "glad to be out of it. Hated sucking up to a useless wanker of a boss, and attending endless meetings. If I need a status meeting nowadays, I just look in a mirror."

"Do you always work alone? Or do you sometimes collaborate?" I asked.

"Always alone. I did one app a few years back with a designer, and it was a bit of a disaster, all style over substance, so since then, I do it all myself. So what made you go into law?"

I pondered his question. "Money really. Corporate law is a well paid profession, and I wanted to escape my background. I wanted to aim high, and I enjoy the intellectual rigour of law. I didn't want to be involved in criminal law because I hate grisly stuff, and family law is often emotionally draining. I like the detail of contract law, and the fact that its usually done in shiny, neat offices rather than police cells or prisons."

James smiled at me, "I admire your ambition, I wish I had more of it. I'm happy just sitting coding apps and dreaming up games."

"You did ok out of it," I said, sweeping my hand to indicate the apartment, "this place is fantastic."

"Yeah, I'm pretty lucky," he agreed.

I spent the first evening in my new home watching telly on the big flat screen in the living area. James had shown me how to use the coffee maker, and dishwasher, so I insisted he sat down while I cleared up after dinner, and made us both coffee. By nine, I was yawning, so bade him goodnight, and went to bed.

The next morning I was up at my normal time of half five. I wandered through to the kitchen to make tea, and discovered James boiling a kettle.

"Morning Elle, sleep well?"

The Debt

"Morning, yeah great thanks. Is there enough water in the kettle for two?" James nodded. He looked even more dishevelled in his dressing gown and pyjamas, with his beard sticking out like bed hair. He pulled out another cup and threw a tea bag into it.

"So what's your agenda for today?"

"I'm gonna check out my new gym, pop into my new office to say hi, and explore my surroundings. Anything you need me to bring in?"

"Don't think so, I'll text you if I think of anything. I've got stuff in the fridge for dinner tonight, so don't worry about food."

"Ok, thanks, just let me know. I'm gonna take a shower now and head out." I took my tea back to my room and drank it while staring at the view from my window. After a luxurious shower, I dried my hair as I watched the stylist do, and applied a touch of makeup. I decided that trousers and flats were best bet for the day I had planned, so dressed in neat but trendy trousers and a simple cashmere jumper. As I wasn't sure what time the gym would open, I went back to the kitchen and made another tea. James wasn't around, so I sat quietly at the island and read through the bumf on the gym that HR had given me. It all looked pretty straightforward. I would have unlimited use of the facilities, and only pay for personal training. I checked the opening hours, finding that it opened at six. I would be able to do a workout in the mornings and still be at my desk by seven thirty, perfect. I finished my tea and placed mine and James cups in the dishwasher before heading down.

The lift stopped and the doors slid open while I was looking at my map of the area, and I automatically

316

began to walk out, bumping straight into someone stepping in.

"I'm so sorry," I began, before noticing we were not in the lobby, and I had just bumped into Adonis himself. "I thought I was on the ground floor." I said lamely.

"Just be more careful," he snarled, before studiously ignoring me for the rest of the journey down. Must be the man James warned me about I thought. James didn't tell me he was sex on legs though. I surreptitiously studied him as he exited the lift. Short dark hair, bespoke suit, and a face that would be handsome if he smiled.

I was indeed five minutes away from the Canary Wharf tower, which rose majestically to top the surrounding skyscrapers. I followed the directions to the gym on the lower ground floor. It was a health enthusiasts dream, row upon row of state of the art equipment, complimentary towels, pristine changing rooms, and a full list of fitness classes. I booked in for an orientation session the following day, and picked up a class timetable. I exchanged my voucher from HR for my gym pass at the desk, and wandered around for half an hour, checking out the changing room and the machines.

My new office was based on the 34th floor of the tower, so at nine, I went up there to introduce myself. The receptionist was a pretty Asian girl, called Priti, who seemed efficient and welcoming. She introduced me to a few of the other lawyers, all of whom seemed friendly enough.

"I can show you where you'll be working," said a geeky, skinny man who introduced himself as Peter Dunn. "They told me you were starting Monday, so

your desk is all ready."He showed me through a large
open plan office full of people to a corridor of glass
fronted offices. Pushing a door open, he revealed a
large office with four desks. Two desks were occupied
by men. Peter explained that he sat at the far end, and
the final desk was earmarked for me. I introduced
myself to the other two.

"I'm Adrian Jones, and he's Matt Barlow. So your
the ex trainee we have to get up to speed then?"

"That's me. I hope you don't mind having a newbie
around," I said, hoping to disarm them. I knew that
nobody liked babysitting newbies.

"I'm sure we'll cope, and it'll be nice having a bit of
eye candy around, eh boys? This firm has an ugly
secretary only policy," Adrian sniggered.

"I'll do my very best to look pretty gentlemen, just
don't forget I'm not a secretary." I smiled to make them
think I was teasing.

"If you wear a tight blouse I promise I won't get
you making tea," quipped Matt.

"I'll see what I can do," I laughed, "as long as you'll
be able to concentrate on your work if I'm in here with
my cleavage on show."

"She's gonna have every hotshot in the tower
salivating over her, you have no chance," laughed Peter,
looking amused at the adolescent behaviour of his
colleagues. I had fully expected sexist banter, and it all
seemed quite harmless. Certainly my office mates
seemed friendly enough, and I was confident I'd be able
to handle them.

I didn't hang around long, as I wanted to explore
the whole area. I discovered the vast shopping complex
beneath the tower, looking out for decent lunch places

and a dry cleaners. I found wine bars, restaurants, and pubs for evenings out, and a gorgeous deli for supplying food for evenings in. I stopped off at a Starbucks for a coffee, and settled into a sofa to check my map.

"May I join you?" My head snapped up at the masculine voice. Adonis from the apartment block was standing in front of me.

"Sure," was all I could manage. I went back to my map. I could do rude too. He coughed slightly, which made me look up. He was staring intently.

"You just came out of Pearson and Hardwick," he said.

I stared back, "yes," I replied, giving nothing else away. He unnerved me, which I didn't like. I hoped he didn't work for them as well. He blew on his coffee before sipping it. I watched his mouth. He had the sexiest mouth.

"So what were you doing there?"

"I beg your pardon?" How rude was this man? Out of all the ways to frame a question, he had to pick the worst.

"Are you a secretary?" I almost spat my coffee at him.

"No I'm most certainly not. It's none of your business why I was there." I watched as his eyes flashed. I couldn't work out if he was laughing at me or angry.

"I suppose it's not, I just saw you in their offices. I was in there signing a contract," he said.

"Are you a client?" I asked, suddenly wary of upsetting him.

The Debt

"No, I was there with my own legal team, they had drawn up a contract for the other party. So are you going to tell me why you were there?"

"I start work there Monday, I'm a lawyer for Pearson and Hardwick, just moving over to corporate. Went there today to introduce myself."

"So are you going to introduce yourself to me? Seeing as you nearly knocked me over at home and work two floors below me in the tower?"

"I'm Elle Reynolds. I just moved into the apartment, James' new flatmate. Have you lived there long?"

"About two years. I'm Oscar Golding, and it's very nice to meet you Elle." He leaned forward and shook my hand. His hand was surprisingly warm and soft for such a harsh looking man. I wanted to get a smile from him to see if I was right about him being more handsome. I gave him my best beaming smile, hoping he would reciprocate. He just about managed to turn the corners of his mouth up when his phone rang. As soon as he saw the screen, he scowled and excused himself. I went back to my coffee and my map.

I picked up a box of Krispy Kremes before heading home. James came out of his study when he heard the front door.

"Thank god you're back. I was going boggle eyed at my screen in there. What you been up to?" He made coffee and set out the box of doughnuts while I told him about the gym, my office, and the shopping mall.

"I bumped into our downstairs neighbour this morning, quite literally. He really is a strange one. Snarled at me in the lift, saw me in Starbucks this afternoon and managed to piss me off again."

James laughed, "how did he manage to piss off a jolly little thing like you?"

"Said he saw me in the Pearson and Hardwick offices and asked if I was a secretary." James' eyebrows shot up.

"Why did he assume you were a secretary? Stupid man."

"Quite. He really is quite unpleasant. Never smiles either." I sipped my coffee, and smiled at James demolishing the pile of doughnuts. "I did make sure he wasn't a client though."

"Clever move. Never a good idea to make a client feel like an idiot." We both laughed.

James made fajitas that evening, which were delicious. Afterwards I had a long hot bath before putting my pyjamas on and joining him for a bit of telly and a glass of wine before I turned in.

Thank you for reading this sample of A Very Corporate Affair Book 1, available from all good booksellers.

The Debt

10631871R00174

Printed in Great Britain
by Amazon